GAURAIN

BOIS de BARRY

g. Ingoldsby

INFANTRY

ENGLISH & AUSTRIANS

Cavalry

VEZONS

OY

RGEON

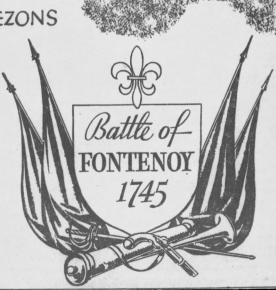

Battle of
FONTENOY
1745

ENCH CAVALRY

"   INFANTRY

IGLISH & DUTCH CAVALRY

"   "   " INFANTRY

EDOUBTS

A DAY OF BATTLE
A Novel

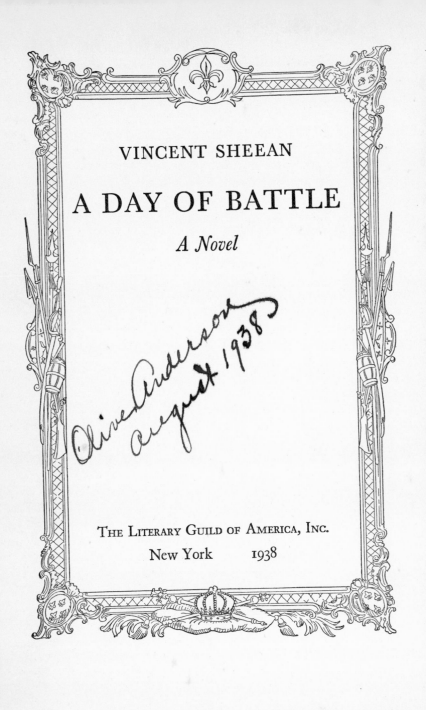

VINCENT SHEEAN

A DAY OF BATTLE

A Novel

THE LITERARY GUILD OF AMERICA, INC.

New York   1938

PRINTED AT THE *Country Life Press*, GARDEN CITY, N. Y., U. S. A.

FOREWORD

THE WARS of the eighteenth century between France and England, with allies variously arrayed on either side, were a vast panorama of shifting power. France, decaying from within, began the long contest in 1743 with an empire which was still very great, a navy as powerful as the English, a treasury filled by years of prosperous peace. When these wars ended, Canada and India had passed from the French power forever, the American continent north of Mexico had been turned over to an English-language civilization, the French navy had been crippled beyond repair, and England emerged as the first naval and imperial power of the world, ready for the immense development which the Industrial Revolution was to make possible.

The wars were differently named, and the allies on the French or English side were not always the same. Prussia, rising like England to new importance, was on France's side in the first war (the War of the Austrian Succession); in the second, the Seven Years' War, Frederick the Great took his logical position beside England, and France's ally was her old enemy, Austria. As between Prussia and Austria the opposition was also one between the rising and the falling power, between the past and the future. In the forests of America—as in Europe and the Orient—the clash of world forces brought men to battle; the struggle in America was called the "French-and-Indian wars."

At one point upon the immense panorama of the century the historic process seemed halted or even, for a time, reversed. For a year or two it seemed that France —and with her most of the lost causes of Europe, the exiled Stuarts among them—had vanquished the traditional enemy. Most of all did this seem to be the case after the French victory at Fontenoy in Flanders on May 11, 1745. In the battle of Fontenoy an army of mixed nationalities, commanded by the German Maurice of Saxony, and relying heavily upon the exiled Irish, Scots and English who made up the Jacobite Irish Brigade, met and defeated an equal army of English and Hanoverians, with Dutch allies, led by the Duke of Cumberland. The battle was hailed as the greatest of French victories; Te Deums were sung throughout France; the Stuart family and all their partisans picked up hope. Charles Edward Stuart ("Bonnie Prince Charlie") was so encouraged by Fontenoy and by the sanguine temperament of his Irish and Scottish friends that he made his expedition to Scotland later in the same year and brought his family's part in history to an end at Culloden. In the peace that ended this war France obtained no advantage; after the next war she was shorn of her overseas possessions; the forces that produced the French Revolution were gathering momentum while the empire and the navy fell away and the court, dominated by Louis XV and Mme de Pompadour, spent its whole energy in a flight from boredom.

Fontenoy is only a pin point upon the movement of that wonderful century, but like any other pin point, it is full of life when examined under the microscope. It was a victory of lost causes; it raised hopes which were never to be satisfied, seemed to reverse the current of time and history. Those who took part in it had little notion of its significance. To the veteran commander, Maurice of Saxony, it was an exercise in military tactics; to Louis XV it was a chance of military glory and a gift of love to his new mistress, the young and tender Jeannette who was so soon to become Marquise de Pompadour; to the men who fought it was a grim duty favored by circumstance; to the exiled Irish, Scots and English on the French side, it was an opportunity to carve their way back to their island homes under a Stuart king. Except in the case of the Marquis d'Argenson, who was in some degree sicklied o'er by the pale cast of thought, none of the principal personages of the day reveals an awareness of the movement of the century. Their letters, diaries and other papers, which have been preserved in great number, betray an unconsciousness of historic current, a concentration upon immediate detail, which is worthy of the present time. To look at the losers in their moment of victory, to reflect upon the lost cause when it seemed to win, and to feel by some system of imaginative transference what men and women felt on the day of Fontenoy, was the hope of the author in beginning the book. Invention has had little to do with this novel and evidence a great deal; it is a kind of history. But since reversals of the current of time are a phenomenon of not infrequent appearance, there may be Fontenoys today or tomorrow, and the battle seems to the author not a tangent from the historic process, but a part of its general curve.

V. S.

A DAY OF BATTLE
A Novel

THE DARK RIDGE of the hill lay smooth against the even gray of the sky, and a line was marked along its blackness by small yellow lanterns. The lanterns shed no light. They only indicated, in opaque and beautiful blobs of color, the limit of a frontier and the track of sentries. In the clear, warm night, upon which the stars were only now growing pale, no fires had been lighted. Men slept in bivouac without discomfort, in the places allotted them for the morrow. All was ready; everything had been done. From Barry Wood, here on the left, across to the village of Fontenoy and on in a curving line to the banks of the river, the troops were aligned in what the Marshal called a very good position, fortified by occasional redoubts and comforted by the power of numbers. The great curve lay still under the paling stars; in the gradual paling light the men lay sleeping. Their sleep was a still, invisible cloud that contained them all, the cloud of the breath of life that would come or go, cease or continue, upon the luck or prowess of the bodies that shared it in their thousands. The sleeping stillness on the hill and the plain enfolded them all for some moments yet, beneath the line of yellow lanterns; but the first far trumpet was already blown, and was taken up now, again

and again, back and forth, echoed and re-echoed for a
blinding moment of sound. Patrick Cusack in the first
company of Dillon's regiment blew mightily; Rory Mac-
Naughton blew in Lally's; Michael Gilcannan, wiping
the cobwebs of sleep from his eyes, and wishing he had
not drunk so much red wine on the night before, reached
for his trumpet and blew a blast for Clare's; the army
was awake. The light of fires sprang up here and there
across the land that lay between Barry Wood and the
far-off river, where the French King lay in considerable
luxury and as much safety as a battlefield could afford.
Between that camp, at Calonne on the other side of the
Scheldt, and the left point of the crescent at Barry Wood,
men stirred and dressed and clamored for their soup
while the air grew clear with dawn. The yellow lanterns
were collected and extinguished.

It was a French army, but the men in it were of all
nations. There were blackamoors from Virginia in some
of the Irish regiments; there were Scots and English;
there were Germans, Livonians, and Swedes in the
French regiments; there was a whole regiment of Piedmontese. The talk that filled the air was in every language, and at the tent of Lally-Tollendal, pitched behind
the ridge at the extreme left near Barry Wood, there were
to be heard the brisk alternations of French, English,
Gaelic and German as the Colonel prepared himself for
the day's business. There was a special edge to Lally's
eagerness, for his regiment was new and had never tried
its strength in a real engagement; seven months before

it had not existed, and its scarlet coats were fresh on the bony backs of peasants brought from Clare and Kerry and the bleak hills of Connaught. The veterans shifted from other regiments were few among them, the French-born Irish fewer still; they talked among themselves in the Gaelic, and had learned enough of French commands and English speech to get along, and no more. But when Lieutenants O'Kearney and Piers Butler spoke to each other it was in English, for they were gentlemen.

"What make of war is it," O'Kearney asked, "where they put the Irish in the reserve?"

"Wait," said Butler, "and you'll see. I heard the Colonel talking last night . . ."

Lally sat over his coffee and bread with a map which he had made himself. He took pride in his gift for strategy, and had been able to make a very useful suggestion to the Marshal no later than the night before, after a survey of the lines between the villages of Fontenoy and Antoing; the Marshal had listened to good purpose, and a new redoubt had been run up there hastily to strengthen the French position. It was Lally's way to put himself forward, to ensure an appreciation of his talents, and to offer his opinion in and out of season, but much in this vein was forgiven for the sake of his intelligence and courage. The word adventurer gave him deep offense, but the thing was in the whole stamp of his person: he had the look of it as he sat there over his coffee, his black brows frowning over the sketch he had made of the army's position, his hair already larded and whit-

ened with flour, his epaulettes gleaming. He had waited
a long time for this moment and did not intend to let it
find him unready. Indeed he had hardly slept all the
night before, his mind busy with schemes of action in
which, naturally, whatever the aim to be pursued—and
he was remarkably single-minded in that respect—the
virtues of Lally's regiment and of its chief should have
their part. It was a good regiment, and a whole winter's
effort and all the money Lally could extract from the
treasury had gone on its drill and equipment; it should
hold its own with Dillon's and Clare's and the rest of
them in the coming day; and if he understood the land
correctly, it was just here, down the Mons Road, that the
English would most probably advance, just here where
Lally's and the rest of the Irish would be on hand to
greet them. Lally was French-born, of a French mother,
and had indeed only seen his father's country once, but
he was an O'Mullally of Tullenadally, and the liquid syllables were not more Irish than he felt himself to be. His
encounters with the inherited enemy had not always been
fortunate, and he had a black memory of Dettingen, but
this was another day.

"You see, O'Hegarty," he pointed out, "there is the
one road they can come on; every other approach all the
way around is protected by redoubts. We spoke of it last
night, and somebody said another redoubt would have
protected this one too. The Marshal said he agreed, but
he did not think any troops on earth could approach on
this road through the artillery fire from both sides. I do

believe it, O'Hegarty. That is what the English will do."

He looked across at his lieutenant colonel with snapping ice-blue eyes, profoundly pleased.

"We are here in the right place, for once," he said. "Glory be to God! Why do you sit there with your long jaw stuck out, O'Hegarty? Don't you see what this means to the regiment?"

"I don't see much advantage," said O'Hegarty, "in being posted at the weakest point of the line."

He was an older man than Lally, and had a long, sad jaw on which the beard showed blue under the fresh-shaved skin.

"I'll not argue with you," said Lally. "If I didn't know what you could do I might doubt you, O'Hegarty, but I know you'll be all right when the time comes. What is it then, Hennessy?"

"There's a messenger come who says he is from the Marshal himself," said Hennessy from the front of the tent. "I told him you were at breakfast but he——"

Hennessy was a lieutenant, young and rawboned and with a look of being permanently unsuited to uniform, so that not the best of tailors could make a coat fit him. He spoke with a broad Irish accent and rolled his r's at leisure. Lally cut him short.

"Let him come in, man, let him come in at once," he said. Then he added to O'Hegarty: "It's a sin and a shame the way that Hennessy lets his red arms stick out of his shirt like a scarecrow on the road. Is there no cloth in the regiment to cover him?"

A shining figure came in and saluted: a young man in the white uniform of the French King's household cavalry, with his boots and his lace and epaulettes gleaming, his hair shining with grease and powder, his whole person gleaming and shining like a reproof to the dull red skin of the ill-graced Hennessy.

"It's Mézières," said Lally, getting up. "My dear Mézières, this is early work for such as you. Sit down and drink some coffee with us. You will have had better coffee in the Marshal's camp, but still——"

Mézières sat down but refused the coffee. He was very young and looked very English, with the skin and eyes that had made his mother and aunt the beauties of the Stuart court at Saint-Germain. When he replied to Lally it was in English.

"I have messages for the other colonels and for Lord John Drummond," he said. "The Marshal wishes to see you all in turn, at your convenience, within the next hour."

"How is the Marshal?" Lally asked. "Did he sleep?"

"No," said Mézières stolidly. "He did not. He was in great pain all the night through. He was unable to put his cuirass on this morning and when I left he was trying to get on his horse. I do not think he will succeed."

Lally and O'Hegarty made noises of commiseration.

"If the Marshal cannot command," Lally said, "we have lost our best chance of victory."

Mézières was unmoved. He seemed to have schooled

himself to impassivity at a very early age, perhaps in defense against the delicacy of his own face.

"The Marshal will command," he said. "They are preparing the wicker basket to carry him in if he cannot get on to his horse. So long as he is alive he will command."

When he had satisfied Lally's curiosity further, Mézières saluted and went out. Lally mimicked his set face and stiff salute after he had gone.

"Did you see him, O'Hegarty?" he said. "Did you get a good look at the cut of him? I don't know what his kind are doing in the French army at all. He ought to be over there with the English. He's a pure and absolute Oglethorpe if ever I saw one. Did you ever see Fanny Oglethorpe, O'Hegarty? That was his aunt, the one that came over with the Old King. When I was a child I saw her one day, driving in her carriage in the Forest of Saint-Germain, and she wasn't a day under forty then, but she had a face on her like fresh peaches in new cream."

He dropped the Irish turn of phrase which he affected in talk with his officers. He had just remembered the Marshal.

"You will pass the regiment, O'Hegarty," he said. "I will ride first to Drummond, and then to the Marshal. There is no possibility of action for two or three hours, I believe. Keep the men in position."

He was roaring for his horse before he had reached the door of the tent. O'Hegarty watched him go with grim admiration. Lally was forty-three, but had the grace and agility of youth, emphasized, perhaps, by the deliberate gallantry of his manner, his flying leap to the saddle, his way of pulling a horse up so that it pranced and curvetted before the gaping men. There was something in all this that flaunted and flared, something O'Hegarty would have resented in anybody else. With Lally there was no means of telling where exaggeration began, but at such moments as this, when he mounted and rode away, it gave his personality an emphasis which could have been pushed into caricature with little additional effort. If it had been pushed just that little more, he would have been the joke of the brigade instead of its favorite; as it was, the men cheered when he passed.

O'Hegarty sat quiet for a minute. He was a good soldier and knew it—as good a soldier as Lally—and yet he sat here, at fifty, under the orders of a man seven years younger. He asked no better; indeed he had waited long enough for this commission and counted himself lucky to have it; but he could not help observing that patience and hard work were not of themselves enough to take a man far in the army of the Most Christian King. His commission he owed to his quality—Lally needed a man like him in the new regiment—but even so, he thought grimly, he might never have got it if the O'Hegartys had not been Connaught men from the neighborhood of Tuam, not far from that Tullenadally which supplied the O'Mullallys with the other part of their Gallicized name. It brought him into the network of kinship, clan relations and place relations (a man from the same place in Ireland, if you met him in France, was almost the

same as a relative) which governed the brigade.
O'Hegarty had been in the brigade since his thirteenth
year, when an uncle had brought him over from Galway
in the hold of a ship stinking with fish and sick men; his
life as he now accepted it had begun then, and his life
before that was a kind of dream whose irreality was shut
away by the terrible stink of that ship. On the other side
of the stink he remembered places and people, the water-
fall where he used to bathe in summer when he was a
child, his mother's voice, the names and faces and ways
of talk of a score of O'Hegartys, the priest's flogging and
the frequent calamities that were spoken of in the place
(death, prison, hunger); he remembered all this, and
could hold his own in reminiscent talk when he had to;
but it was exactly like the talk of all the others—it had
happened before the great stink of that ship, and belonged to a region of the imagination which, by much
talking over, had come to wear the name of Ireland, but
had not necessarily a close connection with any fact.
O'Hegarty was a truthful man, and would not have mis-
represented the events of his actual life even in the most
garrulous tavern session, but about that legendary life on
the other side of the great stink he was capable of much
harmless romancing.

"The French have poor, weak milk," he would say.
"In the part of Ireland I come from, the milk is so rich
you can lift the cream off the top with the flat of your
knife, thick as butter." Or: "There's poor flowers in any
of the best gardens, and I have seen them all, Versailles

and all of them. We had finer flowers growing wild in the part I come from, big as your head, and the smell of them——!"

He believed what he said, for his memory of everything before the journey over was drenched in imagination. Since then the imagination seemed to have become extinct in him, and he was a notably hard-working, hard-fighting, literal-minded officer who looked upon questions of drill, pay, rations, billets and promotions as an officer should. The fortunes of Lally-Tollendal filled him with amazement but no envy, for Lally was obviously made to be fortune's favorite, and had early learned to fence and dance, make speeches and go to court; Lally had fought duels and gone on a mission to the Empress in far-off Muscovy before O'Hegarty had risen from the ranks; Lally was also his chief. O'Hegarty occasionally wondered what would be the end of that chief, what dangerous destiny—not in battle, which would have been ordinary enough—awaited him, clever as he was, among all these French grandees who were so much cleverer, with their splendid, terrifying palaces and their exquisite, incomprehensible women. O'Hegarty had seen Lally perform feats of skill and bravery that moved him to admiration, but they had not aroused in him the sheer wonder that was stirred by the sight of the same Lally among a group of French court ladies at a review.

"There he stood," O'Hegarty told Byrne and Kelly afterwards, "bowing and scraping with the best of them, his tongue loose at both ends, and the ladies laughing and making up to him with their lips pouting and their eyes full of mischief. It was a fine and wonderful sight, I tell you, but it's not safe. They'll be the death of him. It's all right for a Frenchman, but not for a Mullally."

The fact that Lally's correct official style was Comte Arthur de Lally de Tollendal, and that he had been bred to these airs and graces, had no influence on O'Hegarty's mind. A Mullally was a Mullally, even when crossed with another breed and transplanted.

He rose and squared his shoulders. He had the regiment to pass.

"Did you see the French officer, Hennessy?" he asked. "Well, then, are you not ashamed of the way your coat is cut? The first man you should kill in battle is the tailor that made it. Never mind. Before the day's over you may not be needing a coat."

Hennessy's face, neck, ears and even his offending wrists turned a darker red.

"I saw the French officer, then," he said, "and I'd rather have me own coat, sir, for as long as I'll need it."

§

The French officer had no love for the Irish. He picked his way among them with fastidious care, for they were a troublesome lot and quick to take offense. He had seen Hennessy and knew the type: another of these clumsy, rawboned louts, he thoughts, who were "officers" for incomprehensible reasons and could scarcely be distinguished from their men. Eugène de Mézières at twenty had all the prejudices of his birth and upbringing. He was Catholic and Jacobite, but thought the savage bigotry of the Irish a drag upon the Stuart cause. He disliked their noise and dirt, their boasting and their drunkenness. He was both a French gentleman and an English gentleman, and for all their touchy pride, the Irish did not seem to him to be gentlemen at all. He made exceptions for Lally (who was, after all, a Frenchman) and for such officers as Dillon and Lord Clare (who were the same as Englishmen); the rest were, in his eyes, a barbarous rabble who could be useful in hand-to-hand fighting and in scarcely anything else. He was often among them, as his knowledge of English marked him out for such service, but in his opinion there was no section of the army, except perhaps the Highland Scots, which showed less relation to the civilized part of humanity. He rode among them now, remote and shining in the early gray light, as unlike them as some visitor from another species. There was no road, and he picked his way among them, his horse sometimes slowing to a walk; for they were sprawled all over the hillside and into the edge of Barry Wood, the whole six regiments of them, shouting, bustling, eating their food, larding their hair, polishing boots or weapons. The ground was alive with them, and there were no clear lanes drawn as in the French camp for the passage of messengers or wagons. They ate where they had slept, in the long grass that had been beaten down by many feet, in the poppy fields or among the rocks. Each man had his bread and meat, and the company kitchens handed out soup and wine. The sergeants were hurrying them up, but it looked to Mézières as if no order might ever come out of such confusion, the noise and movement of five thousand men who were not overused to discipline. He made his way to the tent where he saw the colors of Dillon. There, at least, he could be brief and waste no effort in talk: for Dillon was as brisk an officer as any in the army.

Mézières dismounted and spoke to the sentry. A red-coated officer stood in the door of the tent.

"Come in, Mézières, come in and give us your good news. The Colonel expects you."

Mézières gravely saluted the elder officer, who was O'Neill, lieutenant colonel of Dillon's regiment. O'Neill was a massive, weather-beaten man in the middle forties with a great saber scar across his cheek, and the gleaming young aide-de-camp looked like a child beside him. It was this that made Mézières's face even more wooden, his shoulders even straighter, as he stepped inside the tent and saluted again, this time to James Dillon himself.

"The Marshal's compliments, sir," he said, "and he would be glad to see you within the next hour."

"Very well," said Dillon. He made no move to get up or to treat Mézières as other than a messenger. There were no coffee cups on the table in front of him. "How is the Marshal?"

"He is not well. He slept very badly and is in pain."

"I am sorry to hear it. Thank you, sir."

Mézières saluted again and went out. He had known the business with Dillon would be brief. Dillon was as professional a soldier as the century had produced, the son, brother, and grandson of soldiers, born at Saint-Germain (which is to say, in the brigade) forty-six years before. He had inherited the regiment when his brother went back to Ireland to accept the family title and estates with the Hanoverian allegiance. This Dillon, called the Chevalier de Dillon, was like the rest of his race, a stubborn and hardy fighting machine with no gift for words; sixty-nine of the clan had been attainted of treason in Ireland in 1691, and the French and Spanish armies had benefited thereby for two generations. James Dillon, like his brother Henry before him, picked on officers who were rather of his own kind, the massive O'Neill, the captains Shortall, Fitzgerald, Kennedy, MacNamara, to all of whom Mézières granted the tribute of uncomprehending respect in matters of war; they were, as his mother the lovely Oglethorpe had said, "half brute and half machine," a type of soldier especially valued in an army weakened by intrigue. Mézières observed that they were more orderly, even now, than Lally's men: in another half-hour they would be drawn up stolidly to wait until the artillery preparation was over and they could do their work. He thought, suddenly, as he had thought once or twice before, that these men actually enjoyed fighting. It was a reflection that defied human reason; it could not be true; and yet there was some basis for it in

the behavior of the Irish regiments, as of the Scots. For
the hand-to-hand work of bayonet and sword, these were
the men—above all, Dillon's were the men, for all had
been born to it, most had been in the brigade since they
were children; their lives were passed in a brutish rou-
tine in a foreign country or a series of foreign countries,
and the actual point of battle, the killing of the enemy,
appeared to arouse in them some savage joy unknown to
other troops. They were at their worst in ordinary camp
or garrison, troublesome, acrimonious, undisciplined. A
strange race, Mézières reflected, with not much talent for
living, at least according to the principles of the land of
their exile: perhaps they were different in their native
island. In France it appeared that they could do two
things well: they could kill and they could be killed. A
commander like Maurice de Saxe, who avoided battles
as much as possible, and held it to be a fixed truth that
campaigns could be won without a single life lost in
direct fight, kept the Irish in reserve for what they could
do best. "A commander like Maurice de Saxe"—but had
there ever been a commander like him?

Mézières thought suddenly of the Marshal and his
heart was constricted with pain. He had seen the Marshal
trying to get on to his horse, half an hour ago—a miserable body shapeless and useless with dropsy, commanded
by a mind that would not give up. It was certain that the
Marshal would not be able to get on that horse, and that
he might never ride again. He would have to direct the
movements of the army from a wicker basket they had

made for him, a kind of bed-chair that could be drawn by four horses. Every movement was agony to that huge body, and yet it would be moving about the field, Mézières knew, until the day was over. A hundred officers of the staff would willingly have given their own lives for the Marshal's, or so Mézières thought, deprecating his own devotion. As it was, the only relief came from a wretched little doctor who "tapped" the dropsy from time to time, and the first soldier of Europe was an inert, suffering mass, while dozens of worthless red-heeled courtiers from Versailles swarmed over the camp in their futile activity. Whether it was worse to be "half brute and half machine," like Dillon's men, or all red heels and gold lace, like the carpet soldiers of Versailles, Mézières did not feel called upon to decide, but he had no sympathy with either. His admiration went rather to the sword that was wielded with civility but effect, and after the Marshal, who was unique in his eyes, there were a number of French officers who deserved it. Among the Irish there was one, Lord Clare.

Clare, who was known among the Jacobites as the Earl of Thomond, received Mézières with cool friendliness and held him in talk for a few minutes on the hillside, the two of them dismounted beside their horses. Mézières had more extended instructions for him than for the others, for Clare commanded the whole brigade with the rank of lieutenant general, and occupied its center with his own regiment. He was tall, well made, with bold, handsome features and a courteous manner; he could quote a poem or pay a compliment; he could be almost as fluent as Lally when it was required; but he was no courtier. If Lally was the favorite of the brigade, Clare was its pattern of excellence and its notion of what a high officer should be. He had distinguished himself in numerous actions, most notably of late at Menin and Ypres; the Marshal attributed the capture of both those towns chiefly to Clare's efforts at the head of his own regiment. Clare was the chief of that part of the house of O'Brien which had remained Catholic (the greater part) when the branch of Inchiquin accepted Protestantism and the Hanoverian allegiance. The O'Briens claimed descent from the half-legendary king Brian Boru, and thirty-four of them had been attainted of treason in 1691 for Jacobitism; there was no clan among the Irish more given to pride of race. These considerations did not occur to Mézières, who was unfamiliar with the particular distinctions the Irish made among themselves, but he saw in Lord Clare an officer of mark in the army, a man of high importance among Jacobites, and a friend of his own mother's. His manner with Clare was less rigid than with any other of the Irish officers, and at the same time more deferential. He delivered his messages, answered a few questions, and waited to be dismissed. The General was subjecting him to a good-natured inspection.

"You remind me a little of Madame de Mézières," he said, "although I suppose you have heard that often enough. I hope she is well?"

"She was very well when I heard from her last," said Mézières. "She has returned from Rome to Versailles."

"Yes," said Clare. "Yes. I heard she had been in Rome."

He paused reflectively, letting his eyes rest on Mézières's horse rather than on the young man.

"She found everything as usual in Rome, of course," he said.

"I think so, sir."

"She heard nothing—that is, nothing new, nothing in the matters that interest us?"

"I think not, sir."

Clare suddenly looked straight at Mézières and some movement of comprehension altered the expression of both their faces very slightly; they were communicating upon a matter of no direct interest to this army, and army rank ceased to influence their way of speech.

"They are rather timid in Rome," Clare said, smiling without contempt. "It is their way. I suppose you have heard our affairs discussed with more courage nearer at hand."

"I think I may say so, my Lord."

"A great deal depends upon this day," Clare said with force. "You understand that, of course? If we win today the Marshal can easily conquer Flanders. The Channel is open. It is a moment that cannot be allowed to pass. If it does pass it will never come again. Do the young men understand that?"

"I think so, my Lord."

"Do *all* the young men understand it?"

"I think a great many do, my Lord. The one who should understand best of all does, and he will not let it pass if he has to cross the Channel alone."

"When did you see him last?"

"Three weeks ago, in Paris. He is still there, I think. He would have come here in the army except that the Marshal would not allow it."

"Of course not," Clare said. "If he is ever to be king over the English he must not bear arms against them in battle. Tell me, Mézières, you know much better than I: is he ready for anything? He will not be afraid to take the field even if his own father forbids it?"

"He is ready for anything, my Lord. But he has no money. All supplies from Rome have stopped, and the French are unwilling even to recognize his existence."

"Yes," said Clare. "Yes, I suppose that is so. But if we win today—and certainly we must win—there may be great changes. Even his father in Rome must realize what a difference this will make. The French, too. They ought to know . . ."

He stopped for a moment, frowning at the ground.

"Well, today will show," he said. "Tell him, Mézières, when you see him, that O'Brien of Thomond and Clare is ready to follow him if it is permitted for an officer of France to do so. I wish I could say more than that, but I hold the King's commission."

"He will understand, my Lord."

§

Alexander MacCarthy of Drisbane watched Mézières
come and go with somber dislike. That was the kind of
French officer that made an Irishman, particularly a Mac-
Carthy of Drisbane, regret his service under the French
colors. Stiff, foppish, haughty and overdressed they were,
shining and gleaming in their white and gold and silver,
much too fine to pass the time of day with an ordinary
brigade officer, but able—this was the worst of it—to engage Lord Clare in an indubitable conversation of equals,
lasting no less than ten minutes. In the intervals between
his resentments, which were many and fierce, Alexander
MacCarthy of Drisbane regarded Lord Clare as the greatest captain since Julius Caesar. For Clare ("the Gineral",
they called him) to waste his time on one of these up-
holstered messengers from headquarters was, in Mac-
Carthy's view, an injustice, especially as "the Gineral"
had cut him short that very morning in the recital of a
grievance.

It was a serious grievance, too, but long-winded and
involved in the telling. Alexander MacCarthy was the
youngest captain in the regiment; his uniforms were
made by a good tailor; he had a dark, sullen sort of good
looks which made him violently attractive to some
women; and there had been a girl in Ypres named
Arlette who experienced this attraction, even though she

was the official property of another captain named Mac-
Guire. MacCarthy, without much interest in the matter
beyond his own pleased vanity, had found it convenient
to pass certain hours with Arlette, and had been discovered by MacGuire on an occasion which left no possible
doubt as to the extent of the damage. MacGuire and
MacCarthy had fought, at first with their fists and afterwards—when MacCarthy was armed again—with their
swords. MacCarthy had pinked the elder officer slightly
in the right arm. All this was a banal affair, usual enough
in the brigade, and would have been hushed up and forgotten in the ordinary way. But it so happened that
MacGuire had a fondness for Arlette and was unable to
forget or forgive her treachery. He had told his story to
another officer; MacCarthy had told his to several; and
a first-class feud had grown up which threatened to em-
battle half the regiment. In the course of it the ancestry,
habits, characters and accomplishments of the various
participants had been thoroughly canvassed aloud, and
much offense given and taken on all sides, so that the
original cause of the dispute no longer mattered much to
anybody. Arlette was forgotten by all but MacGuire, and
a complicated system of clan relationships came into
play to support the honor, as it was called, of the quarreling partisans. Some hint of this imbroglio had come to
the attention of Lord Clare, who had begun to watch the
black looks exchanged between his officers and had actually detected Alexander MacCarthy in the act of tripping
up a fellow officer as he was about to enter the com-

mander's tent. It was soon after this disgraceful episode that Clare had invited MacCarthy, with quiet courtesy, to explain himself, and had then cut the explanation short.

"That is enough," he had said. "I don't want to hear any more. Your brawls in taverns and brothels do not concern this regiment. Do you understand that? This regiment is about to be engaged in an important action. Its officers can have no private quarrels. MacCarthy will shake hands with MacGuire and forget this matter until a more opportune time. Are you raw children or are you gentlemen holding the King's commission?"

So MacCarthy looked sullenly upon Mézières, who—at the age of twenty or not much more—could apparently be treated by the commander with more respect than a true-born MacCarthy of Drisbane with a grievance.

"That Frenchman there, Mézières his name is, can get all the time he wants for his chatter with the General," he said to Davoren, one of his lieutenants. "This army is overrun with favoritism and intrigue and black doings altogether."

"It's family influence," said Davoren wisely. "That Mézières is half an Oglethorpe. His mother was one of the Oglethorpe sisters that used to be at Saint-Germain. They would be talking of the Chevalier, no doubt."

"Chevalier be damned," said MacCarthy, fuming. "The Chevalier and his whole family have been the curse of the world, the curse of the true religion, the curse of Ireland and the MacCarthys of Drisbane. Would we not be at home now, taking our ease, if the Stuart family had been worth two sous to the devil that hatched them? Get the men formed for Mass, now, Davoren, and don't talk to me about the Chevalier. Let them say their prayers if they have any. They'll need prayers this day."

Masses had been said since the first trumpet call here and there along the swarming hillside and down to the cleared edge of Barry Wood. The priests hurried through the service and scampered off to another point to repeat it, for the six Irish and one Scots regiment were devout enough in religious practices when they remembered them, especially on a day which seemed likely to be the last for many men. The religion of the Irish and Scots had come to be so involved with their racial, economic and political memory that it assumed completeness in such rites as the Mass, symbolized the whole of their heritage and destiny. They had suffered "for the faith" and were now about to fight for it: "the faith" comprised the lands they had lost, the imprisonment and death of their relatives, their devotion (grown lukewarm with the passage of half a century) to the Stuart family, the tradition of struggle and the nostalgia of exile all together. To the direct religious or magical impulse, which in many of them was very strong, there was added such a powerful concatenation of personal and family feeling that they were bound by "the faith" as by the life of their bodies. To MacCarthy of Drisbane, kneeling now in the front rank of his men before a small improvised altar on the hillside, "the faith" was inseparable from the whole life, multifarious and vehement, in which he so strongly asserted his right to share, and redeemed it from horror, lifted it from disgust—for there was horror in MacCarthy's sullenness, disgust in his black resentment—as it dignified its end in a promise of eternity. He was glad, now, that he had shaken hands with MacGuire.

"Lamb of God that takest away the sins of the world," he prayed, "give us peace."

The Kellys, O'Briens, O'Sullivans, MacDermots, MacCarthys, O'Neills, Plunketts, Burkes, Wogans and Moriartys that knelt before the mumbling priest on the hillside repented them, with the swift, wholehearted but momentary repentance of their kind, for all the brawling, theft, indecency, cruelty and dishonesty of their lives. "Lamb of God that takest away the sins of the world," they said, "give us peace."

§

Mézières found the kilted Scots an even stranger breed than the Irish. For one thing, he could hardly understand their speech either in English or in French, and never attempted to talk to any but their highest officers. Their costume seemed to him ridiculous, their indiscipline disgraceful, and their music, with which they accompanied all their movements in peace and war, an offense to the ears. It was his duty to inform their commander, Lord

John Drummond, that the Marshal had heard ill reports of them from the night before.

"It has been reported to the Marshal," Mézières said, "that certain Scottish troopers visited the enemy camp last night, and that certain of the Scottish troops of the enemy visited the encampment of your regiment, sir. The Marshal calls your attention to the obvious danger of this. He asks you for an expression of opinion, and suggests that the men who have associated with the enemy be kept out of the line today."

Drummond laughed grimly.

"The Marshal does not know our Scots," he said. "There is no means of keeping them within rigid lines or under rigid rules. If a Macdonald of Clanranald knows that there is a cousin of his in the opposite camp he is quite likely to pay a visit, for the sake of a drink and a talk. There is no harm in it. My regiment is full of Macdonalds and Stuarts, and there are plenty of both among the enemy. Lord Crawford's regiment on the other side is made up of clansmen who should be with us."

"The Marshal was informed that this visiting back and forth was on a remarkable scale, and that scores of men passed the lines in both directions."

"It is quite possible," said Drummond. He was only thirty, but his expression could be as forbidding as that of a commander twenty years older. "As I have said, these men are relatives. Crawford's regiment—they call it the Black Watch, I believe—is posted at the other end of the line, but even if they came our way there would be no slacking in the fight. The men who were drinking and playing the pipes together last night would kill each other with great fury if they met in battle today. This may seem strange to you, Chevalier, but I am responsible for the regiment."

"Very well, sir," said Mézières.

Drummond suddenly unbent. He had met Mézières in circles that were sacred to all Jacobites.

"I received a letter from Prince Charles last night," he said. "He sends his best wishes to all his friends for this day, and mentioned you among them. When did you see him last?"

"Three weeks ago, in Paris," Mézières said. As in his previous talk with Lord Clare, he dropped the parade manner of the French King's officer and spoke as the eagerness of his years and the freemasonry of the cause demanded. "He was very well and aching to be with us here. The Marshal did not want it."

"The Marshal was right," Drummond said. "It is not here, in Flanders, that the Prince should fight. He must go to Scotland, and by God, Mézières, if we have any luck at all today, he will go to Scotland."

"Scotland?" Mézières echoed. "I know many say so, but I wish it could be England."

"England is a harder nut to crack," Drummond said. "If we could have gone last year, with a French army, when we were all together at Dunkirk, it might have been a different story. But it's Scotland now, or nothing.

How is he living, Mézières? He tells me there are no more supplies from Rome."

"None," Mézières said. "My mother was there not long ago, and says the court refuse to speak of him. It is a sad business."

Drummond swore briefly under his breath.

"They are full of whys and wherefores at Rome," he said. "They think of what the Pope wants, and what the French want, and what the Spanish want, when it's clear that all we any of us need is a chance to fight. Get us a ship and a few men, and perhaps a little money, and we'll set the Prince on shore in Scotland and the rest will take care of itself. King James won't refuse to speak of him then. It's today that will decide, Mézières, it's this very day."

The exultation in his voice showed that he, at any rate, was already sure of the outcome and had passed on to the further certainty of an expedition to Scotland. He was an officer valued in the French army, and had risen through the grades there before he raised his own regiment of Scots; but behind his years of regular service, and the years of devout education at Douai, he remembered the gray walls of Drummond Castle and the misty hills. Like the Irish, some of whom were in the third generation of exile, Drummond and his Scots pinned their hope of a return home to the fortunes of the family that had caused their exile. The obstinacy of this hope, after so many years, struck Mézières afresh, every time he met with it, appealed powerfully to his imagination, filled him with the youthful fervor for a lost cause. His own Jacobitism was a mere sentimental heirloom from his mother's family, a thing of songs and stories and personal attachments, but Drummond's (like Clare's or Dillon's) had the reality of a demand for food, for land and life.

Prince Charles Edward, Mézières was thinking as he rode away: it all depended upon Prince Charles Edward. These men in their thousands would be restored to their homes, or would live the rest of their lives in exile, as the luck or ability of a very young man in a Paris lodging-house might decide. Mézières had been taken to Rome as a child, by his mother, to kneel before King James III and his Queen Maria Clementina in their mimic court; he had met Prince Charles then for the first time, when he was ten and the prince fourteen. The obstinacy of Jacobitism seemed to have affected even the physical character of the Stuarts, for Charles was more strongly Stuart than his father: his Polish mother and Italian grandmother had not altered the inherited type. When Mézières saw him first he was wearing the Stuart tartan —this on a terrace over the roofs of Rome—and although most of the talk around him was in Italian, and his parents called him Carlo or Carluccio, there was no mistaking his nationality.

"You are Mézières," he had said directly. "Do you like to hunt?"

Mézières at the age of ten had not yet developed that taste, but Carluccio had followed foxhounds in the

Roman Campagna since an even earlier age. The "little Italian," as the Hanoverian English called him, seemed to have seized upon everything in his own character and surroundings that could strengthen his connection with the far-off country from which his grandfather had been driven years ago. And now—without a word to his father, the timid and dilatory "King"—he had abandoned Rome, some months before, and taken the road to Paris with intentions that were clear to everybody in Europe. Upon his course would depend the fortunes of many men who had already lost much for his family, and who now, in the later years of an unlucky cause, had hardly anything to lose, everything to regain.

Mézières had seen him often in Paris—lighthearted, impatient, without fear, the perfect rallying point for a desperate enterprise. From the moment he left Rome, "Carluccio" had been launched upon his adventure in the plain view of all Europe. The Hanoverian English watched his every move, reported upon his comings and goings as if he had been a hostile army instead of a single, penniless and inexperienced blade of twenty-four; the Russians, the Prussians and the Spaniards all had their eyes on him; and the French court kept him dangling, now friendly and then cool, as it suited them, while they protested blandly to the English ambassador that they were unaware of the young man's existence. In this long moment of his enterprise—a moment lasting almost a year—Charles Stuart was surrounded by all the romantic nonsense of Jacobite tradition, its disguises and passwords and mystic signals, in the pretense of a secrecy which had long since ceased to exist. In the salons of some French court ladies he was treated like a sovereign, but at the court itself he was not even received. He lived in a Paris lodginghouse most of the time, conspiring twenty-four hours a day, and although the details of the conspiracy changed almost from hour to hour, its general aim was always the same: that expedition of which Drummond had spoken, the invasion of England or Scotland or Ireland which was to restore the Stuarts to their own. To practical politicians like Frederick II, watching this comedy from Berlin with sardonic attention, the whole thing seemed absurd, a groundless fantasy, the invention of another age; to the French ministers it was a possible, but very minor, weapon, which just might be used if it was needed in the world-wide struggle against England. But to the Drummonds and Clares and the other remains of Stuart power, it was the last hope of a cause which even they felt to be lost, and appealed to them all, in its very desperation, as a cry for life in the midst of engulfing death.

Mézières rode back through the Irish and Scots regiments and wondered how many of them would be permitted to go when the time came. They could all be counted upon for their emotional loyalty to the Stuarts, but they were regular regiments of the French line, and could not be detached for such knight-errantry except as the French court might direct. This depended upon the course of the war in Flanders and at sea, in Germany, in

Austria, and beyond the ocean in the Americas and the east. If it seemed advisable to Louis XV's ministers to use the weapon of Jacobitism in a direct attack on England, these Irish and Scots regiments would be the first to go. They understood it well, and thought of the coming invasion as a reward that might be expected for this day's doings. Mézières saluted them monotonously, for the names and faces of many among them were known to him now; they were, in spite of their service under the French flag, Carluccio's army.

"Do you see the fine French aide-de-camp riding on his horse?" said Trooper MacGinnis of Roth's. "That's a friend of Prince Charles, they say, and will be with us when we all go overseas again."

"God bless him," said Trooper O'Sullivan piously. "Could you give us a hand with this bloody firelock, then, and see have I jammed it?"

§

Mézières had been with Carluccio at two of the masked balls at Versailles the winter before, before the campaign started—with Carluccio and with Sullivan, Kelly, Clancarty, Glengarry, and the dozen Irish, Scots and English exiles who surrounded him. Those were among the last festivals of the French monarchy in which the nation wholeheartedly shared; they celebrated the marriage of the Dauphin to a Spanish infanta. Paris was decorated throughout the month of February, and there was dancing in the streets at night, with fireworks and free wine. At one of the masked balls, given on the seventh of February by Mesdames de France, the King's daughters, Charles Stuart had been invited on condition that he did not unmask, and had danced until four in the morning, protected by an incognito that deceived nobody. At the second, the great ball of February 25, he had not been invited, but the same was true of most of the other hundreds of men and women who invaded Versailles from Paris on that night. After the court's supper *à grand couvert* the doors had been opened at the marble staircase and in the chapel courtyard for the masquerade; for this no cards were necessary. The attendants at the two entrances required one person in each party to unmask and give his name; the rest of the party was counted but not named. In this way the Duc de Gramont had taken in Charles Stuart and seven or eight of his friends, including Mézières. They had passed on and lost themselves in the enormous crowd that packed the Grand Gallery and the neighboring rooms. Turks, Armenians, Chinese, Romans, in every extravagance of costume suggested by the taste of the day, chattered, danced, ate and drank in half the salons of the palace, making free with the splendors to which many of them had never penetrated before. It was a mob such as Mézières had never seen at Versailles —a silken and scented mob, good-natured and full of easy enthusiasm, but a mob. The light flashed over their fantastic heads from a million candles, reflected in a thousand mirrors. On one occasion Mézières, who had been pressed into service by the Princesse de Conti, tried to make way for that lady to pass from one room to the next. His failure to do so induced her to remove her mask; her face would clear a way, she thought—as indeed it might; a face of pomp and ceremony, with old eyes hard as diamonds. But she had been completely unrecognized; one or two of the crowding maskers had even the effrontery to laugh.

"It is easy to see," the old lady had said, "what bad company we are in here tonight."

Mézières laughed now when he remembered that incident. But there had been other, less humorous episodes of the crowded evening. It was on that night that he had first heard the name of Mme Lenormant d'Etioles, and had become aware of a new power unfriendly to the interests of Charles Stuart. It had been the matter of ten minutes—ten minutes of movement and byplay at a masked ball, with consequences that still bore upon the destinies of many men.

Mézières was standing with Carluccio at the upper end of the Grand Gallery when the Queen, Dauphin and Dauphine made their entrance. The Queen was unmasked, ablaze with diamonds, her plain Polish face reddened with happiness. Her son, dressed as a gardener, walked beside her; his bride was on her other side, dressed as a flower girl. For this trio the whole assembly came to attention and homage. The Queen made her journey down the gallery and back again; when she had returned to her starting point and taken her chair, Carluccio slipped forward to speak to her in Polish. He did not remove his mask, and she made no sign of recognizing him, but replied in that language which was unknown to all others at Versailles. Mézières saw, heard, and approved. Marie Leczinska had little power at Versailles, but such as she had might be worth conciliating. The Polish vocables crackled in the scented air; it was like a language of horses, Mézières thought; still, to speak it seemed to give the Queen pleasure. At a sign from Carluccio he drifted away and left them to this exercise, in the hope that some good might come of it.

As he moved down the vast room, an aimless spectator, amusing himself by guessing at the identities behind some of the flimsy disguises before him, he came upon a figure he would have recognized in any crowd; it was the long chin and potbelly of Binet, the Dauphin's chief valet. Mézières knew him as most of the youths of the Dauphin's age at Versailles knew him—a grave and worthy personage, devout in religious practices, dignified at all times. On his arm was a delicate white hand, a very youthful hand, which came from the black silken anonymity of a domino beside him. The domino was like a thousand others there tonight, but the white hand that protruded from it was exquisite.

"Ah!" Mézières said. "My friend Binet! Congratulations, sir, congratulations."

Binet, who was dressed in the Versailles version of a

mandarin's costume, with his face powdered yellow beneath his mask, nodded solemnly.

"You may well say so, Chevalier," he said. "Madame, this young man, whom I shall not present to you, is a bad example to all our youth. Mark him and avoid him."

The black silk domino laughed. Mézières could get no glimpse of the lady concealed within it, for her hood was up and her mask on.

"I am maligned," Mézières said. "You know me for a model of virtue, Binet. You are only afraid to present me to your friend."

Binet bowed solemnly. His manner said: move on, move on. But Mézières, stirred to curiosity, dawdled awhile.

"Come, Binet," he said, "you know everything. Tell me, which of all these masks is the King? Or is the King here? I have been wondering."

"So have many others," said Binet stiffly. "I am afraid I am unable to inform you, Chevalier."

Mézières saw the white fingers of the young hand tighten a little on Binet's Chinese silk sleeve. What was old Binet doing with a lovely lady whose identity had to be so thoroughly concealed? The black domino stood close to the mandarin, as if for protection.

"You are not kind tonight, Monsieur Binet," Mézières said, bowing. "But you still have my congratulations."

He looked boldly into the eyes of the mask beneath the black hood as he passed on. The blue eyes that looked back at him were brilliant with excitement or fear. He had not taken three more steps before his elbow was lightly touched and a familiar voice whispered at his ear.

"Dangerous company, Eugène," the voice said. "Very dangerous company. The lady is not for you."

He turned to face a veiled sultana whose brown eyes, much blackened at the edges, were laughing at him over folds of white gauze.

"Solange!" he said.

"Do you know who the lady is?" the sultana asked.

"No. Do you?"

"I shall tell you her name, my young friend. Put your head down. Closer. Closer. She is called Madame Le-nor-mant d'E-ti-oles. Madame Le-nor-mant d'E-ti-oles. Does that mean anything to you?"

"Nothing whatever. I never heard the name before."

"Remember it. You will hear it again."

"Why, Solange? You are making mysteries. I only looked at her because she was with Binet, and because she was so completely hidden under her domino. She has a pretty hand."

"No doubt," the sultana said dryly. "I believe she has many points of beauty. They are not for you, however. You must console yourself with your Solange, for the moment."

Mézières smiled down at the sultana.

"That will be easy, Madame," he said. "Above all since I have nothing to console myself for."

"You can always be depended upon for a doubtful

compliment, my dear. Ah! Here we are! Now we shall see something!"

She took Mézières's arm and pressed it, directing her own gaze, and with it his, to the gallery on the opposite side of the room. The mirrored doors there had just opened to admit an extraordinary procession of figures: eight yew trees trimmed into the peaked shape familiar in the Versailles gardens. They were all exactly alike, and at first from this distance, they all looked like genuine trees set in motion. A second look was needed to discern the black masks amid the foliage, the arms that moved beside it.

The yew trees filed out and stood for a moment looking down at the crowd. Applause and laughter greeted them, and then a long, low murmur of sound, the murmur of hundreds of voices saying in undertones what Solange now said to Mézières: "They come from the King's apartments. One of them must be the King."

The eight yew trees paused for a moment to enjoy the sensation their entrance had made. Every pair of eyes in the room turned towards them and sought to distinguish one among them, but in vain: their costumes were so cunningly devised, and the men beneath the foliage were so much of the same size, that the eight remained, even in movement, exactly alike. They turned and came down the stairs to the ballroom in solemn procession, and the crowd surged towards them. There was great laughter and some cheering.

"Watch closely," Solange said. "See what becomes of your pretty domino now."

Mézières stood back against the wall with the sultana while the crowd moved towards the eight yew trees. He knew now what she meant, and wondered a little to see the grave, devout Binet employed on such an errand. Binet and his mysterious black domino (Mme Lenormant d'Etioles? the name was unknown) stood motionless for a little and then drifted slowly, with the rest of the crowd, towards the yew trees. The yew trees were separating. One had already found a lady and was taking her to the other end of the Grand Gallery to dance. Another had stopped to talk with a friend; two or three were exchanging quips with the crowd. The others were swept apart by the press of people, lost into the mob, but lost with a difference; for wherever there was a yew tree there were at least two or three ladies bent upon conquest. What Solange had said was accepted by all there as the truth—one of these yew trees must be Louis XV.

Mézières watched the fate of the yew trees with the interest of a courtier and the contempt of a very youthful philosopher. These women of Versailles, he was thinking —what a shameless lot they were! There was hardly one of them who would not lie, steal, break vows and submit to any indignity for the privilege that was called "the King's favor." When that favor, bestowed with a semi-marital monogamy, was shifted from one to another of the ladies, there was an agitation over the whole country, a stirring and a restlessness throughout the administration, for "the King's favor" was the source of all power, and every appointment depended upon it. These symptoms were still as nothing to what they were to become, for the King was only thirty-five and his open adultery was still too recent to have grown into a system of government. He had, in fact, publicly declared only three of his liaisons, those with the Mailly-Nesle sisters. Of that strange harem dynasty the eldest, Mme de Mailly, was now forgotten in her convent; Mme de Vintimille and Mme de Châteauroux were dead. The court remembered all too well how the two who were now dead had cracked the whip: Mme de Vintimille with her thirst for military adventure and high politics, Mme de Châteauroux with her desire for power in all things, great and small. The emotions of the Châteauroux reign were recent in all memories. It was only six months since Louis XV, falling desperately ill at Metz, had become reconciled to religion, sent Mme de Châteauroux away, confessed and received Communion, to the horror of all those at Versailles who did not belong to the devout circle of the Queen and the Dauphin. His reformation had not long outlasted his illness: he was dying in the odor of sanctity in August, but by November, when he returned to Paris to be acclaimed as "Louis the Well-Beloved" by his delirious subjects, he was already prepared to recall Mme de Châteauroux to her functions at court. Death was quicker: Mme de Châteauroux had been seized of a fever in early December and died before she could see Versailles again. That was little more than two months ago, and since then not a day had passed without its crop of rumors. Such an interregnum could not long endure: the King must have a mistress, and every clique at Versailles had its own candidate for that exalted position. The efforts made by grave men of affairs to put forward their female relatives did credit to their patriotism. The industry of the Duc de Richelieu, who was uncle to the Mailly-Nesle sisters and claimed responsibility for their good fortune, had never been more assiduously employed; the ladies themselves were not backward in displaying their charms; but the interregnum continued. There were still two Mailly-Nesle sisters to be conscripted, Mme de Flavacourt and Mme de Lauraguais, but time passed, and neither was installed in the official place at Versailles. Stories of the King's adventures in Paris were circulated: he had taken to going to the public balls, meeting many women not of the court. It was said that his nature, so secretive, shy and tortured by boredom, had had enough of duchesses—that the new mistress, whoever she was to be, would come from some unexpected place, and would owe everything to him. There were persistent rumors of unknown women seen at Versailles, women of the bourgeoisie, even women of the people. No courtier could soberly suppose that Louis XV would install a woman of the inferior classes in the palace as his avowed mistress, and yet some such enormity seemed to grow steadily more possible as time passed and the court ladies—crippled as they were in every act of life by considerations of rank, precedence and etiquette, and weighed down, moreover, by the greed of innumerable relations—obtained from him nothing better than a yawn. Somebody totally new, somebody who had perhaps never seen Versailles before, and would be immune to the fearful jealousies of rank and family, might seize upon this vacant moment and turn it to lasting advantage; that was the possibility that hung over the whole assembly, tonight as for weeks past, like a threat.

"Don't waste time dreaming of your black domino," Solange said to Mézières. "You will see what becomes of her."

And indeed she seemed directed by Binet with purposive insistence towards one particular eddy in the crowd, an eddy in the midst of which one yew tree stood as if waiting. It was done in another moment: Binet and his companion reached the yew tree. The crowd closed about them; when Mézières, eagerly standing on tiptoe, glimpsed Binet again he was alone.

"The yew tree has gone," he said aloud, "and so has the black domino."

"Only to dance," said Solange wisely. "They will vanish altogether soon."

Mézières looked down at her and speculated.

"You know a great deal about everything, Solange," he said. "How did you acquire such a wealth of knowledge?"

"The lady has friends," Solange said, her brown eyes

wicked over the folds of gauze. "Surely you have learned by this time that I also have friends?"

She directed Mézières's gaze again by a look, and he saw the yew tree and the black domino again—for the last time that night. They were passing through a doorway at the further end of the great gallery; now they were seen no more.

It was then that the damage was done—so quickly that at the moment it seemed nothing; Mézières did not think of it until weeks later when some of its consequences became apparent. As he stood there with Solange, wondering why she had seemed so lovely to him only a year before, he saw that Carluccio had come some distance down into the room and was beckoning for him.

"You must excuse me for a moment, Solange," he said, "I am being summoned."

Carluccio in the black velvet of an Italian Renaissance courtier was waiting.

"Mézières," he said in the conspiratorial tones developed by his daily adventures, "you stopped and spoke with Binet and a lady. Who was that lady?"

"I do not know her, Monseigneur. I believe her name is Madame Lenormant d'Etioles. That is what I have just been told."

"Thank you," said Prince Charles. "Amuse yourself if you can."

He turned and made his way back to the head of the great gallery, where Marie Leczinska was still sitting; he must have left her side only a moment before. Mézières watched him return to her, still masked, and bend down to speak. The Queen's heavy face reddened slightly as she listened.

That was the moment of the damage, Mézières thought —when Carluccio, having learned the name of Mme Lenormant d'Etioles, repeated it at once to the Queen: this on the night when Mme Lenormant d'Etioles entered Versailles, and, according to some of the stories, the King's bed, for the first time. There was no doubt in anybody's mind before the evening was over that the King had been one of the eight yew trees, and that that particular yew tree had soon vanished from the scene in charming company. It might have been left to other, even busier tattlers, to repeat the tale to the Queen. It was Charles Stuart's bad luck, his incurable venturesome meddling, that made him the first to repeat what was to become public knowledge a few days later. All through March and April the name of Mme Lenormant grew steadily more familiar, until it seemed that the very curtains at Versailles murmured it in their rustling. Carluccio might have waited before casting his voice on the losing side, the side of Marie Leczinska, the Dauphin and the Jesuits, in a contest against the powers of youth, beauty and love. Mme Lenormant had those powers on her side, as all now knew; and although she had not yet been officially installed at Versailles, it was only a question of time, and very little time at that; she would soon be there. On this very day, May the eleventh, when the army was to engage in an action of first importance, every officer in it knew that the first news of that battle would go straight from the King to Mme Lenormant d'Etioles. So much had become clear since the night of the masked ball at Versailles.

Mézières, as he rode along through the last of the Irish lines, pondered on the bad luck and bad judgment of Charles Stuart, and saw again the glittering confusion of the great gallery on that night, and the dark figure of the masked prince bending to speak, and the trimmed yew tree and the black domino vanishing through a doorway. These were the meaningless misfortunes, the pointless little catastrophes with an unending chain of consequences; men might die in shoals for this, or starve or grow weary of life, because an enmity had been aroused that need not have been aroused at all. This Mme Lenormant—Mézières had caught a glimpse of her once afterwards and thought her exquisite—would soon have, if she had not already, more control of the acts of men, many men, than the ministers in the King's council. She could hurl armies, perhaps, with that small white hand Mézières had admired on Binet's arm, but she would never hurl them for Charles Stuart.

§

The army was formed in a deep crescent, almost a triangle, the apex of which was near the village of Fontenoy, with wings resting on Barry Wood at the left and

the town of Antoing on the right. It was a position classically correct, classically chosen, surveyed and reinforced for a classical battle in open country. Indeed its
main lines had been drawn up thirteen years before by
today's commander, Maurice de Saxe, in his *Rêveries*,
and by awaiting the Anglo-Hanoverian-Dutch army in
this place he was obeying all his most cherished maxims
—leaving nothing to chance, taking every advantage of
country and numbers, giving battle only when the probability of victory was strong. The Irish regiments held the
left of the line, with the Royal Corsicans at their extreme
left, behind Barry Wood; next, mounting towards the
apex of the triangle, came the Swiss Guards and the
French Guards; the center—the curving apex of the triangle, the middle of the crescent—was held by some of
the best infantry regiments in the French army, those of
Courten, Aubeterre, Dauphin, Beauvoisis and Diesbach;
beyond the curve, down in a straight line to Antoing and
the river Scheldt, were two dragoon regiments, the regiment of Biron, and the Piedmontese. Behind the wall of
men thus formed, in straight lines filling the plain, were
the household troops, bodyguards and cavalry regiments,
the gayest of the pennons and the richest of the uniforms: Fiennes, Fitzjames, Clermont, Brancas, Maison
du Roi, Gardes du Roi, Mousquetaires. In that vast body
of cavalry and consequence, great names and gold lace,
there were far more officers than would have been
needed for an army twice the size; there were five
princes of the blood royal, with their suites, two cabinet

ministers, a handful of marshals and lieutenant generals, and the King himself with the Dauphin and a horde of aides-de-camp, courtier-soldiers, cooks, chaplains and valets. The dead weight of hundreds of spectators and critics was stored away on that plain; Mézières, as he rode back from Barry Wood, saw the flash and glitter of their first movements in the early morning light and groaned. In that splendid incubus lay the weakness of the army.

After he had passed through the Swiss and French guards Mézières cut down into the plain to reach the field headquarters of the Marshal. He passed through Fitz-james' Horse—a regiment of Irish, Scots and English Jacobites—and back across the lines of French cavalry to the position the Marshal had fixed upon, behind the village of Fontenoy on the Antoing side. As he drew near that nerve center of the army, the proportion of red-heeled and gold-laced aides increased: the ducal do-nothings were busy, galloping from the Marshal to the King and back again. Lines were drawn carefully here, and broad lanes were kept free for the passage of wagons and messengers. Mézières was kept constantly saluting, and although he had all the young soldier's contempt for the red heels of Versailles, his face did not lose its pre-ternatural gravity. Before the Marshal's tent, a sturdy canvas affair with carpets and silk hangings inside, there clustered a great hum and buzz of officers, half of them in and half of them out of the fore part of the tent which served as anteroom. Mézières saw his man, Valfons, one of the Marshal's most competent aides, and went up to him to report.

Maurice de Saxe had spent the preceding night at the Charterhouse on the Scheldt, outside of Tournai. Rising at three in the morning, he had crossed the river and come down to this tent, his field headquarters, where he had taken to his bed again for an hour. He was suffering from dropsy, from fatigue, and above all from the anxiety brought on by the presence of innumerable self-appointed experts and carpet soldiers from Versailles. He had done his best to prevent the King from being present at the campaign, and had failed: Louis XV had suddenly taken it into his head to make a showing as a warrior, for the sake of his new charmer or out of a hitherto unsuspected vanity, and no cautious warnings could deter him. With him had come all the ragtag and bobtail of the court, and the Marshal, who was already beset by the jealousies and pretensions of a much too noble staff, found his most careful plans endangered every hour. He was not in the best of humors, had slept badly for nights past, and was more fully aware than anybody else in the army of the extent to which his entire military career depended upon the outcome of this day.

Maurice was forty-nine years old now, and his soldier's mind was rich in theory and practice, but he had never commanded an army in open battle before. He had seen open battles in his first youth, when he served under Prince Eugène against the same French regiments that he now commanded. He had fought in many a skirmish and hand-to-hand fight from Flanders to Russia and back again, had conducted siege and defense, march and countermarch, and taken his part in actions under the orders of other men; but the full-dress battle, the play for mighty stakes, had never been his to order as he willed until today.

It was his principle, of course, to avoid battles. He held that the best campaign, the most successful, was the one in which fighting and loss of life had been most skillfully avoided. He believed that the same advantages could be obtained by strategic moves without risking the lives of many men. But when a battle became necessary —as it now was, with the Anglo-Hanoverian-Dutch army bearing down to the relief of Tournai—it was his system to seize upon every conceivable favoring circumstance, to put the enemy in every possible aspect of inferiority, so that the outcome was as certain as anything depending upon human beings could be. His system of thought was far removed from the aristocratic notions of "chivalry" which obsessed a good many of the boudoir soldiers around him, and it made him impatient and angry to hear the scented dukes, fresh from their conquests at Versailles, talk in terms borrowed from the romances of the court.

"Pig-dogs," he would call them when he spoke to his valet, or to his friend Löwendal the Dane, or to any of the intimates with whom he caroused liberally when the necessities of his position permitted.

For he was gross and lewd, was Maurice, according to

the standards of the people among whom he found himself now; he liked what was called "low company," and enjoyed himself more with strolling players, prostitutes, ordinary soldiers, Germans, Swedes and the like, than with the ladies and gentlemen who held rank at Versailles. He had never learned to speak or write with easy correctness in any language, and although his long association with Adrienne Lecouvreur had given him some acquaintance with the French classics, at least for the theater, so that he could quote Racine, Corneille and Voltaire at length, his culture hardly went deeper than that: he could never spell the simplest sentence through without errors, and had found no time to read since his first youth. True, he had written a great deal—he had gifts for expression, and kept up an enormous correspondence for years—but always without regard for the elegancies of his adopted country. In fact, those elegancies had come to be associated in his mind with the bowing and scraping, the meanness and bad faith of the Versailles courtiers, so that he scorned the one with the other, and a good many of his bizarre misspellings and bits of bad grammar seemed half deliberate, as if he were thumbing his nose at the whole civilization into which he had been transplanted.

As he lay on his bed now, swollen to shapelessness with dropsy, and gasping sometimes with the pain of it, his blue eyes alone kept the cold fire of his youth. His big nose, flattened at the end, was red now, and his square, protruding jaw had a burden of flesh about it. The cold, relentless, daring and unconquerable eyes were the same. With those eyes he had turned Adrienne's blood to water, years before, and whipped the country squires of Courland into obedience to his will; Elizabeth Petrovna and many others had been afraid of their incandescence; in the decay of his body the eyes retained the bladelike flash of power, so that one who had known him twenty years before would have acknowledged them when everything else had become unrecognizable. They were the eyes of eager appetite, unyielding, thrustful will, restless and exploring ambition: the eyes of a King's bastard forever looking for a throne. If he had been born within the halo of a wedding ring—brought up, like his brother of Saxony, in the easy comfort of legitimacy, with a future arranged at birth—he might have lasped into the simple swinishness that was native to part of his character; food, drink, and companions without pretense, the requirements of a great deal of his nature, would have been enough, perhaps, to dull even his talent for generalship. But he had been brought up as a King's son without the rank or income of a King's son; he had lived in a court without a set position there; he was immensely conspicuous from birth, having been "recognized" as one of his brood of bastards by old King Augustus, but derived from his position only the bitterness of poverty without its obscurity, the discomfort of greatness without its power. When he remembered Dresden now, it was without affection or nostalgia. He had been intensely unhappy there—and the drinking or fighting to which he was driven by the rebellion of his temperament had only brought him fresh disgrace. He was expected to behave like a prince, a proper and dutiful prince, although every privilege or responsibility of a prince had been taken from him. He was expected at the same time to be grateful for any small favor that was bestowed upon him by his father's grace, since bastards, after all, had no legal claim; and between the two extremes of these contentions, the dutiful prince and the nameless bastard, he had lost whatever equilibrium he might have had by nature. He had become "wild," as his father said—"that wild man"—chasing over Europe in search of a place, a position, at best (and he strove hard for it) a throne; offering his sword to this one and that one, his person (which was desirable) to whatever lady could best advance his cause; until he had so embroiled the affairs of eastern Europe that his father was glad to buy him a regiment in France and settle him into the French service by way of amends. This was the best Augustus of Saxony and Poland had ever managed to do for his "wild" son, and that was years ago. Maurice today, although he obstinately kept to the Lutheran religion, because it was his mother's (had she not died, at last, in a Lutheran convent?) and retained some use of the German language with his intimates, called himself a Frenchman. It was Adrienne who had made a Frenchman of him.

He was accounted a bold, loose and heartless man with women, taking them and throwing them away, concerned less with their own feelings in the matter than with the feelings of the calf that was slaughtered to make his dinner. And yet he had loved Adrienne, not only in the first ardor of their insatiable youth, but afterwards, when her passion and her disease were combining to waste her life away, and he had turned to a variety of other charmers, and she wrote six letters to his one; from those later days, when the actress and her faithless lover had become the fable of the court, and Paris was alive with stories of her misfortunes, he had kept every one of her despairing letters. He, who kept nothing else at all, kept these yellowing sheets of paper, each one of which was a cry of the misery of love—touched up, it is true, with the language of the theater, with literary conventions and rhetoric, but with the heartbeat in them still, distinct and painful: kept them, and sometimes even read them.

At night when the pain kept him awake he could see Adrienne in the darkness still, now and then, and could feel the hot rush of her tears. He did not speak of her, but her shadow came sometimes between him and the almost innumerable women (actresses, court ladies, prostitutes, among whom his indifference made no choice or preference) who succeeded each other in his bed. His extraordinary brutality with women was due most of all to the vividness with which two among them, his mother and Adrienne, had impressed themselves upon his sluggish imagination. He had been loved by two women with the utmost fanatical devotion: Aurora von Königsmarck in her convent, centering every wish of her earthly existence upon him, and Adrienne in her theater, the incarnation of all the ill-fated heroines of poetry, flinging her live heart and her burning genius beneath his heavy feet. He had been loved by Phèdre, by Iphigénie, by Electra (the Electra of Crébillon, but still Electra); his mind would have had to be far more brutal than it was to survive the experience unchanged. His speech and writing, coarse, illiterate though they were, were filled to the end with poetic allusions, scraps of plays and bits of verse, in every one of which an attentive ear could hear the far-off accent of Adrienne. He kept a troupe of players constantly with him in the army, and often seized, in these field performances by strolling comedians, some hint of the tragic voice and noble gesture of the past. For the rest, he took his pleasures in the simplest animal fashion, an oafish and unthinking brute, and wanted no others. When he was asked why he did not marry, he said: "A wife is not suitable furniture for a soldier." As time went on he grew to dislike the company or even the embraces of "ladies", and to confine himself more and more to the poor and uncultivated women, obscure provincial actresses or prostitutes, who were prepared to accept him as they found him. He was forty-nine years old, and Adrienne—the rare and noble Adrienne, whose like could not appear more than once in a century—had been dead for fifteen years. She had died in his arms, with M. de Voltaire on the other side of the bed to take careful note of it, and had been hurried away by night to an unknown grave. Her frail human body, burning with love and tuberculosis, had been destroyed with quick-lime, lest the people of Paris (who worshiped her) might dig her out again to find if she had been poisoned or murdered. So, in a dark storm of rumors and accusations, she had made her departure, and by this time the prudent silence of her friends and enemies had caused her to be very nearly forgotten. Except by M. de Voltaire, that is, who forgot nothing; and by the faithful D'Argental, who had loved her without return; and, on sleepless nights, or in the theater, or at moments which recalled the fading magic of his youth, by Maurice.

Last night, in his cell at the Charterhouse of Tournai, he had hardly slept at all. The hideous discomfort of his disease would have been enough to keep him awake, without the thought of the coming day's battle, with every detail of the arrangements he had so carefully drawn up for its conduct. He was well aware that this was to be, in all probability, the great day of his life, the day upon which he would prove or disprove, once for all, the genius that had been so liberally attributed to him by his friends for twenty-five years. He regarded this as an irony of injustice, since generalship was to be shown as much by avoiding battles as by winning them, and yet his practical mind, the mind of a realist, conceded that such was the way of the world. If he won this day he would be the hero of France, a glory of Europe, his new Marshal's baton gilded with victory; if he lost he would be the Saxon bastard again, the nameless adventurer, and could take the road to the east, unregretted. He had no

doubt which it would be. He would win. He had been
preparing for this battle for all the forty-nine years of his
life, and everything he knew of war and men would go
into it. Once, when he had been half asleep for a few
minutes, he woke suddenly to the thought of Aurora and
Adrienne. How proud they would have been, he thought,
Aurora in her convent and Adrienne in her theater! Both
had spoken a great deal of "glory," had urged him upon
the courses of fame and conquest; Aurora had dreamed
of nothing else since his birth, and Adrienne, although
she valued him chiefly as her lover, had recognized and
fed the necessities of his ambition. She had been proud
of him, too, although she made reiterant passionate pro-
test against everything that took him away from her;
illogically, she rejoiced in his fame and begrudged him
the long absences in which he won it; she would have
had reason for pride in the coming day. For a moment
he seemed to see the two women together, as they had
never been in life—the lovely, quiet face of Aurora in her
nun's habit, and Adrienne's unhappy splendor in a
theater dress covered with diamonds. Of the two, he
could see now, Aurora had been much the more beautiful. Adrienne was not beautiful, but she burned and trem-
bled with a life somehow intensified, so that her voice
and eyes and the movements of her long hands quick-
ened the pulses of those who beheld them. For a moment
he seemed to see Aurora and Adrienne together, looking
at each other across the space in which his huge, uncom-
fortable body now lay, and in their very different ways

they smiled at each other, as they had never smiled in life. But that was gone in a moment, and he wondered at his own fancy; for they were dead, both dead, and had been dead for fifteen years. They had died in the same year, and he had never seen them together like this in life or in death. He supposed it was one of the oddities of insomnia, and due to his disease, upon which he bestowed a few vigorous German curses as he turned painfully in his bed.

But when he turned towards the wall, and closed his eyes, and tried again to sleep, he seemed to hear their two voices speaking in quiet, unmoved, friendly tones, as they had never spoken in life. He heard them at first as two familiar sounds, intermingled, two sweetly familiar sounds.

"Damn me," he said aloud, "that's Adrienne." And "Damn me, that's my mother."

He stirred and groaned, and for a little while the voices were unheard. But just as he was drifting off to his half-sleep again (he had had no real sleep for many days and nights) they reached his ears, the gentle voices of the women who had loved him.

"Madame," Adrienne said, in the melancholy, penetrating tone he could never forget, "I know how much you have given for this day. I have not given so much, but believe me, I am also deeply concerned. I would have given as much as you if I had lived."

"You gave more, Madame," Aurora's gentle voice replied. "Each of us gave a good deal. We gave our lives.

Yours was a greater gift because there was no reason for your love except love."

"Damn me," said Maurice aloud, "I am going crazy."

He turned over again, carefully, painfully, every inch of his bloated flesh threatening to burst as he shifted it. He opened his eyes wide. The cell was bare, empty and dark.

Adrienne and Aurora, Aurora and Adrienne.

Suddenly the tears came into his eyes for no reason and flowed, for one moment, as from a spring. He cursed heartily as he rubbed his eyes with the back of his hand. How many years had it been since he had wept? He could hear the two voices again, fading as they spoke, as if their owners were retreating slowly from the dark cell.

"Do not weep, Maurice," Adrienne said. And Aurora said: "Do not weep, Maurice."

He turned his head against the pillow and blubbered, for some minutes, like a child.

When the fit had passed he was quite calm, and the thought of Adrienne and Aurora left him. He began to consider the question of the redoubts. Would it not have been better to build one more redoubt near the Mons Road? The position was difficult, much too difficult for a rational commander to attack, and yet he was persuaded by experience that the English might, in fact, attack just here where they could never be expected. Upon the more open positions all around the crescent from Fontenoy to Antoing he had lavished the best efforts of his best engineers. The redoubts and entrench-

ments there constituted a position which he did not believe any army now effective in Europe could possibly
take. There had been one weak point, but the keen eyes
of that Irishman, Lally-Tollendal, had detected it in time.
He reflected for one moment about Lally, with whom he
had many characteristics in common. Twenty years ago
he had been rather like Lally, all fire and fury, but he had
always possessed a fund of common sense which seemed
lacking in the Irishman. Lally was, in fact, not much
younger than himself (what were six years?) but Lally
had his limbs, his strength, his youthful agility. Maurice
could feel every part of his own stuffed and unwieldy
body aching against the hard pallet. When he remembered what he had been like twenty years ago he groaned
aloud. He had been able to make the cork ooze out of a
bottle by pounding it on the bottom with his bare hand;
he had been able to hold his body out straight from the
jamb of a door; he had been able to outride and outwalk
and outfight and outfornicate any of the roisterers of
Paris when he first came there, in the roistering days of
the Regent. Well, he was now a Marshal of France, commander in chief; in twenty-four hours, perhaps, the hero
of Europe—and the Regent, well, the Regent, too, was
dead.

Maurice speculated briefly about hell, a district which,
if it existed at all, the Regent must now be honoring with
his presence. By whatever creed you estimated him, God
could certainly have very little traffic with the Regent.
And yet, as Maurice remembered fleetingly, he was a

man of charm and wit; he was damned good company, better than a pot-faced Jesuit any day.

The question of that other redoubt bothered him. He shifted and groaned, groaned and shifted. Would this young fool Cumberland drive his Englishmen through that one impossible place, where no redoubt had been built because no redoubt was necessary?

What did he know about Cumberland? Nothing much. Twenty-four years old; fat as a pig already; a fierce disciplinarian, hanging men in numbers because they stole a hen or robbed a baker's shop. Maurice had no great love for that fat family from Hanover which now governed England. A gross, thieving, murderous lot they were, in his opinion, and although he had no personal reasons for saying so, his family tradition in the matter was clear. His own uncle, Philip von Königsmarck, had been foully murdered in the night at Hanover as he was about to visit his mistress, the Electress Sophie. No clear evidence had been brought to light, but George, the Elector, afterwards George I of England, was held to be guilty of that deed. Maurice sometimes wondered if it were possible, for George (like the rest of his family) was lazy, fat, voluptuous, self-indulgent, perhaps too lazy and gross to mind what lovers his wife had. Somebody, anyhow, had murdered Philip von Königsmarck, and had afterwards locked his despairing mistress up for thirty years. Aurora, Philip's sister, had filled Europe with her lamentations, and had gone from court to court demanding aid and vengeance; she had visited the court of Augustus II once too often on this mission, and Maurice was the result. Maurice had been taught to hate the Hanover family, and did so, in a good-natured way; but he often wondered whether he would have existed at all if they had not driven his mother out to beg for aid against them. Now, at any rate, the fat people from Hanover had prospered exceedingly. The son of that unlucky Sophie, Königsmarck's mistress, now governed England as George II; her grandson, Frederick II, was King of Prussia; another grandson was this same twenty-four-year-old Duke of Cumberland whom Maurice was to meet in battle tomorrow. The breed was weak in brain and character, strong in sheer, naked luck. Well, Maurice had his luck, too; and twenty-five years more of life than young Cumberland—a life so tumultuous that it counted for ten of any ordinary princeling's. These legitimate princes, he thought suddenly, these pampered favorites of destiny——

The thought made him grind his teeth and curse again, for he had remembered the worst, the very worst examples of that kind, the French princes of the blood. They afflicted him like gadflies, like physical pains and aches, like a swarm of insects. The less important they were the more they claimed the privileges of importance; the farther removed from the throne, the more insistent upon its prerogative. Clermont and Penthièvre and the like—Maurice could not think of them calmly. Some of them owed their rank as "princes of the blood" to the illegal fancies of Louis XIV, imperious and doting in his old age, determined to make his bastards rank above all subjects and directly beneath the royal family itself. This subterfuge was not to the taste of Maurice, especially when he was required to give its beneficiaries the tributes of respect which had been denied to him. But even the others, those of the Condé and Conti branches of the Bourbon family, were offensive enough in their pretensions, requiring the commander in chief of the army to call upon them, demanding a rank and state in the field which made their presence a perpetual encumbrance. Without its King and princes, without its highest nobles and without its general dependence upon Versailles, the French army would be, Maurice considered, the best in Europe. It was weighted down at the top, made immobile by an excess of splendor. He groaned when he reflected—as he did a thousand times a day—that his most careful arrangements, his most exactly planned systems of defense and attack, might be upset at any moment by the foolhardy intervention of some princeling whose only claim to consideration was that his father or grandfather or great-grandfather had been a King's son.

Maurice's legs moved in the bed like painful great bolsters. They were fat with water. His arms themselves were scarcely more at ease; and his body, his vast, shapeless body, was wrapped round with layer upon layer of the dreadful bloating blisters of his disease. He was old. Adrienne was dead and Aurora was dead. He was forty-nine, and at forty-nine other men might be young; but Maurice was old. When he went to sleep at last the tears had dampened his pillow a little—suddenly, for no reason, as he thought of the day that was coming, the great day of his life, of the wretched ruin of a body that he brought to it, and of the women who had loved him; of Adrienne and of the smile on her face.

§

The Marshal's tent was the gathering place for all such elements in the upper ranks of the officers as wished to curry favor, observe, carry tales or urge recommendations —as well as of those others (a minority) who had regular business there. The big silken anteroom was never without its crowd of courtiers and hangers-on, for the military system of the time permitted many an officer to hold high rank without definite duties, without troops to command or a station to encumber. Among them, as Valfons took Mézières through the crowd, were the Duc de Richelieu, the Maréchal de Noailles and some of the greatest nobles in the kingdom; for the word had gone round, only that morning at the break of day, that the King was determined to give the Marshal full and unquestioned command in the coming battle. More than ever in his life before, Maurice de Saxe was in favor, and the dignitaries of Versailles were willing to pay their court to him this day before the King himself.

Richelieu was the great dandy, the peerless exquisite, of the day, and carried his vanities even on to the battlefield. He had regular, small features, of which the nose and chin were to sharpen with time; his eyes, wrists, ankles and calves were his pride, and he directed attention to them by every artifice known to the valets of Versailles. His face was painted and powdered as thickly as any lady's, and his large blue eyes were surrounded by the black pencil marks of mascara. His white chin was decorated by a small, star-shaped patch of court plaster, a *mouche de toilette,* either to hide a spot or to exhibit the whiteness of the surrounding skin. His dress was rich in the extreme, and he wore decorations in diamonds; one of his ears, in the fashion of an earlier day, was ornamented with a heavy diamond ring. His conquests among the ladies were innumerable, for such extravagances in dress and toilet were held to enhance, rather than to detract from, his masculine charm. He was immensely vain, gossipy, malicious, pretentious and unprincipled; he had personally arranged the supply of his nieces to the bed of Majesty, and gloried in it; he was director of the masques and pageants of Versailles, and fancied himself not only as an arbiter of elegance and squire of dames, but as soldier, poet and philosopher. In none of these capacities had he shown a trace of talent, but he had looks, fortune and a great name; best of all, he had the royal favor; and with such advantages talent was unnecessary. He might almost have been invented to impersonate (with a shade of caricature) the dominant character of the regime—glittering frivolity and incompetence supported upon the serfdom of a nation.

Richelieu was talking.

"I told the Marshal," he said, "that I did not agree with his choice of regiments for the first line. I told him frankly. Some attention must be paid to the rank and traditions of the army . . . The cavalry is the main thing. All this emphasis upon infantry and artillery is new and strange to us, foreign to the genius of our military establishment. We shall see whether I am not to be proved right. Give me an open field and a cavalry charge. That's what I said to him. All this trench building and redoubt building and artillery preparation—it's of a piece with the other innovations the dear Marshal has wished upon us. Like his other invention, marching in cadence. Now who ever heard of such a thing? Turning the infantry regiments into a sort of machine, one-two-three-four! Ridiculous, my dear sir, ridiculous. Turenne, Condé, Henri IV—they never heard of it; search our history and all history, and you will find no record of such a thing as marching in cadence. Go on back to Julius Caesar and you won't find it. I tell you, the Marshal is a genius of some species, we all concede that; he is full of ideas and knows his profession pretty well; but his passion for innovations will be the death of us. It isn't only the army that is affected, either. The whole nation must in time be affected, to the point of disloyalty, by this insistence on ordinary infantry and artillery methods. Where are the nobles of France? In the cavalry. And for all the use the Marshal makes of us, we might as well not exist. Oh, yes, I know he uses us at times, but he invariably bases his action upon the other arms, not upon us. I told him frankly that I did not agree with these conceptions. I am not one to conceal an opinion."

From the diamond in his ear to the high red heels on his shoes, Richelieu shook with unaccustomed seriousness. In the ordinary traffic of his life—court ceremonies, social assemblies, and the bedrooms of the ladies—he was no fool; he even had a kind of wit—enough, that is, to make malicious epigrams and clever compliments. But when he attacked a subject demanding thought in its soberer forms, a comprehension of principle or basic theory, he became supremely, lucidly foolish. Even the officers who now clustered about him, although they were too conscious of his position at court to evaluate his mind with any exactness, grew uneasy beneath the flow of his speech.

"The Marshal is a very great soldier," one of them murmured, avoiding Richelieu's eyes.

"Certainly, certainly," Richelieu said. "But can he be as great a soldier as Condé or Turenne? That is obviously impossible. And unless he were a greater general than either of them, why should he be permitted to interfere with their principles of campaign? You understand that there is nobody in this army more devoted to the Marshal than I am. I think I may say that he would not be a Marshal today if I had not shared the common opinion of his merit. But he has brought ideas into this army which do not accommodate themselves to our tradition. We have not seen the last of it, either. These changes will lead very far."

There was a gleam of amusement in more than one pair of eyes just then. M. de Richelieu in the role of prophet was a novelty indeed. He might have continued to air his opinions almost indefinitely, for he was in a rarely earnest and public-spirited frame of mind; but at this moment a stir among the officers nearest the door to the inner tent notified the company that some of the Marshal's early callers were leaving. It was, in fact, the Marquis d'Argenson, Minister for Foreign Affairs, who had overcome his dislike for Maurice de Saxe enough to pay him a visit of ceremony thus soon after the dawn. D'Argenson smiled at Richelieu: for the brilliant fop, in spite of his shortcomings as a philosopher, had the trick of ingratiating himself with most people, and had taken some pains to ensure D'Argenson's regard. The company stirred, moved restlessly, and reformed again in other groups; Richelieu had been summoned to the inner tent as D'Argenson left.

D'Argenson moved like a man of weight and consequence. Slowly, smiling to left and right, with a careful judiciousness in the rationing of his smiles, he made his way through the antechamber and on to the open plain encumbered with the tents and bivouacs of an army. A broad lane had been made through the army, passable for carriages, and the Minister's carriage and footmen waited near the Marshal's tent. D'Argenson stood and surveyed the scene in the early morning light while his carriage drew up to receive him. The whole plain and the small hillsides to the left were alive with men; there were tents and bivouacs all the way down to the river Scheldt on the right. There had been a pearly mist over this lower plain since the dawn, but the sun was coming on now with a promise of brilliance, warm and clear, and the smoky mist was rolling away towards the north, where the English lay; there were clouds flecking the early blue sky with small lamblike bits of white, in which there was no threat. D'Argenson watched a lark rising from some hedge or coppice behind the tents to the right; rising until it was lost in the gray-blue light of the early morning.

A lark in a hedgerow, he thought; that was what all these people, these Maurice de Saxes and these Richelieux, missed altogether. They missed the lark in the hedgerow as they missed the early springing of the columbine, the flowering of the hawthorn in a country lane, the singing of birds in a dark and silent garden. They did not notice such things. They were busy with the advancement of their own and other people's fortunes in the struggles of Versailles or those even stupider struggles in which men murdered each other in numbers. D'Argenson disapproved of all wars, or so he thought, although he had had his share in making this one. He could see no particular advantage in victory, and certainly none in defeat. War had been an almost constant condition of life in the days of the old King, Louis XIV, and France was no better off for it. If it had been possible to keep the peace . . .

But it was not possible. It was to this conclusion that

D'Argenson's mind returned fifty times a day. It was not, it had not been, possible to maintain peace at a time when all Europe was in turmoil and France was threatened at every turn. He had no quarrel with the Queen of Hungary, whose legal or illegal claims made the pretext for the present outbreak; in fact, from what he knew of her, he thought she seemed a capable and spirited young woman. Her family was, it was true, an inherited danger to France, but it was above all her friends who constituted the new, the permanent, danger: it was those rapacious English, with their ships roaming the seven seas, whose hunger for colonies had begun to be the nightmare of every French minister with a knowledge of geography. At this very moment, D'Argenson thought, there might be battles going on in Canada, in India; nothing was safe against the English. The world was their theater. If France was to hold Canada and India the English must be defeated now, decisively enough to keep them in check for years to come. And yet D'Argenson— a gentle, philosophical pessimist by nature—had no real faith in the final result of the struggle. He was professionally bound to believe that the war would be a striking victory for France and her allies; that a Stuart king would probably be enthroned in England as a result; that the threat of an English conquest would be permanently warded off for Canada and India; that the power and prestige of France on the continent of Europe would emerge strengthened from the contest. Yet he did not believe it. He was too profoundly aware of the insecurity of the internal structure of France: he knew too much about Versailles and the decaying, incompetent and extravagant administration of which it was the visible ornament. In so far as he hated anything, he hated Versailles. "What am I doing here?" he asked himself often. "Why do I not go home and cultivate my garden?"

His carriage drew up and he stepped into it, saluted by a dozen officers. As he leaned back on the cushions, his severe, pedantic head stood out against the panoply of all those uniforms and pennons. He was no man of war. The carriage turned and was driven down the broad lane towards the right, in the direction of the Scheldt. He was no man of war, and as his carriage passed through the busy lines of those who made war their profession, he mused over his own part in all this and was dissatisfied. He knew himself to be better educated and more capable of comprehending the shape and relations of events than those who governed with him. Why, then, had he been unable to prevent this almost meaningless struggle? Almost meaningless—in appearance. D'Argenson knew—and he was probably the only man in the field who did know—that courses of immense importance might be guided for decades to come by the results of the struggle. The French empire was to remain French or it would become English: it was as simple, and as grandiose, as that. But the general shape of this antithesis between a decaying France and an expanding England was unknown to those who engaged their lives so eagerly in battle. They thought they were fighting for altogether different reasons—for the Austrian Succession; for a balance of power in Europe; for a dynastic or nationalistic principle. The Irish and Scots were fighting "for the faith"—more specifically, for the right to resume their land holdings and civil rights in their own countries. To many of the men—probably to most—in the French army there was no question of why the battle was fought: it was fought against the King's enemies, at the King's pleasure, and for no reason. D'Argenson, who knew the reasons and could perceive with all the acuteness of a subtle and sensitive mind how far the struggle involved the interests of the whole world, disliked his own part in the proceeding intensely. Presently there would be a great deal of blood poured out in these peaceful Flemish fields, and he would have to see it; he was revolted by the sight of blood, and yet he would have to conceal his revulsion; he could not avoid an uneasy sense of semiresponsibility for what was happening, and yet he knew the struggle to be inevitable and told himself so with monotonous regularity.

That lark, now, rising from a hedgerow over a field of battle . . .

Well, it could not be helped.

His severe, pedantic head nodded and fell slightly sidewise on the cushions. As the carriage jolted along towards the river, through the lanes of busy men clearing up breakfast and examining their firelocks, the Minister for Foreign Affairs slept.

§

Louis XV had established his field headquarters in a peasant's house at Calonne—the largest house to be had in the village, with barns and byres encircling it. Even so, it was neither commodious nor clean, and the efforts of an army of servants, equipped with bales of silken carpets and hangings, wagonloads of china, silver and glass, had barely been able to make its one principal room habitable to Majesty. The innumerable gentlemen in attendance were billeted in the peasants' huts round about, some of them in the barns; the servants slept with the cows and horses or in the farmyards. The smell of manure hung heavy over the village, and gallons of the costliest scents from Paris warred in vain against it. The King and all his suite were compelled to have frequent recourse to their smelling salts, which was, indeed, the only weapon most of them employed throughout the campaign.

They had been settled at Calonne for three days. The village had the advantage of being on the safe side of the river, with the whole army on the other side between it and the English; it had a bridge, fully guarded, so that the King could pass over into his army and yet be ensured of a quick retreat. The luxury of the encampment in this miserable Flemish village, with its thatched roofs and its heaps of manure, was immense, but its comfort was almost nonexistent. The King was accompanied by fourteen high court officials (the Grand Chamberlain, the First Gentleman of the Bedchamber, the Captain of the House Guards and the Captain of the Hundred Swiss, the Grand Equerry, the Grand Almoner, the Grand Quartermaster, the Grand Master of Ceremonies, and so on); there were five princes of the blood royal, most of them now camped on the other side of the river with the army; there was the Dauphin himself and all his suite; there were seven aides-de-camp, four ordinary gentlemen, the Treasurer of the Household, and a political secretary, as well as three cabinet ministers; there were the King's four first valets and his four ordinary valets, his two hairdressers and two linen-valets, four servants of the bedchamber, two footmen of the antechamber, a footman in charge of watches and clocks, two footmen in charge of the King's personal luggage, one ordinary footman in charge of the trunks, three pages of the bedchamber, and eight footmen with specialized duties such as the care of silks and bedclothing. Besides these, there were five servants in charge of the royal wardrobe; a tailor, a cravat maker, two apothecaries, an ordinary doctor and a surgeon; two almoners, a chaplain, a confessor, an auxiliary priest and clerk of the chapel; and sixty-nine servants of the department called "the King's Mouth" (La Bouche du Roi), which was charged with getting the King's food prepared and transported to its destination. In addition to these there were twenty-eight cooks, assistants and waiters in the bread section, eighteen in the wine section, and seven in the section devoted to coffee. There were almost innumerable servants in the various departments which took care of transporting all the rest, caring for the carriages and horses, and providing the King and his immediate suite with mounts. There were about six hundred horses for carriage and riding purposes, couriers and officers of the household; there were three hundred more for the kitchens. The guards, both Swiss and Musketeers, amounted to a small army in themselves.

This was the King's campaign kit, and represented a considerable reduction from the establishment which accompanied him on more peaceful journeys from one house to another in France. Modest though it was, not all of the establishment could be housed at Calonne, and was consequently spread through a number of villages around Tournai. Such as could be housed at Calonne—and everybody who could find a place there did so, in order to be near the seat of Majesty—were packed in like the vermin that inhabited the straw on which they slept. The smells of the place were appalling, so that after the King had been in residence for three days the scent of honest manure had come to seem worthy of regret. The Minister of Foreign Affairs woke up with a start when his carriage entered the village street; he coughed and reached for his smelling bottle, which he kept to his nose from then on.

He had not slept well the night before, and, rising at three in the morning, had dressed and made his way across the bridge to call on the Marshal. It was now nearly half-past four in the morning, and there were signs of great activity in Calonne. Every house in the village was disgorging its temporary inhabitants, who made their toilets in the street without attempt at concealment. They were all sleepy-eyed, tousled of head, scratching bitterly. No amount of silk or scent had been able to disguise the basic material of a Flemish peasant's bed, which was verminous straw. The cooks were at work; smoke arose from every chimney in the thatched roofs and from the open fields beyond; the guards were dressed and on duty. The mist had completely lifted now, and the rising sun shone with ironic splendor upon a scene of luxurious dirt and discomfort.

D'Argenson's carriage halted at the door of the thatched house which was the King's present residence. The guards saluted him; he descended with dignity, feeling a little faint and sniffing strongly at the bottle. He had to stoop to get through the door, which was hung with folds of exquisite Venetian tapestry in colors of rose and gold.

Inside the room, which was long and wide for a peasant's house, every effort had been made to produce the proper setting for a King. A fire was ablaze in the enormous chimney at one end of the room, and supplied its only means of ventilation. The floor had been covered with layers of thick silken rugs, into which the high heels of D'Argenson and the others sank without a sound. The walls had been hung with silk, pale blue and silver and gold, with bits of the rose-and-gold Venetian tapestry at the two doors. The same treatment concealed the ceiling, above which the peasants who ordinarily inhabited the house had a loft for sleep. A smaller room leading off this main one had been converted into a bedroom for the King, and the loft had been used by members of his household.

There was a great tapestried chair beside the fire, and a table of worked ebony and ivory beside it, for the use of the King. There were two other tables and a number of gilt-legged chairs disposed about the room. The whole place had been repeatedly sprayed with scent, and some incense had been thrown on the fire, so that, although the air was thick and heavy, it was a little less noisome than the air in the village street. Its peasant owners would never have known the room—but they were in no danger of seeing it; they had been packed off to sleep in any ditch they could find, with a gold piece to comfort them.

Into this transformed chamber there had been crowded as many high officers and nobles as could get in. There was no means of excluding them: certain positions carried the right of admission to the King's antechamber, and the holders of those positions could not be prevented from exercising the privilege without attacking the whole system of prerogative and ceremony upon which the court was built. D'Argenson made his way forward through the crowd towards the fireplace, bowing with studied courtesy at almost every step. In front of the fire he encountered his brother, the Comte d'Argenson, Minister of War, and bowed lower than ever.

"Good morning, Monsieur le Marquis," said the Minister of War.

"Good morning, Monsieur le Comte," said the Minister of Foreign Affairs.

There was no great love between the brothers, and indeed the Comte d'Argenson, a born intriguer and an adept at court methods, resented his philosophical brother's intrusion into the world of great affairs. They were the sons of that D'Argenson who, owing his rise to the old King, had served for years as Minister of Police under the Regency. They had been born to a family tradition slightly different from that of the ordinary territorial nobility, and although the Marquis yielded to tradition only halfheartedly, and was forever asking himself why he occupied any post in a court he despised, the Comte was made of sterner stuff: he wanted power and position, and would stop at nothing to obtain them.

"You are up and about at an early hour, Marquis," said the Comte, his cold voice giving the words an edge of accusation.

"I have driven across to the army," the Marquis said defensively. "I did not sleep well, and I thought I might look at the positions there. I called upon the Marshal."

"Indeed," said the Comte even more coldly. "Our paladin has had a very bad night, they tell me."

"He is ill, very ill," the elder D'Argenson said. "I do

not pretend to understand military matters, but I cannot help wondering how such a man can command an army in battle."

"Your doubts are shared by most of the officers in this army," the Comte said. "It is a misfortune for any army to go into action without confidence in its chief."

"Confidence?" the Marquis echoed. "I don't know. The men have plenty of confidence, I am told. What the higher officers may say is another matter."

"I did not think, my dear brother, that the time would come when you would be heard defending the Maréchal de Saxe."

The younger D'Argenson's voice was hostile with irony and dislike. His elder did not reply, but stood gazing down into the fire, sniffing at his salts. When he spoke again, after a pause, it was as if he was thinking aloud and confiding his thoughts to the blaze at his feet.

"I do not like bastards and adventurers in general," he said in an undertone. "I do not like intriguers and all those who have their way to make in the world by means of intrigue. I do not like unmeasured ambition, or people who take service under a flag which is not their own, or courtiers—or even courtiers. I do not know what I am doing here. I really do not know."

"Perhaps the problem may be solved for you, my dear brother, in the course of time. Perhaps there will come a time when you are no longer here."

"I know, dear brother, that I can count upon you to

hasten the coming of that time by every means in your power."

The two looked at each other for once, their eyes clashing like swords. It was the Marquis who looked away, sighing and warming his little porcelain salts bottle in the palms of his two hands.

"Has His Majesty risen?" he asked in an ordinary tone of voice.

"His Majesty has risen," the Comte said, with scorn for his brother apparent in voice and look. "I believe his toilet is now proceeding. The room he occupies is so small that the usual attendance at the levée is impossible."

"These are the hardships of war," said the Marquis. "We just bear with them. If forty courtiers are prevented from seeing the King get out of bed, they suffer that privation in a good cause."

There was an irony in this that was a little too much for the Comte, since he was unable to see against what precise point it was directed. He took refuge in a plain snort. His brother's affectations of philosophy were those he found hardest to bear.

"At the last I heard," he remarked vulgarly, "His Majesty was on the *chaise percée,* in which position he was questioning some officers about the dispositions for the day. You could verify this if you chose. You still have the entrée."

"Still," said the Marquis a little sadly. "I think you choose your words well, brother."

At this moment there was a movement in the crowd which filled the room, talking in undertones. A number of valets and footmen had penetrated by the main door —that opening on the village street—and proceeded through the crowd with a small gilt table and two golden trays held high. The rear guard was brought up by another servant carrying a great silver coffeepot. The procession vanished behind the rose-and-gold curtain at the other end which concealed the opening into the King's bedroom. The crowd closed in again upon its passage.

"Do you bring any news from the Marshal's headquarters?" the younger D'Argenson asked, less for the sake of information than to give the impression, to the crowd in the room, that he was talking amicably with his brother.

"Our outposts report that the English and Dutch are moving," the Marquis said. "They were held back by the mist, but they have been moving steadily since an hour or so before dawn. It will be another two hours, probably, before they can reach the point of attack."

"We have already heard that," the Comte said impatiently. "We are not entirely without information. But is there anything new?"

"Nothing, except that the Marshal tried to get on to his horse and failed. He will be obliged to cover the ground in that wicker affair they have made for him. He is resting now. Richelieu and Noailles and some others were there."

"More than one officer in this army," the Comte said darkly, "believes that the command would have been better entrusted to Richelieu or Noailles. It is a sad day for France when there is no French general to command the French army, when we have to borrow the bastards of Germany to lead our troops."

"You do not say that when you see the Marshal."

"Perhaps not. Neither, my dear brother, do you. But it seems to me you mentioned something of the same or a similar kind not long ago."

"I do not see much difference between a German bastard and a French one," the Marquis said. "We have suffered quite enough from the ambitions of the nameless. They are all born with a grudge against the world and a determination to get their revenge. No; it is not the Marshal's nationality that I dislike. It is his character. He is devoured by ambition, he is crude, self-indulgent, ignorant, and, except on professional questions, exceptionally foolish. His vanity passes belief. He . . ."

"Enough," said the younger brother. "I am familiar with your opinion. The fact remains that he has the King's confidence, and that must be enough for us, for the present."

The Marquis sniffed his bottle absently, staring into the fire. How true it was, he was thinking, that nobody in the world of Versailles deserved the respect of a philosopher! As he had spoken of the Marshal he had himself been aware, in some underlying commentary of the mind, that the same words could have been used with equal truth of almost any other man holding rank or power in the kingdom. They were all devoured by ambition; all were crude and foolish except in some matters of limited professional competence. Richelieu, for instance, knew how to arrange a court ball or a spectacle— that was a sort of competence—but what else could he do? If the whole court were swept away, the Marquis thought, every useful function it performed could be performed by others, and perhaps better performed at that. Merit had so little to do with the organization of the state—was in all cases so subordinated to considerations of royal favor and inherited privilege—that it was only sheer chance, some exceptional combination of accidents, that threw a capable man into high office. The Marquis resolved to write on this subject to his friend M. de Voltaire: a full-blown literary letter, elegantly phrased and decorated with learned allusions. He could savor some of the phrases now in his mind. Decidedly, decidedly, he thought, he would be better off when that time of disgrace came upon him—the time mentioned by his brother, when he would no longer be here—when he could retire to the country and write literary letters and cultivate his garden. Why he clung to office at all, why he had ever made an effort to compete in the intrigues of the powerful, he could never fully understand. He supposed it was because he had been born a D'Argenson: office attracted the breed. He shuddered with distaste and looked sidelong at his brother. That treacherous ape, he reflected, had issued from the same womb as himself and owned an even greater share of the D'Argenson appetite for power. All the larks in the world, rising at one time from an infinity of hedgerows, could not distract him from the steady pursuit of his aims. It was a kind of strength. There was no indecision in it; no dilemma of conscience could arise. The Marquis sighed, and knew himself to be beaten. He was without that strength, and dilemma was the permanent state of his mind.

A murmur over the crowd in the room made him look up hastily and assume a more attentive posture: there had been a stir at the rose-and-gold curtain at the other end. The King was coming in. The men in the room, obeying the signals of the lackeys, rearranged themselves in a moment so as to bare an open lane over the silk carpet from that doorway to the fireplace. The rose-and-gold curtain was drawn and Louis XV entered.

He was thirty-five years old, and had been King of France ever since he could clearly remember anything. The constant pressure of a position so splendid, so unrelievedly public, had produced two contrary effects in him, so that he exhibited some of the phenomena of a double personality: he could be more dignified and gracious than any other prince in Europe when he was on parade, for his experience in playing the role was unique; but he was driven, by the demands of temperament, to compensatory devices of almost incredible complication to achieve some form of private life and activity. The division between the public and private personality —which in Louis XIV had scarcely existed—had grown more pronounced in Louis XV with every year. His shyness, against which he had had to struggle since infancy, was perhaps partly due to the tremendous shadow cast by his great-grandfather, and to the priestly injunctions and admonitions which had constituted his whole education; but it was also the result of a just opinion of his own inadequacy. The other notable influence upon every act of his life was a dread, morbid in its intensity, of being bored. Shyness, boredom and the sense of his own inadequacy drove him into almost fanatical secretiveness; he would conceal everything he possibly could conceal, express an opinion only when it became unavoidable, and make a decision at the last possible moment. His double personality, the opposition of public and private character which steadily sharpened, led him into curious courses. He would officially instruct an ambassador, and then secretly instruct the same man in an opposing sense; and he would further complicate the business by secret instructions to another agent, unknown either to the ambassador or to the French ministers. In this way he had several lines of policy running at once, and could flatter himself, in some morbidly compensatory way, that nobody but himself fully understood the diplomacy of the state. To baffle and mystify his own ministers gave him the pleasures which his self-esteem, so early undermined and so very uncertain, could not afford him. In the same way he tended more and more to construct a sort of private life for himself in the small rooms—"les cabinets" —of his favorite apartments at Versailles, with small supper parties of guests chosen without regard for their public rank. More and more he withdrew a certain part of his existence from the remorseless open splendor which had been wished upon it by the Grand Monarque. The Grand Monarque had been an absolutely public phenomenon at all times, even in bed. It pleased Louis XV to evade or diminish as many as possible of his responsibilities towards the system of monarchical parade, and, when he had duly constructed a kind of privacy behind the labyrinth of small rooms he favored, to permit therein every familiarity in speech and manners. He had even discovered that he had some talent for cooking, and looked forward to the day when, with this private part of his life duly guarded and secret, he might be able to cook a meal for himself and his chosen friend of the moment and eat it with her, unseen by any foreign eye.

This passion for secrecy—inevitable though it was in a shy, amorous, sensitive and superstitious temperament exposed to such conditions of life—had already impaired the prestige of the monarchy by encouraging gossip; it was to develop, in time, into a disaster for the system Louis XV represented. Even though he did no more than cook a stew or play a game of cards in the private little rooms where he spent his evenings, the court and the people at large came to believe that he had withdrawn from them to indulge in unnamable orgies. No Frenchman held it to be a serious misfortune if the King kept a mistress: in fact his first ten years of decorous monogamous marriage with Marie Leczinska had been regarded with considerable astonishment. His virtue, supported on religious fears, was phenomenally slow in succumbing to the attacks to which it was continually subjected at Versailles. But when it did succumb, he took steps which shocked the court and, eventually, the nation: he openly separated from his wife and openly lived with one mistress at a time, in a sort of substitutional matrimony of a kind the French had not seen before. These courses were due to his religious fears, which were deep, ineradicable. When he separated from his wife he separated from the sacraments of the Church, which he did not dare approach again except by way of deathbed repentance. His respect for the Catholic morality and the institution of the family was unshaken by any of his own lapses. He would not, for example, have children by anybody but his wife, and although at least one accident had been suspected, he denied it passionately. He lived "in sin," cut off from the sacraments of the Church, filled with a sense of guilt which further increased his shyness and secretiveness, but at least he avoided hypocrisy. If he had been a better hypocrite he might have had a dozen mistresses and his wife as well, all at the same time, without unduly disturbing the nation. His ancestors had known how to do this; he did not. His dual nature pursued its course, until he came in time to have two lives, one secret and withdrawn, the other as pompous and public as the regime could contrive. In this second—the pompous, public life—he met his wife and children upon terms of the utmost politeness, in the presence of the whole vast, bedizened court; in the secret life which he was only now constructing, he was to develop in time the talents, manners, habits and good humor of a rather self-indulgent butcher or baker.

It was difficult for a man like D'Argenson, much given to reflection, to understand how a complex but unthinking nature like that of Louis XV could go on from blunder to blunder. D'Argenson believed, and recorded his belief, that the ineptitude and extravagant stupidity of the regime were leading towards some kind of catastrophic collapse. He failed to perceive any awareness of this fact in the language or acts of Louis XV. The King was lazy and grew lazier every year; he was intelligent enough to perceive that things did not always go well, that trade was bad, the Parlement of Paris troublesome, the currents of popular opinion often hostile; but he made no effort to understand more than the surface of the difficulties, and any expedient was good enough to use in overcoming them. D'Argenson's attempts to introduce a more thoughtful attitude towards the problems of the moment were treated with cold impatience, and the King made no secret of the fact that such talk "bored" him. Since "boredom" was the one thing his autocratic temper refused to accept, D'Argenson's days were already numbered, and before long he would be given ample opportunity to live in the country and cultivate his garden.

Things had not yet come to such a pass, and as Louis XV advanced through the room, nodding or smiling at the courtiers who bowed before him, he drew up before the D'Argenson brothers.

"So, Monsieur le Marquis," he said, "they tell me you have already visited the army this morning. Is there any sign of the English and the Dutch?"

"None that I could see, Sire. I was told that they were moving towards our positions, but there was nothing to show it. I believe they were held back by the early mists."

"They will no doubt be upon us by seven or eight o'clock. I think we must attend to whatever business there may be at once, so that I can cross over to the army before they arrive."

The Dauphin, a fat, pious boy of eighteen, who had followed his father across the room, nodded his head and smiled eagerly. Clearly he, too, intended to be present at the battle. Both King and Dauphin had chosen to wear a kind of court version of the white uniform, blazing with decorations. The Comte d'Argenson spoke, weighting his voice with all the gravity he could command.

"I know Your Majesty's decision," he said, "but as a loyal subject I must ask again if there is any possibility of reconsidering it. France cannot afford to risk the lives of her King and Dauphin on the same day."

"I am going to cross the river as soon as possible, and my son will accompany me," the King said impatiently. "We have already gone into all that. My place on this day is with the army. If you have papers to be signed, letters for the courier, or any business of importance to put before me, let us get through it immediately."

The Comte d'Argenson bowed and produced his portfolio. The King sat by the fire, in the great chair prepared for him, and looked at the papers without reading them through. When the Comte had finished the Marquis began; a secretary appeared with another portfolio, papers for the morning's courier to Versailles; the Chamberlain appeared with a sheaf of appointments to be signed. There was in all this, perhaps, a suggestion that the King might not be able to sign papers when the day was over. If so, Louis rejected the suggestion by instinct, for he put at least half of the papers aside to be examined later, and signed only those which seemed to have some urgency.

The Marquis d'Argenson watched him, as always, with a mixture of awe and bewilderment. So much had been given to this King that it was a perpetual astonishment to discover how little it conduced to his happiness or to that of any other human being. Louis XV was thirty-five years old, exceptionally handsome, and no less perspicacious than most of the people among whom his life was spent; he was a good horseman, had kept his body straight and strong, and moved with grace; he was as well educated as the times demanded, perhaps better than most princes, and could take pleasure in such things as drama, music and the talk of cultivated men and women; he had an excellent memory and considerable instinctive judgment of human characters and motives;

he still exercised his undoubted charm upon so many of his subjects that the name "Louis the Well-Beloved" could be applied to him without irony. In addition to all this, a long period of peace under the guardianship of his old tutor, Cardinal Fleury, had put the treasury in a condition to withstand almost any extravagance; he had autocratic power, as nearly without checks or curbs upon it as any western Europe had seen; he was—since the illness of last summer at Metz, which had so nearly taken him off—popular, immensely popular, so that no amount of gossip could, as it now appeared, detach the people from him. And yet in spite of these and a thousand other advantages, every gift that human history had rolled up across the centuries and heaped upon him, he was a man who could hardly bear to look anybody straight in the eye. Even now, when D'Argenson looked at him, he evaded the older man's eyes, glanced down or into the fire. Except in occasional flashes of anger, he was incapable of either a direct look or a perfectly direct speech. The instinct for secrecy was so strong in him that he appeared to veil his face as he veiled his thoughts, and nobody—neither mistress nor friend—was ever able to say with confidence: "I know him."

D'Argenson wondered and was silent. He saw the King write a small private note and put it in with the dispatches to go off by the morning's courier. No doubt His Majesty thought this, too, was a secret from all those around him; yet D'Argenson knew, the whole roomful of courtiers knew, and a very large proportion of the population of France was beginning to know, that these secret missives, to which the King gave as much attention as to any state paper, were addressed to a woman of no rank or family, to a simple bourgeoise in a country house at Etioles. This woman, this Mme Lenormant, whom D'Argenson had not even seen, who had never publicly appeared at court, was the object of the acute (but, so far, still discreet) curiosity of all Europe. It was known that Louis had bought an estate in the south for her, with an extinct marquisate attached to it, at a place called Pompadour, and that he proposed to issue the papers conferring the new rank upon her as soon as he returned to Versailles. D'Argenson had seen the superscription on one of the royal letters only yesterday: it had said À Madame la Marquise de Pompadour, and was sealed with a little device from one of the King's rings, with the motto Discret et Fidèle. What was more, the decorators were busy at Versailles furbishing up the apartments that had once housed the Duchesse de Châteauroux. All this was secret: a court secret, which is to say, known to innumerable people. D'Argenson had the usual sources of information open to a courtier who was also a cabinet minister, but he had another and more illustrious informant on this subject, his faithful correspondent, M. de Voltaire. M. de Voltaire was a friend of the mysterious new lady from the bourgeoisie, as he had contrived to be of almost every lady who could be of any use to him for years past, and he did not fail to impress upon D'Argenson the frequency with which he

enjoyed her society. What new powers and dangers were
to be released by this woman from nowhere, whose passion for the King was said to be intense and was certainly reciprocated, D'Argenson could not begin to
guess, but he felt in this, as in other manifestations of the
life around him, the tremors of approaching change, the
shifting and cracking and crumbling of a system that
had once seemed as solid as the earth itself. Involuntarily
he sighed as he watched the King seal that private letter
to an unknown woman, a creature of obscure origins, a
woman almost of the people. Philosopher though he was,
at least in intention, D'Argenson could not altogether
escape the feelings of the caste to which he was born.

Louis heard the sigh and looked up, annoyed. For a
moment his disdainful blue eyes opened and passed over
the Foreign Minister like a chilly wind. Then he rose
from his chair.

"I think we have disposed of everything that needs
immediate attention," he said stiffly. "It is time to go."

§

The King rode with a small suite and a handful of
guards. The Dauphin, a much less practised horseman,
followed with his own suite at a gentler pace. Those who
attended the battle in carriages—there were four or five
of them allowed to do so—brought up the rear of the
party from Calonne. D'Argenson, accepting this igno-

miny, consoled himself with the reflection that even
Maurice de Saxe, the most notable soldier in Europe, the
commander in chief, was compelled to do the same. The
greater part of the King's traveling court, his swarms of
servants, pages, guards and officials, remained at Calonne
to wonder, tremble and fear throughout the day.

There had been scattered musketry fire audible from
the outposts beyond Fontenoy shortly before five o'clock
in the morning, and a serious artillery preparation began
shortly afterwards, when the general disposition of the
enemy forces had become discernible. When the King
reached the battlefield it was nearly six o'clock, the mists
had entirely cleared, the sun was bright and promised to
be warm, and the din of the batteries on both sides was
intense. The army lay in its triangular position with the
apex at Fontenoy and the two arms reaching towards
Barry Wood and Antoing, and so far little damage had
been done by the enemy's guns. But for the noise and
the puffs of smoke that rose in the morning air, there
was nothing yet to show that the attack was at hand.

Louis XV was in high good humor. As he rode along
he read a lesson in dynastic history to his surprised suite.

"Since the battle of Poitiers," he said, "no King of
France has been personally present at a battle with his
Dauphin. And since St Louis no King of France has ever
won a decisive victory over the English."

"Your Majesty will be the first," said the Duc d'Ayen
promptly.

"It is possible," Louis said. "I have studied the position

and think it is good. Some of you object that the Marshal has not put up enough redoubts, others that he has put too many, and still others that he has distributed them badly. I trust his judgment, and count upon every officer in this army to do the same. Some of you have objected that this position offers no possibility of retreat. I agree. There is nowhere for our army to retreat to except into the river. All the more reason, gentlemen, for expecting victory. We shall win here or die, for we have no alternative."

"Your Majesty's retreat at least is assured," D'Ayen said. "That we must insist upon."

"I shall not take it," said Louis without bravado. "Now that I am here, I shall stay until this battle is over, whatever its outcome."

D'Ayen and the others protested, but without much force. There was stealing in upon them the conviction that something had happened to their King, something which had shaken him out of his comfortable do-nothing habits and made him anxious to display the courage which they all knew him to possess. The woman, whose name had never yet been pronounced aloud in court circles, must have brought about this change, somehow, must have talked to him of victories and triumphs, inspired in him the wish to emulate his ancestors instead of being weighed down by them. However it had been done, it had brightened that shy, bored, secretive character into something approaching the gaiety and courage of Henri IV, the ambition of Louis XIV. The mood might

not last, but if it could survive even one day it would
have an inspiriting effect upon the troops.

They cheered him wildly as he rode through them
towards the position he had chosen to occupy, well up
towards the apex of the triangle behind Fontenoy. He
rode well and swung his feathered hat at the lines of
men; the long, ringing cry of "Vive le Roi!" was taken
up at one point as soon as it had died down at another,
so that it never seemed to cease. These men, recruited by
every method the skulduggery of the age had invented,
came from the jails of Paris or the starveling fields of
Auvergne, some willing to serve and some far from
willing at first; their lives were brutal and debased, their
pay, clothing and rations barely sufficient to maintain
them; when they left the army—if they ever did—it was
only to return to the peasantry and the unceasing exac-
tions of the landlord, unless they vanished into the slums
of Paris; they had little in past or future to cause gratitude or loyalty towards Louis XV. And yet when he
passed they cheered wildly, comforted in some obscure
way by the thought that the King was to share their danger, and that if they died today it would be under his
eyes, perhaps with him. The professional soldiers among
them—those who, by whatever accident they had fallen
into the army, were resigned to staying there for the rest
of their lives—were especially susceptible to this emotion,
and many a leathery old face in the line regiments was
wet with tears as its owner yelled himself hoarse for the
King. Louis himself was deeply affected; perhaps he

knew that such devotions were not his due and would
not come his way again; those closest to him observed
that for a good while he seemed unable to speak as he
rode down the line.

The position which had been agreed upon for the
King, after numerous consultations of officers in the preceding two days, was the clear plateau near a small
church called Notre-Dame-aux-Bois, behind the main
body of the army. Before taking his place there, Louis
rode as far as the furthest line regiments towards Fontenoy (the regiments of Beauvoisis and Dauphin),
cheered all along the way, and then turned to the north
again, riding through an open space bordered on the
right by the infantry regiments of the line and on the
left by the cavalry regiments of Brancas, Clermont-
Prince, Fitzjames and Fiennes. From the cavaliers, conscious of their tradition as guardians of the throne, Louis
received an even more tumultuous welcome, with plumed
hats thrown into the air while the horses stamped and
jingled their trappings. In the open plain behind the first
regiments of Irish—Lally's and Clare's—the King and his
suite galloped off to the left, towards the household cavalry and the place appointed, Notre-Dame-aux-Bois.

By this time the cannonading was heavy, for the
French had been able to discern three important targets:
a battery of ten pieces on the hill of Bourgeon, south of
Fontenoy, held by the Dutch with ten squadrons in support; the dark lines of the advancing Dutch infantry beneath the hill of Bourgeon; and, on the other side of

Fontenoy, between the hamlet of Vezons and Barry Wood, very slowly in motion across flat, marshy land, the red coats of the first English.

Louis XV took his place at Notre-Dame-aux-Bois with visible impatience. He was behind the entire army, with fifty thousand men between him and the nearest enemy. The regiments of the Maison du Roi, Gardes du Roi, Mousquetaires and Gendarmerie were aligned on either side and in front of him; behind him was a quick and easy retreat across open fields to the Scheldt bridge and Calonne. He would have preferred a somewhat closer acquaintance with the dangers of battle; no military glory was likely to be won at this carefully guarded post of observation, with a spyglass and a smelling bottle as his only weapons. He was well aware, however, that the Marshal and most of the higher officers did not want him to be present at the battle at all, and had permitted him even this mild display of martial ardor against their better judgment. He would have to be content with it; and in any case it could not be denied that the place was fairly high, commanded a good view of the gently sloping plain which was the field of battle, and might even, later on, when the English artillery became more effective, get to be fairly dangerous. He did not want to make a nuisance of himself, and his sense of his own ability, accurate as always, told him that he would be no use to anybody in the front lines.

He dismounted and walked up and down on the plateau, inspecting the field through a glass. To amuse himself—and perhaps to add to whatever tender missive he would be sending off to Etioles later in the day—he made a rough sketch of the semicircle before him, the French regiments lying in their carefully studied positions on the higher part of the plain, the first of the English and Dutch emerging at two points beyond them. They would never be able to form a proper line, Louis could see at once. The Marshal had explained all this to him on the day before, but he was now able to see it for himself, and took pleasure in pointing it out to the officers with him.

"The English are coming through a narrow space," he said, "in which they will not have room to deploy properly. Barry Wood there is too thick and too extensive for them; besides, I believe, it has a hill in the middle; they will have to leave it alone. They must come through where they are now; can you see the red coats? They will have the woods on their right and the village of Vezons on their left; they don't get much open ground, and the slope is against them. It will be very difficult for them. I don't see the Dutch so well—they're off beyond Fontenoy, at that hill, which is, I believe, called Bourgeon. They must wait to see what the English do; yes, decidedly, they must wait for the English. And they must keep up their communications along a fairly extended line with all sorts of interruptions in it, villages, marshes, hamlets. Yes, decidedly, gentlemen, the Marshal has chosen his place well. I wonder what has become of the Hanoverians? We don't see them."

He talked with unusual animation, gesturing, pointing out places on his sketch or on the panorama before them, offering his glasses with extraordinary affability to any officer who happened to be at hand, and laughing sometimes as he talked. His officers tried to keep up the tone he had decided to adopt, although many of them had no such high opinion of the dispositions the Marshal had made. The battle might have been a spectacle arranged for the royal pleasure, and the plain before them a theater; it was in this way—since he could not fight—that Louis elected to take it.

Before them, on the slope which led to the lines of cavalry beyond which the Irish were drawn up, an untoward excitement caught their attention. Half the men in the front lines, turning their backs on the enemy, were cheering; the cavalry regiments behind them were foaming with plumed hats shaken in the air. In a few minutes they were able to discern the cause: Maurice de Saxe's "cradle" was on its way up to Notre-Dame-aux-Bois.

The "cradle," as Maurice called it, was a wicker basket affair on wheels, a sort of bed and carriage in one, light and mobile, drawn by four horses, and capable of covering the ground at a surprising speed. The commander in chief was half lying and half sitting in this contraption as it whirled along, his vast bulk spreading over many cushions. It came up to Notre-Dame-aux-Bois full tilt, with the aides-de-camp galloping beside and behind it. The discomfort of such motion to Maurice's body must have been extreme, but he ground his teeth together and ordered the driver to make haste. When the "cradle" reached the open space on which the King and his suite were standing, it drew up, and the Marshal's aides prepared to help him out of it. This was prevented by Louis himself, who could move swiftly when he chose.

"You will not think of stirring, Marshal," he said. "I beg of you, stay as you are. You are in sufficient pain as it is."

"With Your Majesty's leave, I will," Maurice answered. His face had beads of sweat on it, brow and cheeks and chin, from the effort of endurance. He could not restrain a slight groaning sigh as he stretched himself a little more comfortably on the cushions that had now, mercifully, come to a halt.

"I wish to assure you, Marshal, in the presence of these gentlemen," Louis said in a loud voice, "of my complete confidence. Neither I nor any officer of my army will endanger the victory by negligence of your orders. All who are here must obey you, and I shall be the first to give the example. Command me."

"Your Majesty's first duty is to run no risk to a life so precious for France and the world," said Maurice, partly through clenched teeth. The necessity for such speeches, at a time when his pain and his impatience caused him great suffering, was a hard one. He stumbled on: "If I dared to give orders to Your Majesty, the first one would be to expose yourself as little as possible, or not at all."

"We are very well placed here," Louis said, smiling a little. He knew Maurice disliked the rhetoric of these public exchanges—which were bound to be repeated at once by all who heard them, and were often, indeed, written down before the actual words had grown cold in the air—but they were a kind of obligation on King and Marshal alike. Once the appropriate "historic word" had been said and overheard by a considerable number of people, it was possible to talk in less exalted terms.

"What has happened?" Louis asked eagerly, in his ordinary undertone. "I can see that there are some red-coats in the hollow opposite there, near Barry Wood, and I can see that the Dutch have established some sort of position in the distance to the south, beyond Fontenoy. But exactly what has taken place?"

"We have full information," Maurice said. "We even have copies of Cumberland's most recent orders, those issued yesterday afternoon and last night. The allied armies began to move at two o'clock; that is, one hour before the break of day. Prince Waldeck and his Dutch-men are to take Fontenoy if they can, and Cumberland apparently designs an attack on our left wing, if the flanking movement fails. The flanking movement obvi-ously must fail. He cannot get infantry and artillery through Barry Wood. He has a heavy force, which I think totally useless, detached to Barry Wood. As nearly as we can make out it consists of two battalions of his English under Ingoldsby, with some Hanoverians and some Scottish Highlanders, but they have been there now for nearly two hours and have done nothing. Cumberland himself is in that hollow between Barry Wood and Vezons, with the main body of his English troops and some Hanoverians, but the space is not suited to their maneuvers. We can hardly make out what they are doing, but they seem to be changing formations. Perhaps he is waiting to hear from the Dutch. Certainly the Dutch are waiting for him. If Your Majesty will take my glasses, you can see that the Dutch are quite motionless. See— beneath that hill, to the south. They have not moved for nearly an hour. They have a very strong battery on that hill, which is giving us some trouble. For the present, it seems to be a duel of artillery. We have had no very seri- ous losses yet."

The King listened attentively to all this, which Maurice delivered slowly, pausing to see that each point was un- derstood, and lifting himself painfully on one elbow to indicate the positions with a nod of his head.

"Our plan, then, is to do nothing?" the King asked. "Do we simply wait?"

"We simply wait, Sire. Every advantage is ours in so doing. They must attack us. They have no choice. They can never relieve Tournai unless they do so. It is obvious that they see this as clearly as we do. Cumberland's gen- eral orders last night—of which we have an exact copy; we are well served in such matters—leave no doubt that what is intended is a pitched battle. They will attack us along the whole line if they can. I feel sure that they can never take Fontenoy or Antoing; both are very strong positions. They may be able to cut through the sunken road between Fontenoy and Antoing; that is a possibility; it depends on Waldeck and his Dutchmen. The other point where their attack is obviously coming is down there, where Your Majesty now sees the first redcoats. We are giving them as well-nourished a fire of artillery as we can manage at the moment. Those are English regiments of the line, and the English King's guards."

"The Elector of Hanover's guards, perhaps we should say," Louis remarked with a sidelong smile.

"I did not know Your Majesty had accepted that point of view," Maurice answered. "Very well. The Elector of Hanover's guards. The usurper's guards. Facing them are a considerable number of the Scottish, Irish and English troops in Your Majesty's service, who will be glad to meet them."

"My cousin Stuart has given us good men," Louis remarked. "Still, I do not know that they alone should meet their kinsmen in battle."

"They will not do so," Maurice assured him. "They will be held in reserve as long as possible; they are to the left of the point of attack, and except for Fitzjames' Horse, I doubt if any of the Jacobite troops will be in action soon. No; if Cumberland comes through there, he will meet French troops. But he should not be coming through at all; it is a terrible test for any army. The space is not great and the ground is unfavorable. As they come up the slope they will die in ranks as they stand, the poor devils."

"You need not waste pity on the enemy, Marshal," Louis said, still smiling. "No doubt they will do their best to kill a few of ours, too."

"They will, Sire," Maurice said very soberly. "I would have avoided this encounter if I could. There will be many men killed today, on both sides. Your Majesty has not yet seen the English infantry advance, I believe."

"No, perhaps not," Louis said nervously, looking away from the vast body in the "cradle" towards the plain. "Perhaps not. No, indeed. But I have seen the French cavalry charge."

"You will see it again, Sire."

There was something unduly sober, almost solemn, about Maurice's way of speech this morning, and it did not consort at all with the gaiety which Louis was attempting to maintain. The last words made the King lose interest in the conversation.

"I must not keep you here, Marshal," he said. "We are all under your orders today. You are to go and come as you please."

"With Your Majesty's leave, I will go now," Maurice said. "I should be in two or three places at once, and they are not near together."

"God go with you, sir," the King said, and as Maurice gave the signal for his "cradle" to be set in motion again, the King instigated a cry of "Vive le Maréchal!" to speed him on his way. The "cradle" turned and made off down the slope towards the lines of French cavalry, with its clump of aides-de-camp galloping behind.

The King motioned to his officers to leave him for a moment. He walked alone towards the further edges of the little plateau on which he had been stationed for the day. His face was somber; all the gaiety had been drained out of it. He could not but think of the opposition that had been forced upon him. He was young, strong and brave; he had never felt a lack of courage in any circumstance; he was absolute monarch of the richest and most powerful kingdom in the world; but life had not fitted him for anything but the role of a spectator at this battle. The men who would fight and die today in his name would do so under the orders of a nameless German adventurer, the bastard of Saxony, whose ruined body could not even walk or wield a weapon or sit upon a horse. For some moments the King walked alone, looking down the slope towards the tremendous array of his men and horses, the army of France. When he turned to come back to his officers, who had stood in respectful silence waiting for him, he had composed his countenance and was smiling again. Even a spectator could be of some use, if he was Louis XV.

"Gentlemen," he said cheerfully, "the Marshal explained it all to me, and I think we may be sure that Monsieur de Cumberland will not get out of this so very easily. Indeed not. Ah, my son is arriving, I see. We shall have the inestimable pleasure of explaining the whole thing to him all over again. He cannot begin his education in such matters too soon."

§

It was half-past seven, and the positions of the enemy were still not greatly altered. The English had at first sent four battalions into Barry Wood, and then withdrawn two of them, reforming in the center, and detaching four Hanoverian battalions to join with the Dutch on their left at the village of Fontenoy (the French center). All these movements and countermovements had consumed hours of time, during which the artillery on both sides had kept up a steady din. So far as the officers surrounding the Marshal could tell, the French artillery appeared to be doing severe damage among the English, but the English cannon were not so effective. At about half-past seven the English appeared to be bringing up new batteries into position between Vezons and Barry Wood, and the cannonade was suddenly intensified. It was clear that the object of this was to silence the French fieldpieces—*batteries à la suédoise*—and such was the exactness of the English aim that the object was soon attained.

The effect of the sudden intensification of fire was to bring home to every man on the French left the nature of the struggle. It was not to be a battle of maneuver and noise: the English were in earnest. The losses inflicted by the new English batteries were not severe, but they were conspicuous. Almost the whole of the French light artillery was silenced, its men blown into shreds. Here and there on the field there were individual losses which awed the men who witnessed them and were repeated from rank to rank. Thus the young Duc de Gramont, riding towards his uncle the old Maréchal de Noailles to report, was hailed by one of his attendants:

"Sir, Sir, your horse is hit! Your horse is killed!"

"And so am I," said Gramont, falling.

The explosion had horribly mutilated him down one side, but he lived for another half-hour or so. The old Marshal, his uncle, wept over the bloody fragment.

The men had been instructed to take advantage of every possible cover the ground afforded, which was little enough; they did so; but it was still an open battle, and the carnage of artillery attack, however limited in scope, was horrible enough in that sunny amphitheater.

Maurice de Saxe sat up in his "cradle" in the midst of it and studied the English positions opposite with his glasses. He watched for ten minutes, and the results explained themselves.

"They are after our fieldpieces," he said. "They have wonderful artillerymen, the English. I am not sure, but that should be Ligonier's men up there. It looks like the uniform of his regiment."

He prided himself upon being able to detect this sort of detail at a distance.

"A Frenchman, too," he added. "Killing his own countrymen. Well, there will be enough of that today."

Instructions had already been given to concentrate the

fire of the fixed batteries on Ligonier's position; nothing more could be done.

"I will pass the entire line, from left to right," Maurice announced. "The English will not be able to come through just yet. We still have too much artillery against them. There is not too much time, nevertheless. The Dutch must be doing something by now. We start from the extreme left, gentlemen, riding behind the lines until we get there."

The cavalcade turned back again in the open space next to Fitzjames' regiment of horse, and rode towards Notre-Dame-aux-Bois. Before they reached it they wheeled round to the north and sped along behind the troops of the left wing, the Irish brigade backed by a line of French cavalry. The ground was uncommonly even, a smooth plain affording very little cover for men, but also permitting the greatest freedom of movement for horses. Riding at this pace, the Marshal and his party soon passed beyond the range of the English guns; all that part of the army which lay behind Barry Wood was protected, and the men had no enemy to contend with but their own impatience and curiosity. They cheered the Marshal as he passed, and many of them shouted "What is happening? Has the attack begun?" The officers riding with the Marshal sometimes shouted replies: "Nothing yet. Only artillery." The regiments at this end of the French lines had been in formation for about three hours and had so far seen nothing but the blank

wooded hill in front of them, although they could hear
plenty of cannonading from further south.

Maurice did not attempt to enter Barry Wood, where
his "cradle" could not have gone far. He was satisfied
that the redoubts he had established there would hold;
there were two battalions of the Eu regiment in them,
and the irregulars called Grassins strung between; the
English had so far sent only four battalions into the
wood, and these four appeared to be doing nothing, perhaps waiting for further orders. No; it was not in this
thickly wooded hill, where no troops could move freely,
that the battle would be fought. In his mind Maurice had
already sketched out, from what he had seen just now,
the nature of the combat. It would be that most dreadful and destructive of operations, an advance of English
infantry. He knew those troops, and although he admired
their steadiness beyond anything he had seen in warfare,
his heart misgave him when he thought of what they
might do. It would be hand-to-hand, in open field, and
in this kind of operation there was nothing like the inhu-
man steadiness and discipline of the English. He was
glad he had some English, Scots and Irish of his own to
oppose to them. The French infantry, although capable
of great outbursts of fury, had not the rocklike quality
needed to withstand an English advance.

The last regiment on the left flank of the army was
the Royal Corsicans. They seemed, at present, so far away
from the theater of operations that their officers openly
wondered if they were ever to see any fighting. Maurice

consoled them grimly. It was his opinion that no part of the army would be without some experience of bloodshed today. He passed the regiment and went on to the Irish.

The first of these was Bulkeley's regiment, with Dillon's, Berwick's, Roth's, Clare's and Lally's following in that order. He had already spoken to their commanders, earlier in the morning at his own tent; he now passed the troops in review. They were big men whose red faces and blue eyes gave them the look of another race. Maurice sighed; these were savages, perhaps; certainly very few of them had ever heard of Racine; but they would be needed today.

"I shall leave one of my young men here with you," he said to Lord Clare, "so that I can get a quick report of your doings in about an hour's time, when I am down beyond Fontenoy. Who shall it be? Mézières! Will you stay here, please, with Lord Clare, and join me at about nine o'clock at Fontenoy or beyond, wherever I happen to be? You understand that I am now passing the whole line, so you will have to ride until you find me."

Mézières accepted the mission without enthusiasm. From the present look of things, the Irish brigade was not likely to see much action for some time; it lay entirely protected by the woods, with the advance guards of Clare's and Lally's actually in the trees. From this position the steady cannonading to the south was an irritation to the nerves, and nothing more.

Lord Clare accompanied the Marshal to the end of the

Irish brigade (Lally's) and took leave of him when he passed on to the next regiment, the Swiss Guards. Mézières, as instructed, turned back with Clare.

"The Marshal is a great man," Clare said as they trotted along towards his own regiment. "When I am unable to sit on a horse, and very nearly unable to move, I doubt if I shall want to be commanding an army. Does that thing he travels about in—the 'cradle'—cause him much pain?"

"Severe, I believe," Mézières replied. "It is the best that has been contrived, but of course it causes great pain. He will probably have to be tapped again before the day is over. That seems to be the only thing that gives him relief."

"I wish we could rejuvenate him somehow and take him with us on the day that is coming, across the water. There is not a tactician like him in Europe. With half an army, and the people themselves no doubt rising on our side, we should soon turn the Hanoverians out of London and put the right King back again."

"Do you think that this day's victory, which we all expect, will be followed by an expedition to England?"

"To England, or Scotland or Ireland. I believe Prince Charles wants to land in Scotland, where our friends are most numerous, and march south. By God, Mézières, it will be worth something to see that day come. You don't know what it is like to spend your whole life in exile, with strangers holding your lands and sitting at home in your place."

They reached Clare's and dismounted. Alexander MacCarthy of Drisbane saw them coming and commented sourly to Davoren, one of his lieutenants.

"There is the young French whippersnapper again, riding along with His Lordship as friendly as you please," he said. "Is it a battle, then, or is it a teaparty? Divil an Englishman do I see at all, but only a fine party of French gentry that should be at home putting more paint on their dirty faces."

"There's English somewhere beyond," Davoren remarked. "The French would not be firing off all those cannon for nothing."

"They'd do anything to make a noise," said MacCarthy. "Have you not heard them yelling 'Vive le Roi!' and 'Vive le Maréchal!' and the rest of it? They're a noisy, fussy, dressed-up race of monkeys, Davoren, and it's a sin and a shame that a true-born MacCarthy of Drisbane should be wearing out his life in their service. I'd almost rather serve the English, the black Protestant heathen swine that they are."

Davoren was used to this sullen growling and could keep it going almost indefinitely, disagreeing just enough to lead his captain on. It served to pass the time; and occasionally MacCarthy, by dint of incessant complaining, with exhaustive objurgation and expletive, talked himself into what was almost a good humor.

The day was already warm, and the grassy shade in the outskirts of the wood was pleasant after a long, hot ride. Mézières sat under a tree and stretched his legs. Clare had no need of his services, and the men were at ease; it was a moment of peace and relaxation. The guns suddenly seemed far away. Mézières was half asleep. Lazily he watched a spider on the branch above him, and his head nodded back against the tree trunk. Poor Gramont! he thought suddenly. Poor Gramont! Dead by now, certainly; no man could live long with such fearful wounds. The shell had shattered him all down one side; on the shining white and gold of his uniform the blood had seemed startling in its redness. Mézières had not seen blood shed before, and at first he had felt slightly sick. He did not intend to allow this feeling to overcome him again whatever happened. Nor would he take refuge in smelling salts, like the fine gentlemen of Versailles.

Gramont had taken them all to the masked ball at Versailles, the one at which Mézières had seen Mme Lenormant. Gramont had been at many a supper party the winter before, with Prince Charles and the rest of them, gay as a cricket, full of stories, making them all laugh.

The spider on the branch hung perilously by a leg, and Mézières put his head back on the moss to watch it. The sound of the guns grew fainter and fainter, and the hum of Irish voices in unceasing conversation could be heard no more. The Chevalier de Mézières, rolling slightly to one side, fell sound asleep.

§

The girl came through a door into the garden and stood there with her lips slightly parted in surprise, staring at him with half-frightened eyes of an almost unimaginable blue. This was the way she often entered his dreams—through a door into a garden. When he first began to dream of her, four years or more ago, she had been exactly the same age as she was now. Details of her appearance had altered considerably since then—her hair had grown fairer, until it was now like a cloud of light—but her age was always the same. He knew she was a girl of sixteen, although this detail had never been mentioned in any of the talk which sometimes took place in that unknown garden where his vision always found her.

She had a face of angelic delicacy, the skin so fair that it would have seemed an outrage even to touch it. Her very fair hair was drawn back, loose and unpowdered, from her exquisite brows, and was tied somehow behind so that it was never tousled or disarranged. She wore a dress of a silvery-dull blue (this detail had often changed in the past four years) with a kerchief of white lace over her bosom. When she spoke, which was seldom, it was always in English, for she was an English girl. Her name had changed several times. At present, and for a year or so past, it had been Mary.

Mézières had never known anybody like her in real life.

He met her only in sleep. Sometimes he would not dream of her for months on end, and then she would appear nearly every night for a time. He never reached a greater stage of intimacy with her than a touch of the hand, and these dreams—which were puzzling to him in any case— were most surprising in that there was no eroticism in them. They were of a purity unlike anything in his experience, and he had once been amazed to find that they came to him oftenest when his life was least pure. He had dreamed of Mary all last winter at Versailles. Sometimes he was not himself present in the dream at all—it took the nature of sheer vision, and Mary walked or even talked in a garden from which he was absent. Lately he had grown to accept the recurrence of Mary as a part of his life, and puzzled no more; she was there; this was enough.

When he had first begun to think about it, he wondered why she should be English. He had never been to England and knew few English people except the elderly Jacobites who were his mother's friends. Perhaps she was English because his mother was English; but this suggestion did not seem particularly sensible, as nobody less resembled Mme de Mézières than the Mary of his dreams. In time the girl's Englishness—like her fair hair and skin, her eyes, the garden in which he repeatedly saw her—came to be accepted without question.

He had never, even in the beginning, questioned her in dreams. It was only afterwards, when he was awake and wondering, that he had puzzled over the thing at all.

In the dream it was always natural, inevitable, final and perfect, so that any idea of connection with his actual life of every day did not arise. She never referred to his waking life; she gave no warnings, admonitions, or commands; she belonged to a life apart, to which he was admitted only by leaving his ordinary existence behind. Very often she did not speak at all; very often she spoke only of the things that were under her hand, the growth of the flowers, the shape of a shadow cast over the grass, the bird's nest in the yew hedge.

Somehow he had become aware that this garden in which he saw her belonged to a great, quiet house, with spacious rooms and spacious days arranged in quiet order. He had never seen the house; they had not discussed it; and yet he knew, by the prescience of the dream, that it was this sort of house. Mary could not have come from any other. When he was awake he sometimes speculated about the house, from tales he had heard of other English houses, and thought it might be not unlike Westbrook House in Surrey, where the Oglethorpes had lived before their exile. In the dream there was no suggestion of what the house was like or where it might exist—or even that it did exist in the life of every day. It was only his waking thought that dwelt upon the house. Perhaps, as he told himself often, there was no such house, no such garden, no such girl; it was a dream only, and different from other dreams in the single fact that it came back to him again and again.

Sometimes she spoke poetry to him, like a child reciting to please an elder. Her voice was equal and sweet, placing the lovely English words distinct upon the enchanted air. He knew a certain amount of English poetry, and it was the lines that he knew best that she would most often say for him, but she also did say other lines, unknown ones, at times, and it irked him afterwards that he was unable either to remember them or to find them in books. She would look at him when she had finished, straight and grave, waiting for his approval. There was childlike happiness in her smile when it came.

Today she entered the garden and stood there for a long time looking at him, her eyes growing larger and bluer with fright. It could not be, after all these years, that she was afraid of him; and yet there was nothing else in the garden to frighten her. The sun fell clear and warm across grass and roses and sundial. Mézières heard himself speak, very gently.

"Mary," he said. "Mary. It is Eugène. Don't you know me?"

She only looked at him and bit her lower lip.

"Something has frightened you," he heard himself say. "Come, sit here and tell me. Nothing will hurt you, Mary. Nothing can hurt you. Tell me what it is."

She only looked at him, and her eyes began to fill with tears. He tried to go near to her, and in the inexplicable way of dreams, his limbs would not move. A force he had never felt before immobilized him; he could not stir, although he felt the muscles straining to be free. The tears fell at last down her exquisite face, and she still

looked at him with the hopeless great sorrowing eyes of
a child. He strained in agony to reach towards her, but
his body was imprisoned. Even his throat was not free.
He made a desperate effort to speak, and there was a
struggle in his throat.

He woke up, calling out.

"What's the matter with Mézières?" a voice asked indifferently. "Eh, there, wake up, Mézières. You're chok-
ing in your sleep."

Mézières rolled over and sat up. He was beneath the
oak tree where he had sat down a short time ago, and the
same spider clung to the branch above him.

He rubbed his eyes and sat quiet for awhile. The
dreams of the English girl, the English garden, had always made a profound impression upon him since he
had first experienced them in the disturbances of his
fifteenth year. Now that he was twenty, they had grown
to be so much a part of him that he no longer worried
over them. And yet this one had been unlike any other.
It left a feeling of grief behind it out of all proportion to
the events of the dream. Mézières was not far from weeping himself at this moment. How meaningless these
visions were, he told himself; there was no such girl; the
garden, the grass, the roses and the sundial did not exist; that enchanted light and air were not to be found
on earth. And yet he was deeply shaken, mourning in his
heart over the tears of a child he had never really seen.

He tried his arms and legs. They moved as usual. There
was nothing the matter with him—nothing at all. He

could hear the roaring of the cannon towards the south, and the troopers of Clare's moved about among the trees, talking. He got up and stretched. He had no business to be sleeping in the midst of a battle. Perhaps by this time there was news. He went over to his horse, which was tranquilly eating the leaves off a near-by tree, and led it down into the open space towards Lord Clare.

"That fellow Mézières, now," Trooper MacGinnis said to his friend Rory O'Neill, "I seen the thing he did at Dunkirk last March just after St Patrick's Day, and him a slip of a Frenchman no more than eighteen or nineteen years old."

"What was it, then?" O'Neill asked. "I never heard his name before this day. What was he doing at Dunkirk?"

"He was up there with Marshal Saxe, the same as he is today, when the great expedition was preparing against the bloody Englishmen. One day on the shore—it was the first or the second day of the great storm; Fitzpatrick would remember it exactly for he was with me at the time; no more than twenty paces away we were standing, admiring the beauties of nature in her wrath, when this little cock robin of a Frenchman comes along in his fine white uniform and sees a boat capsize out in the mighty waves. It was a terrible storm, you remember, and old Kelly that came over in '15 and has been back and forth twenty times since, a great man for seafaring experiences and terrible stories altogether, says there was never another like it in the entire history of mankind. Well, this Frenchman here, Mézières they call him,

looked out and saw the boat capsize, and the people in
the boat were Frenchmen all. There was some friend
of his among them, or so he thought, for he lets out a yell
of 'Jean! Jean!' as if the hounds of hell were after him,
and off he goes in a minute, flinging his sword and belt
away, and plunges into the horrible great waves that
were destroying the boats of the King's navy. I never saw
such a thing in my life. Fitzpatrick and I stood there,
gaping. We had no will to save the Frenchmen from
drowning—it's a death that's too clean for most of them
—but we could not keep from cheering the little cock
robin when he leaped into that prodigious great sea.
Pretty soon he comes out again, puffing and blowing and
dragging a man that was half dead with him, and when
he gets a good look at the face on him it wasn't his friend
Jean at all, but some common devil of an ordinary
French soldier in a line regiment. So what does he do,
this Mézières, but go back into the raging tempest of the
ocean and fish out two or three more of these half-
drowned Frenchmen. Not a man jack of them could
swim at all, no more than flapping and flopping like a
chicken with its neck wrung, and there was hundreds of
them drowned that day."

"Did you do nothing, then," O'Neill inquired, "except
stand on the shore and cheer for this Mézières?"

"What would we be doing risking our lives to save a
few Frenchmen?" MacGinnis demanded. "There was
plenty of their own men that did no more than we did.
And besides, had I not a great clip on my head from Det-

tingen, and worries and disasters enough of my own? I have a delicate constitution when it comes to anything to do with the sea, and that was a terrible storm, O'Neill, a terrible storm. It destroyed the French King's navy altogether, the great ships cracking up and going down into the depths in thunder and lightning like the end of the world. Nobody minds a bit of a cannon ball or a little bayonet work on the good solid ground, but Jesus, Mary and Joseph keep us all from a storm on the water."

Mézières, unaware of the interest he had aroused, stood by his horse in the open space and hesitated to mount. He was filled with an obscure confusion and dismay; the waves of disorder were let loose in him; he could not escape from the dream. He had to force himself to get on to his horse and ride across the space towards Clare. When he looked up the sky was bright blue and cloudless; the men of Clare's were all about him; the girl did not exist anywhere, and yet his heart was constricted with the urgency of her grief. Why had she wept? Why had he been unable to reach her?

"Mary," he said aloud, "Mary." He seemed to derive some comfort from the syllables of her name. He set his lips firmly and drew up before Lord Clare.

§

"Nothing appears to be changed," Clare said to him, "but I don't feel justified in keeping you here any longer.

You can ride to the Marshal and report that we are in position and waiting. The English are not advancing. Ingoldsby is still in the wood there, not far from our redoubts, but is doing absolutely nothing. Our scouts have seen a good deal of going to and fro, messengers I suppose; and two of the battalions that were sent into the wood early this morning have been detached and sent down towards Fontenoy. The others are motionless. We believe Cumberland is now forming a column, but his movements are a little difficult to follow. I believe they have been thrown into considerable confusion by unexpected difficulties in the ground. The only attack so far is by artillery, and even that does not reach us here. The brigade is, in short, ready and waiting for orders, and nothing has happened yet."

"It seems to be a battle of inaction, so far," Mézières volunteered.

"That won't last," Clare said, smiling a little sadly. "We've got an English advance coming sooner or later; I don't know if you've seen that, Mézières, but I shall be thankful when it is over. We think there is a little more action further south, around Fontenoy, and you may be needed there. Our compliments and duty to the Marshal."

Mézières saluted and turned his horse's head to the south. He had done nothing but ride from one end of the field to the other since before the break of day, and had still seen nothing that could be described as fighting. He was beginning to wonder if all the great battles upon

which his imagination had been nourished since child-
hood were, in fact, no more stirring than this—a mere
confrontation of enemies and calculation of probability.
By the time the clash came, he thought, if it ever did
come, the men would be so tired and stale that they
would not do justice to themselves. He was a practiced
and hardened rider, but after four hours of this even he
was beginning to be saddle-weary; and it was not yet
nine o'clock. He left Barry Wood and came down into
the great swarming plain, the heaving boredom and impatience of fifty thousand men; they were ready to kill or
be killed, to do anything, in fact, except continue such
interminable precarious fear-haunted stretches of waiting
as had been theirs for the past three days. The poor
devils, Mézières thought as he rode along, had been in
battle formation through the greater part of yesterday as
well, and if their lot was to be blood and death it would
be just as well for it to come upon them now before their
nerves snapped and broke under the strain.

He would welcome it himself, now—not in the unre-
lieved romanticism of a few hours ago, when he had
thought it a fine thing to charge with drawn saber and
perform the ceremonial maneuvers of mass murder, but
because his mind was still shaken by the vision of the girl
in the dream. That fragile face in tears was before him
even now, as he rode, and confused his inner simplicities
with the dark surge and thrust of premonition. He was
no more superstitious than most Frenchmen of his age—
which was to say, hardly at all—and yet there seemed

something profoundly unnatural in the recurrence of that friendly vision which had now, on the very day of battle, dissolved in tears and terror. He was still under the influence of the overwhelming powerlessness which had immobilized him in the dream, and exercised the freedom of his arms and legs with some feeling of surprise, some fear that it would be taken from him again. It had been a dreadful limitation of his physical existence, an agony of impotence: the muscles that strained and yet could not stir, the space so small that separated him from the girl and yet could not be traversed. He tried to put these feelings away from him and to abstain from asking what the dream had "meant"—how, indeed, could it "mean" anything when he recognized none of its elements?—but it left him with suggestions of disaster, grief and unhappiness which clouded the usual bright, hard outlines of his mind and made him long for the actual fray to begin, so that he could submerge his half-realized discomfort into the life-and-death turmoil of an immense number of men.

"God," he prayed, in the childlike, personal language which had not been his habit for some years, "let it begin soon!"

It was beginning soon enough for a good many men: dismembered bodies, the bloody remains of horses and of uniforms sometimes strewed the ground over which Mézières had to ride. These were the results of the intensified artillery fire from the English positions. Even so, the casualties were on a relatively small scale and the army, almost wholly exposed to whatever artillery could be brought to bear, was still motionless and still racked with the impatience of waiting. Mézières rode through company after company in which men were stretched at ease upon the ground, sometimes actually sleeping through the steady din of the guns. The Swiss and the French guards, the Courten and the Aubeterre regiments, although fully exposed to the English fire, held their inactive positions with comparative calm. In the cavalry lines behind, there could be seen the convulsions of a vast irritation in horseflesh; the animals resented the necessity for standing still while cannon balls passed over or fell among them; they had less sacrificial discipline than their masters. When Mézières asked about the Marshal he was always told to ride further: "He left here half an hour ago; he may be at Fontenoy." After the Aubeterre regiment—the last of those directly exposed to the English fire—Mézières began to see that the Marshal would, indeed, be at Fontenoy, for there was obviously an action of some intensity going on there.

The village of Fontenoy, which the Marshal had made his key position, the apex of his triangle and the spearhead of his resistant force, lay on slightly higher ground than the plain Mézières was now leaving. It was strongly fortified and defended, and what was going on now, as nearly as Mézières could tell, was an attempt on the part of the Dutch and Hanoverian armies to capture it. Something of that kind, at any rate, was in progress, for the cannonading grew much more continuous as he rode

towards the village and came to the first posts of the
Dauphin regiment. There was an explosion in a clump of
men in that regiment and the torn human flesh was scattered wide; Mézières's horse shied violently; there were
screams that could be heard even above the noise of the
guns and the whistling, smoking confusion of the field.
Mézières rode on as hard as he could; this was obviously
a bad patch; some Dutch battery was working on it; the
going might be easier in a moment. He was right: the
Marshal was there, installed in his "cradle" in front of
the village church.

"Ah, Mézières!" he said briskly; his spirits had evi-
dently improved under action. "What news do you
bring? How are the Irish? How is the left? Are the English moving?"

"No, Monsieur le Maréchal. Lord Clare sends his compliments and his duty to you, and says that nothing is
changed. The English are still where they were, still performing movements of some kind without advancing.
Their artillery fire is strong but does not reach the regiments of the left wing, the Irish and the Royal Corsicans."

"You rode straight here, straight and hard? Good.
Your report is therefore the latest we have. Well, we
hope the English don't make up their minds to move for
another hour or so. I should like to see the air cleared a
little at this end of the line before we attempt to digest
the English. We are having a little trouble with the
Dutchmen, yes, a little trouble; but not very much. I do

not think they will make a very deep impression, whatever old Waldeck does. They do not seem to have much appetite for it, eh, Biron?"

The Duc de Biron, who had relieved Chabannes in the command at Fontenoy, was on horseback beside the Marshal's "cradle."

"They are good troops, sir," he said, faithful to the Versailles tradition of "chivalry" in praising the opponent. "I am at a loss to explain their behavior this morning. They do not move with decision or authority."

"Authority be damned," the Marshal said, grinning broadly. (His actual expression was considerably grosser than the system of notation in another language and age can accommodate; Mézières heard the words with a slight prickle of shock, for such tavern talk was not familiar in his ears, at any rate when used to a Duc de Biron.) "The trouble with them is that they've no stomach for the fire we're giving them, no stomach at all. Damn me, Cronstrom's division hasn't advanced an inch in an hour and a half. And what the devil are the Dutch cavalry doing down there towards Antoing, can anybody tell me? Staying out of range of the guns, that's what they are doing, like a lot of comfortable potbellied burghers as they are. They ought to ride on cows, not horses."

The Marshal was in high good humor, apparently: in spite of the appalling discomfort to which his infirmity subjected him at every moment, he could not resist the enlivening and inspiriting influence of an engagement in which his plans, his long-cherished and secretly elaborated plans, were obviously working even better than he had hoped. He was always made grim and a little fierce by the actual sight of blood and death, but this place, in the heart of the little Flemish village, with a church and a cemetery between him and the enemy guns, was for the moment an oasis in which he could be as coarse and natural and good-humored as he pleased. The Duc de Biron, fastidious and exquisite, replied with chilling politeness.

"The armies of the Princes of Orange," he said, "have distinguished themselves in many battles before this, my Lord. I should not care to speak of their abilities too lightly."

The Marshal ignored the reproof with a frankly derisive grunt.

"Come along now, gentlemen," he said, motioning towards his group of aides-de-camp, "we may continue on to Antoing and then come back. It looks to me as if the only spot of real activity along the whole line is here, but we may as well see."

On second thought he detached Mézières again.

"Stay at Fontenoy," he said, "until our return or until there is a message of importance to bring to me. I shall go to Antoing and return here as quickly as possible, but your services may be useful either to reach me or to get to the left. We have not so many people who can talk the English gibberish."

So Mézières found himself again with nothing to do at the heart of a supreme battle, and wondered if this, indeed, was to constitute the whole of his military experience. The Duc de Biron had no use for him, and did not in fact remain at Fontenoy much longer; he moved a battalion of the King's regiment up to the neighborhood of the village church and then returned to his own division in the plain, leaving the post to be commanded by the Comte de la Vauguyon. Through the ebb and flow of these movements Mézières remained stranded on the church steps, and wondered if he might not be equally useful asleep, as he had been in his hour with Clare's. De la Vauguyon paid no attention to him, and the business of manning the peasant houses, inspecting batteries and entrenchments and redoubts, went on busily without his aid.

He determined to take his place in one of the village houses and see something of the impending attack. There was nobody to control his movements so long as he remained in the village of Fontenoy and waited for the Marshal's return. He could wait just as well in the front line as here, beside the little stone church and its shaded graveyard.

This intention was favored by chance: he saw an officer in the Dauphin regiment whom he knew, a certain Bérac, and hailed him without delay.

"Where are you off to, Bérac? Take me with you?"

"Why? We're holding the front houses there; it's no place for an aide-de-camp in a white uniform."

"Never mind. Just slip me in somewhere so that I can

have a look, there's a good fellow. You might even find me useful if they come close enough."

"Come along, then. But unless they come close enough for you to use your sword you'll have nothing whatever to do but stand and be fired upon. Strange idea of pleasure, Mézières. Where's the Marshal?"

They moved on from the village square in front of the church to the peasant houses beyond, which had been fortified with sandbags and heavily manned. The furthest row of houses was protected by a considerable redoubt and connecting entrenchments, all constructed within the past three days, which made the village into a sort of improvised fortress. The key positions around this semicircular fortress were belching artillery fire, and the gunners, working as fast as they could in simplified clothing, shining with sweat and grime, paid no attention to the white-clad officer from headquarters whom Bérac brought among them. At a largish house near the middle of the semicircle, which had been considerably knocked about already and had one end of its roof demolished and repaired, Bérac entered and beckoned Mézières on.

The room was the usual main room of a Flemish peasant's house—in every respect it resembled the structure at Calonne in which Louis XV had been installed, big fireplace, dirt floor, loft above; but the uses to which it was put were very different. Loopholes had been dug in the solid wall opposite the doorway, and inside as well as out, the walls were reinforced by sandbags. It was dark and smoky in here, with the bitter sharp taste of powder in the air. The guns on either side of the house spoke out with such a roar that the noise filled the room and seemed to mix with the darkness and the tang of powder in an acrid confusion of the senses. Bérac pushed Mézières past half-perceived forms in the darkness until he had reached one of the loopholes.

"Now you can look out," he said, "only be careful."

What Mézières saw was a very gradual slope much fretted and defaced by the explosions of the artillery duel. A young oak tree in his line of vision had apparently been somehow uprooted by a cannon ball and lay crazily askew, neither altogether fallen nor intact. Beyond this he could discern what seemed to be a battery of Dutch guns, somewhat masked by a hasty contrivance of wagons and brushwood, but exposed just the same; brown-gray figures moved jerkily in its neighborhood.

"Not very exciting, is it?" said Bérac. "Let me look. Hmmmm . . . Well, they're as far advanced as they are ever going to be unless they rush us. They must do it sooner or later, so why don't they start? What's this? What's this? Before God, Mézières, I think they're starting. Have a squint at this."

The brown-gray figures in the distance seemed to be on the move—suddenly, with a kind of crouching, side-long rush, the irregular lines of Dutchmen spewed out upon the hillside. The movement had actually begun while Bérac was looking through the loophole. Now the artillery on both sides roared louder than ever. As Mézières watched he saw a cannon ball plow through a whole area of Dutchmen, flinging heads and arms and legs out of its way. The lines of brown-gray wavered and then came on again, urged from behind by some insistence great enough to overcome the storm of opposition from the nearest houses of the village. The roof of the house in which Mézières and Bérac stood was abruptly torn asunder, a whole corner of it swept away while wood and straw and plaster filled the air. The light streamed in from the corner thus opened to the sky, and in the reeking, dust-laden air, filled with flying particles, the grimy faces of the defenders could now be seen. A fire sprang up in one corner of the house and was ignored.

"Give them two rounds," Bérac said, shouting as loud as he could, "and then retire from the house. Remember, two rounds. Wait for the order."

He added to Mézières, in a calmer tone, although scarcely less loudly:

"They might get in on the sides and surround us if we don't retire. We're doing this all along the line."

Meanwhile the French guns were rapidly being withdrawn from their advance positions: they ceased with some rapidity on both sides of the house, although not without strewing the slope with the mangled forms of Dutch soldiery. Bérac waited coolly until the range was right and then gave the order to fire. There was a deafening rattle of musketry. The flames at one side of the house were gaining ground with great speed.

"You'd better get back," Bérac said into Mézières's ear. "You can't do anything here. One more round and we retire. The house will burn, and even if it doesn't it will be no good to them—they'll probably be shelled by their own artillery."

Mézières left the house just as the second round was fired. In the village street outside he could see that other houses were now in flames and being evacuated. The Dutch had not actually penetrated to any part of the village, but in their rush upon it they must have lost heavily. The French were now giving way to a second line already prepared, houses, entrenchments and barricades, and their guns were withdrawn to the more advantageous position. The Dutch would be perched on the edge of the village, at the mercy of the artillery on both sides, and any further advance would have to be made at the point of the bayonet. Most of the houses from which the French now retreated were in flames.

Mézières moved towards the central street of the village, which curved towards the church and graveyard. He had left his horse there, rashly enough, and made his way towards it as fast as he could. The street was filled with the scurrying forms of retreating soldiers, all of whom seemed to be in good humor and shouting with spirits. An occasional canvas stretcher, moving towards the graveyard, passed through the throng without disturbing its tone. The general feeling seemed to be that the Dutch had been well punished for their first step, and would be further chastised in time.

The Comte de la Vauguyon, still mounted, rose in his stirrups to watch the movement of the men from the first row of houses to the second. His excited horse kicked at the sandbags and whinnied. Mézières passed through the barricade just beside it; in another moment there was no more space to pass, and the sandbags stretched from one side of the street to the other. The men who had still to come swarmed over them. The semicircular fortress was re-established, a few yards behind its first outlines.

But the Dutch seemed to have become cautious; they must have entered the outer houses in numbers, but it was seldom that a uniform could be seen. The mass of the Dutch advancing force must be behind the row of houses, burning or intact, which the French had just left. A steady and systematic fire was poured into these now, and De la Vauguyon, hurrying from point to point in his semicircle, urged the gunners on to speedier efforts. The outer line of houses would soon be demolished, and the Dutch could not stay in them or behind them; they must advance or retreat.

Mézières found his horse where he had left it in the graveyard beside the church and turned back to see what he could of the action in the barricaded street. He did not mount, but stood beside his excited animal trying to control its trembling. More than of the destructive clash of the last ten minutes or the din that now again filled the air, he was thinking of the animal. The muscles that quivered beneath that smooth hide communicated their disturbance to his own hands that attempted to soothe them.

"Poor César!" he kept saying. "Poor César! Quiet now, César!"

Before him, and behind the barricade, were the men of the Dauphin regiment in irregular lines four deep; others of the same regiment filled the houses on either side and the semicircle of houses that spread beyond them. The Dutch could not be seen.

Yet now, as he watched and tried to quiet his horse, they appeared at only a few yards' distance, emerging from the houses they had entered or from between the houses, advancing with fixed bayonets and deploying into something like a regular formation as they advanced. They had no chance whatever of making a serious impression on the protected French by firing, and they did not, in fact, fire: they came on as fast as they could behind their glittering steel points. Artillery and musketry spoke at once: the gray-brown forms were scattered; many were dismembered in the plain view of Mézières and all others in the village street; others fell in blood and were trampled upon by their fellows; the lines broke altogether into confusion and fell back quickly beyond the first row of houses, leaving the ground laden with remnants and mutilations of human life. The bright air of the May morning, now hideous with smoke and noise, quivered with screams of agony.

Mézières had never heard these sounds before, except on his father's farms in Normandy when the animals were slaughtered. He now felt sick, very sick. He turned his horse back towards the churchyard and led it gently. Any sudden or untoward motion would have made him vomit just then. At the steps of the church, where he had been instructed to wait, he stood for a few minutes drawing his breath in deep and expelling it sharply; he would have to conquer this queasiness if he expected to get through the day.

There were moans and yells from the churchyard, where those in charge of the French wounded—the surgeons, orderlies and priests of the Dauphin regiment—had installed their clients among the graves. But the street in front of the church, just around a curve from the semicircle of fighting, was swept clean for the moment. Into this empty space, as Mézières waited, the Marshal's "cradle" and its retinue of officers came up at the gallop, instigating a cloud of dust.

"Mézières! Where is Vauguyon? What has happened here?"

"He is just around that bend in the street, Monsieur le Maréchal. The Dutch have advanced. They were allowed to get up to the first row of houses, as arranged, with heavy losses. They have just tried to advance further and have been driven back."

"Good. Let us go on to Vauguyon."

Mézières lost his sense of sick desolation the moment the Marshal's cavalcade appeared. He answered with calm, as crisply as the Marshal had questioned him. Now when the whole party moved forward around the bend in the street he mounted and rode with it.

"What has been going on down towards Antoing?" he asked one of the aides who rode behind the "cradle."

"Nothing," the young officer answered with scorn. "Those Dutchmen in the cavalry are no good. They stay out of range of our guns and haven't moved since they took their position. The infantry have tried to advance but they apparently hadn't any idea of the width of the position. They had to spread out constantly and now they've retreated too—or else they are waiting for reinforcements. It's hard to tell. The Marshal took one look at them and asked a few questions and came back here. This is the only place where they are trying to do anything. Have they succeeded?"

"They took the first row of houses," Mézières said. "I suppose that was according to plan: it seemed to be. They must have lost heavily in doing so. They've tried to come on since, but it's too much for them."

The crowd of mounted officers filled the little street, the horses jostling and jingling behind the Marshal's wicker bed-carriage. The Comte de la Vauguyon sat his horse beside the Marshal and gave his report.

"As you can hear, they are firing here and there all round the position," he said, "but they can't advance any further without a bayonet charge. I don't think they can make one with any chance of success. Of course they can bring up artillery, and undoubtedly are doing so."

"It might be better to dislodge them now," the Marshal said. "The houses they have taken are isolated and will do them no good, but they must not advance any further. I have ordered up another battery for your right redoubt, and there are two brigades you can have if necessary, the Crown and the Royal."

"We do not need them," Vauguyon said with considerable pride. "Unless the English send them reinforcements, we can hold them off easily. You see the results of their last—and in fact only—attempt to charge here. The same thing has happened all around the position."

Maurice de Saxe looked at the writhing or still forms scattered about the village street on the other side of the barricade. His face darkened for a moment.

"Yes," he said, "I suppose so. But Waldeck will not stop now. He will send them at you again as soon as he has got them into line. Have they had much trouble, or do you know?"

Vauguyon seemed to understand the meaning of "trouble" without further explanation.

"They have had great trouble," he said with satisfaction. "Our observers report that their officers have had to beat the men with swords and at times to use the point to keep them in line. They are reforming now, in those houses and behind them, but under our fire all the time."

Maurice de Saxe leaned back on his cushions and a twinge of pain showed in his great, coarse face.

"Almighty God," he swore, "I wonder if any of these poor devils feels any worse from his wounds than I do from this infernal disease?"

There was a silence while the Marshal panted; the sweat dropped from his brow on to the silk cushions.

"Let us get down a bit to the left," he said when the twinge had passed. "There is a place there where I think we can see something."

§

The Prince of Waldeck had experienced the greatest difficulty in getting any plan of attack executed, apparently; after nearly five hours of movement the Dutch army had made only one determined push, that which put them into the outskirts of Fontenoy. The width of the front upon which attack had to be made seemed to have surprised the Dutch exceedingly, so that they found themselves constantly deploying as they advanced, and, fearing to scatter themselves too widely, stopped in their tracks and waited for something to happen. The immobility of the whole Dutch left wing was, for this or other reasons, complete; the cavalry was useless; and the greater part of the Dutch appeared to have been moved forward for no purpose except to sit, wait, and be fired upon.

To the north of Fontenoy, where Maurice de Saxe and his traveling staff had now betaken themselves, no such paralysis had occurred. Waldeck himself was there, and was able to give orders without exposing them to the hazards of transmission by messenger along miles of battle front. It was from here that he had ordered the advance to the outlying houses of Fontenoy, and its success (the only one of the day, so far) had set up a considerable agitation in the Dutch ranks. Across the uproar of the field could be heard the proud blowing of trumpets.

Maurice de Saxe rose as high as he could on his cushions to inspect the Dutch through his glasses.

"Old Waldeck seems to be visible enough," he said, grizzling. "I never understand why these collections of banners and horses can't be wiped out. Good enough target."

Some of the young officers around him winced slightly at such an infringement of the laws of "chivalry."

"They're as busy as a lot of old hens," Maurice went on. "What's this they've got coming? Upon my word, they're getting help from the English. Up to the north there—do you see?—there's a movement of troops coming down towards Waldeck. From up Vezons way. I can't see what they are, quite, but they look to me as if they might be—yes, they are, I do believe, Scottish troops, in their skirts. Look, Mézières—where is Mézières?— look through these glasses and see if you think those men are Scots."

Mézières advanced and looked through the glasses.

"The troops moving down from Vezons are wearing the Scottish kilt, sir," he said.

"So that's it," Maurice meditated aloud. "Well, it's another attack on Fontenoy soon, and a sharper one. We may as well get back and tell Vauguyon to prepare. In the meantime let's have another look."

He rose as high as he could and surveyed the whole visible part of the field. The broken plain between Fontenoy and Vezons was obviously the theater of a good deal of movement, the chief part of which was a movement of reinforcement towards Fontenoy, masked (and also impeded) by the houses and hamlets along the way, the churches, hedges and trees of a Flemish countryside. There was a perceptible tendency towards linking up and solidifying a line, and Maurice's practiced eye could see that within half an hour the English troops which now lay between Fontenoy and Barry Wood, steadily establishing their formations and bringing up reserves under the heavy fire of the French artillery, would be in a position to advance. Meanwhile the Dutch at Fontenoy were to be heartened by the aid of fresh English or Scottish troops. The moment of decision was near.

"Gentlemen," Maurice said, "we have an hour or two of hard work ahead of us." He scribbled for a moment on a pad of paper and gave it to De Chavigny, one of the aides near him.

"Take this to His Majesty at Notre-Dame-aux-Bois," he said, "and answer any questions he may ask, if you can."

Then, to Mézières:

"I think you must go back to the extreme left wing, to Clare that is, tell him what is happening and get his report. You will find me at Fontenoy on your return, I believe, unless I am on my way to the left."

To a third aide, De Pujol:

"Ride to Messieurs De Clermont and De Penthièvre and give them an account of what has happened at Fontenoy; also to the Maréchal de Noailles; tell them we expect the English advance within half an hour; and return here with any report they may have."

He spoke to the others with a brisker and less casual air than before, as if the events he expected were already upon them.

"Back to Fontenoy now, gentlemen," he said. "In a very short time we shall have another attack there. It has taken both the English and the Dutch a good many hours to get started, but I think they are on their way now."

Maurice was right, of course: in no respect was he more remarkable than in this ability to feel the ebb and flow of military movement at moments when it had not yet become apparent to others. To most of the thousands of men aligned across the Flemish plain there was no sign of change in a state of affairs which had been the same for hours; keener observers had not missed the significance of the Dutch push forward at Fontenoy, even though they could see little of it; but Maurice perceived the larger movement of which this attack on Fontenoy was a part, and was aware, by something like a sixth sense developed in years of campaigning, that the crisis of the day was at hand. He turned his "cradle" back towards the village of Fontenoy and lay back on the cushions, closing his eyes. He would need all his strength and decision very soon.

In front of the village church he found the Comte de la Vauguyon, dismounted and eating a bit of bread, as happy as if the day's work had ended.

"You've got another attack coming very soon, in not many more minutes, with English reinforcements," the Marshal informed him. "There will be bayonet work, I am sure. You can't depend on artillery any longer."

"Bayonets, Monseigneur?" Vauguyon said gaily. "Our men thrive on them."

Maurice grunted.

"That's to be seen," he remarked, surveying Vauguyon and his group of gold-laced officers without enthusiasm. "Where would be the best place for us? I suppose around this bend in the street."

"That is a kind of central point," Vauguyon said, finishing his crust of bread with composure. "I will just make a round of all the posts and then join you there. The heaviest attack is likely to come just around the corner here. It's the only street where they can charge with bayonets in numbers. The rest—well, it's houses and sandbags. Not so easy."

Maurice made a sign to his driver and went on. He knew Vauguyon to be a brave and devoted officer, more competent than most of his kind, and there was no use harassing him further. The "cradle" left the little village square and, turning the corner beyond the graveyard, came upon the barricaded street where the "central point" of an attack might be anticipated. There was artillery fire directed here, but it did little damage, coming from afar and badly aimed. There was also a certain amount of musketry firing which grew and fell in intensity from time to time but also suffered from a lack of aim; besides, most of the French lay in relative security behind their barricades. Maurice inspected the little street again and saw no possible improvement to be made. The houses all round had been filled with men, the barricades were heavily defended, there was not another man or another gun to be added. Without troubling to withdraw again around the bend to the church, Maurice composed himself on his cushions for a short wait. He might get a minute's sleep, a moment or two of rest if his disease allowed it.

"Keep the horses quiet, damn you," he growled to the driver, and lay back.

The sky was pure and blue above him. He looked straight up at it for a while, unblinking. Somewhere in the vast indifferent area beyond it, he thought, there was the eternal life in which his mother and all devout Lutherans, like the devout Catholics of his adopted country, firmly believed. Maurice did not believe. He adhered to the Lutheran profession out of sheer obstinacy, because he had been born in it, but he could not credit the tales of an upper heaven and a lower hell between which a brief and unsatisfactory existence was assigned to men on earth. He had not found life on earth at all unsatisfactory, and as he remembered the long tumultuous twisting variety of his own existence through the courts and cities, the beds and battlefields and taverns of all Europe, it did not even seem particularly brief. He would not relinquish it with any eagerness, for he still had a great many things to do, but whenever he thought, as now, of the imminent possibility, it was without the slightest fear of consequences. If the heavenly city of his mother's faith existed, he thought, it must be hugely overpopulated by now, and would acquire a large number of additional inhabitants through today's work. He had more faith in the quicklime that had destroyed Adrienne: thus, he thought, thus we go back into the dust from which we came, and a damned good thing, too —Adrienne and all of us, sooner or later, and that's all there is to it, some by a bayonet thrust and long rotting in a peasant's field, some by quicklime and a pauper's grave, some in darkness and some in light, but all to the dust of the earth again. He closed his eyes and dozed. He heard a cannon ball whistle over him and did not open his eyes.

"Damn me," he murmured to himself, "that one was close."

§

He was awakened by the sharp rattle of musketry and the din of increased artillery fire. Vauguyon was beside him.

"They're coming up now, Monseigneur," he was saying, leaning from his mount towards the Marshal's slightly maladjusted wig on the pillows in the "cradle."

Maurice sat up so quickly that a crash and quiver of pain was felt throughout his vast body.

"Ach, Gott!" he groaned aloud, and straightened his wig.

"English troops and Hanoverians as well as Dutch," Vauguyon informed him. "The English are said to be Scots, of Sempill's Highlanders."

"So, these English Scots," Maurice remarked, adjusting himself as comfortably as he could in a sitting position. "They are bad ones. I shall stay here. Proceed with your own arrangements."

Vauguyon saluted him with a sweep of his plumed hat and was off. The "cradle" stood against the wall of one of the peasant houses some thirty yards behind the barricades, and Maurice had a good view of the restricted field in which the attack would have to be made. By the help of two of his aides he got his pillows into a heap behind him and supported himself on one elbow as he watched.

"I don't see anything—yes, yes I do, by God! Here they come—and God help us, they've put the skirted Scots in the center here, just where they'll have to charge this barricade."

From behind the charred remains of the houses which had been fired could be seen a line of Sempill's Highlanders; they appeared and as quickly filed off to the left to attack the houses there. The fire poured into them as they moved was heavily effective, and yells pierced even that noise-laden air. For a few moments no enemy could be seen through the smoke, but the Scots' place was taken rapidly enough by a file of Hanoverians marching stolidly with fixed bayonets. These formed a column under the intensest fire the French could give them and advanced at the trot.

"Good men!" Maurice said vaguely, so that his aides did not know whether he was speaking of the Scots, the French or the Germans. "It's coming now! Now! Now! Um Gottes Willen——!"

The Hanoverians were almost mowed down as they advanced: they were under artillery and musketry fire from protected positions, and the effect upon them was severe. The column could not be maintained, but its survivors made one wild rush at the barricades with their bayonets before they were called back by a trumpet and their officers' orders. In that small space, with its deadly defenses, an advance of this kind could have been made only over the bodies of a regiment, and apparently Waldeck was not prepared to sacrifice so many lives at once: the Hanoverians vanished over the edge of the slope, behind houses half burned and half standing. On the village street they had left something like a fourth of their number, and groans and yells arose from the shattered remnants of men. The French had had few casualties, and those chiefly from the brief clash of bayonets at the barricade. One of Maurice's aides had been wounded in the arm by a musket ball and was making his way back to the cemetery to the surgeons and dressers. The whole affray had taken about three minutes.

"They can't get through here," Maurice remarked with satisfaction, wiping his brow. "They can't get through here unless they are willing to lose about one man out of two. Impossible. What's happened at other points?"

He looked round him: his supply of aides had been reduced to one, who showed no desire to leave the Marshal. The rest were all acting as messengers, except the one who had just been wounded.

"Monsieur de la Vauguyon will be here in a moment, Monseigneur, and will inform you fully."

"I see, you don't want to leave the old man alone. Hmm. Call one of those officers and say I want to see Vauguyon as soon as he can get here. Hmm. They must have been attacking all around the village, but the firing is dying down now. Yes, it is dying down. I don't think they can have got through anywhere, but find out quickly . . . The thing for Waldeck to do now is attack again at once, but I doubt if he has the stomach for it. Once he's used his English and Hanoverians he has nothing left but his own Dutchmen, and they aren't much good. Hmm. Hmmm. Ah, here's Vauguyon at last."

Vauguyon came riding up, as gaily as if the whole affair had been a tournament.

"They tried all round," he said, sweeping his hat in the air, "and they have retired all round. It's no good. They won't break through here."

"I saw those Germans attack," the Marshal said. "They lost far more than we did. Was it the same everywhere?"

"More or less," Vauguyon answered. "Where the Highlanders attacked it was more equal, but even so they had to fall back quickly. We have had losses, but they haven't made a real impression on us anywhere—haven't captured a house or a gun."

"If they're coming again it should be quickly," Maurice mused aloud. "An attack every hour or so will do them no good at all. And in fact it's a waste of life anyhow; they'll never take this place."

His great coarse face was somber for a moment; the thought of useless waste of life was always a dark one for him.

"Monsieur le Maréchal!"

Pujol, one of his aides, had ridden up on a horse that had galloped hard.

"Monsieur de Noailles sends his duty to you and reports that the English are moving."

"Ah!" Maurice snapped out. "Ah! Ah! That is what I expected. We must get down there quickly. Vauguyon, you'll have another attack soon. Do you need anything? I can move up another battalion from the right, where there is no action at all."

"We should not know what to do with them, sir," Vauguyon said with superb confidence. "But your attack, if I am not mistaken, is coming now. You will excuse me, Monseigneur."

He rode forward the thirty yards that lay between them

and the barricades. Another column—this time of Dutchmen—was coming into view through and around the
ruined houses at the crest of the slope.

"Let us wait just one minute to see what happens
here," Maurice said. "It will not take us long, I believe."

The Dutchmen came on in a rush at first, but after one
round of musketry their ranks broke and there was confusion as their officers urged them onward. They seemed
unwilling to advance further and unable to retire; a second volley did great damage among them, and for about
two minutes they seemed to have been flung into the
open space only to serve as targets both for the French
defenders and for their own officers.

"Poor devils! Poor devils!" Maurice said. "They don't
want it—they've got no stomach for it. Come, gentlemen, let us get down to the center and left quickly.
There seems to be no further cause for anxiety here."

Before the Dutch attack had altogether broken down
and disappeared over the crest of the slope, Maurice and
his cavalcade were leaving the village. They rode down
to the left, behind the impregnable lines of the King's
and Dauphin's regiments, towards the center of the field.

"To my tent," Maurice shouted at his aides as they galloped along. "Turn towards my tent."

Obedient and wondering, driver and aides turned to
the left, behind the Brancas regiment, and reached the
tent which had been set up as the Marshal's headquarters.
They had reached it in a few minutes—cheered now and

then as they passed through the lines—and Maurice, groaning and cursing, prepared to descend.

"Give me a hand, there, Pujol, gently—gently," he said. "Oh, God, take it gently!"

His valet and his doctor came running to the front of the tent and took charge of the vast body as it reached the earth. He could walk, with difficulty, leaning on the valet and the doctor, and made his way inside. There was a clump of officers in the anteroom; one of them, M. de Bauffremont, advanced with a court bow.

"Felicitations, Monseigneur, on the success of the action at Fontenoy," he said unctuously.

"Wait a bit, wait a bit," Maurice said morosely. "It's not over yet. The English will be harder to digest."

Without another word to the men in the room he made his laborious way into the interior of the tent. A gentle buzzing was set up when the curtains fell behind him: what had he come here for? What was he going to do now?

The valet came out and whispered to an aide and went back again. The aide went out to speak to a groom. The significance of these movements was instantly apparent to everybody in and about the tent.

"He is going to try to get on his horse again," they said to each other. "He is being tapped again now, and is going to try to ride. It will kill him—it will surely kill him."

During the next few minutes of waiting Chavigny and Mézières both rode up from their respective missions

and were told to wait—Chavigny from the King and
Mézières from Lord Clare. They stood outside, soothing
their horses and waiting in wonder. Half-a-dozen young
officers, those who habitually rode with the Marshal, were
in the same frame of mind, awed into silence by what
they obscurely felt to be a supreme effort of the human
will. The Marshal's horse was brought round and held
by a frightened-looking groom. The gold and silver trappings of saddle, bridle and stirrups glittered in the morning sun. The horse, a powerful beast from the North,
used to that huge weight and Maurice's heavy hand,
snorted loudly.

Maurice came through the outer room of the tent, leaning as lightly as possible on his valet's shoulder. He was
walking more easily now, but his great coarse face was
pale and beaded with sweat. He reached the horse and
stood there, breathing deeply.

"Now," he said.

His valet knelt and two aides approached to help lift
him. He put his right foot on the valet's bent back and
succeeded in getting the other into the stirrup. It was a
long and painful business to hoist his swollen right leg
over the horse's back, and while the operation proceeded
—with the help of two officers on each side—he cursed
violently in German; but at last he was mounted and
picked up the reins. His face was dead white with pain.

"Just a minute, gentlemen, just a minute," he said,
breathing as deeply as he could. They waited. "Now," he
said.

His horse moved; he kept his seat; he was riding. The spectacle was so cruel that those who watched had no desire to cheer or even to comment; he rode in silence. The aides mounted and followed him.

§

As Maurice advanced towards the center of his army he was halted by an officer in full regalia, grimed by smoke and dirt: Du Brocard of the artillery, dashingly mounted, a figure of action in fury.

"What is is, Du Brocard?" Maurice asked, calming his own voice purposely to reduce the heat of the encounter.

"The English are coming, straight for the Guards," Du Brocard declaimed. "I have commanded the great center battery since the beginning. I now ask your authority, sir, to move the battery so as to allow the Guards freedom of action in meeting the English."

"Certainly," said Maurice equably. "Move it. We don't want it firing on our own men."

"Thank you, my Lord," said Du Brocard, wheeling his horse round.

"Stop him!" said Maurice. "Where the devil is the man going? Stop him! Du Brocard! Somebody else can execute that movement. We need you, and your center battery is very exposed."

"I have commanded it so far, sir, and I shall see that it

is effectively moved," Du Brocard said, turning in his saddle.

Maurice stared at him with great, bloodshot blue eyes. The man galloped off, taking silence for permission.

"There's a damned fool who is going to his death in a hurry," Maurice grumbled. "Why couldn't he let somebody else do it?"

The one military virtue (if it was a virtue) which he had never been able to understand was bravado, and as it was extremely common among the French and the Irish-English-Scottish regiments—much more common than the virtues of patience, foresight and endurance, which he valued higher—there were situations with which Maurice was not qualified to deal. The departure of Du Brocard, the most indefatigable of higher officers in the artillery, to execute an ordinary movement under severe fire, was one of these; Maurice rode along heavily, silently, for a few minutes. He felt as sure of Du Brocard's death as if it had already happened.

They came to a light rise in the ground behind the solid waiting lines of the Aubeterre regiment. The panorama of the attack spread before them. Between the hillock of Fontenoy and the hillock of Barry Wood, both belching death and destruction from their powerful batteries upon the relatively low plain between, the English were advancing in measured step. They were under fire from three sides at once, as they had been for half an hour; they had been under longer-range fire for five hours before that; and yet they moved with deliberate order, closing up their ranks as the men fell. The lines of marching redcoats stretched across the plain from the neighborhood of Barry to the neighborhood of Fontenoy, six deep, as Maurice could just make out; they had doubled their ordinary formation. In their center and at intervals along their lines they had batteries of field-pieces, and their batteries established further back, at Vezons, were indefatigable; the noise of the guns was now at its height. Maurice, for one, had neither seen nor heard anything like it in his whole life of campaigning.

"My God!" he said in an awed undertone. "My God! Do you see them? Do you see them, Mézières? You're half English. Are you proud of them? My God!"

"I see them, Monseigneur," Mézières said, his voice flat and expressionless. "I see them clearly."

Something between awe and panic overcame the greater part of the mounted officers who were able, from one side of the field to the other, to overlook this relentless march into the mandibles of death. The artillery from the two sides, Fontenoy and Barry, plowed great trenches through the living block of the English, and the lines closed up as before and advanced, steadily advanced. The English were neither firing nor accelerating their pace: they were simply marching, and the occasional inevitable disorder in their ranks caused by the path of death was so quickly repaired that they seemed to disregard it altogether, and an inexperienced officer—like Mézières—might not have supposed them to be suffering. Maurice de Saxe, who was perfectly familiar with the movement he now witnessed, even though it had hitherto existed only in his own imagination, brushed the sudden tears from his eyes with the back of his hand.

"Damn me," he muttered, "it's not human. They're not human."

With his eyes cleared he looked again. A movement he had not foreseen was taking place among the French.

"What's this?" he roared out. "Pujol, Chavigny, Puységur, what the bloody hell is this? What is Chabannes doing? Forward, here! What are they doing, the fools? Don't they understand their orders?"

He had seen at a glance what was to become apparent to the others in the next few minutes: that the French Guards regiment, instead of remaining in its position to receive the English assault, was advancing to encounter it. This was contrary to the dispositions Maurice had laid down for the conduct of the battle, and he rode forward as fast as he was able—surrounded and followed by his clump of aides—to investigate.

It was now about twenty minutes to eleven, and the English advance had brought them to a point not more than ten minutes' march from the front lines of the French. The center of the French line was held by the Gardes Françaises, with a sunken road—almost a trench —in front of them, and beyond that a slight hill. The Comte de Chabannes, overcome either by impatience or the fear that his men might not stand still long enough to receive the English charge, was now engaged in moving the Gardes Françaises forward, across their protective trench, to the crest of the little hill beyond. Maurice saw what was happening and pushed on, not to prevent it—it was too late for that—but to get himself into position to command in the clash that was coming. He rode straight ahead, into the Aubeterre regiment which held the northern slopes of Fontenoy, from which he could see the rapid movement of the Gardes Françaises to take up their new position. He cursed heartily as he watched.

"What has happened here, Biron?" he asked, riding up to the Duc de Biron in the front rank of the Aubeterre regiment. Biron, glittering with lace and decorations, replied with icy politeness.

"The Comte de Chabannes wished to move the French Guards forward to yonder hill, sir. He will receive the English attack at the crest of that hill. I have moved a further battalion of the King's regiment up to fill the gap between that hill and us. You see them now taking position."

"Herr Jesus!" Maurice cursed. "Herr Jesus! Why couldn't they stay where they were? They had a good ditch—now they'll only die in it, the blasted fools. Herr Jesus!"

He overcame his anger with an effort.

"Puységur," he said, "ride to the Comte de Chabannes and tell him that I say he has advanced his position without sufficient reason, and that consequently we expect him to justify the act by holding the English there."

Puységur swept his feathered hat from his head and galloped off.

"Mézières! Inform the left that they must not wait: Vaisseaux must attack at once, while the Guards are engaged. Pujol! to Monsieur de Clermont, and tell him the cavalry must prepare to charge at once if the Guards break. Chavigny! To the King, and tell him what has happened."

He growled out one or two orders, so that every aide he had with him was detached one by one. From what had just happened, he had only a limited confidence in the ability of the great nobles of France to obey orders, but they had to be given just the same. He was thus left alone, for a moment, beside the resplendent figure of the Duc de Biron. He took one look at that brilliant man, so cool and elegant in the midst of a murderous din; then he turned his horse's head and rode off without another word. His heavy face was white with pain and wet with sweat. He was galloping against time, towards the center, where the princes of the blood and the dukes in all their diamonds commanded the cavalry of France. They would have to do some work now, for once. Well, there was still the Normandie regiment; he had ordered it up; and there were still the Irish. As he rode along, heavily galloping, biting his lips and cursing the indiscipline of the French nobles, with his huge face deathly white and his body swaying perilously in the saddle, he was like some vast corpse set in motion, and the men parted in terror before him.

Normandie, he was thinking, Normandie and the Irish,

peasants all, crude oafs and brutes like himself; but they would obey orders.

§

Puységur had accepted his mission to the Comte de Chabannes with a gay heart: the moment of conflict found him more than ready. He was a young man of twenty-five, but had seen no battle until this day; and although the general shape of the action he witnessed was not apparent to him, and he could perceive it only as a general glorious confusion of sunlit banners, glittering uniforms and movements of color heightened by the heroic and terrible instant of death, it seemed to him altogether a more pleasurable affair than staying at home and learning, like his stolid old father before him, to administer the dwindling family estate as a good squireen. This was better than the hayricks and barnyards of Puységur any day, so long as he survived it; and he had no doubt that he would survive. He urged his horse on, hurtling across the plain behind the front lines of the Aubeterre, and pushed through them at the end towards the new position of the French Guards, who were still moving forward—excitedly, talking and laughing as they advanced—to the hillock where their commander already had taken his position.

Puységur shoved his way through the men recklessly, regarding their formation as little as they did themselves. His horse pranced through the white uniforms; he shouted good-naturedly at the men to make way. When he reached the little hill where the front lines of the Guards were already standing with fixed bayonets, waiting, he turned and rode down to the center to the Comte de Chabannes. The oncoming English were hidden from view here by the ridge of the hillock; only the latter part of the column could be seen coming up in the distance.

"Monsieur le Comte," he said, sweeping his hat off to Chabannes with a flourish, "Monsieur le Maréchal directs me to tell you that your change of position does not seem to him reasonable, but that now you have done it, he expects you to hold the English here."

Chabannes's face, under its layers of paint and powder, grew dark with rage and humiliation. He looked about him to see which of his officers and men had heard the insulting message; none seemed to have done so. He cleared his throat with an effort.

"My duty to the Marshal," he said, "and tell him that I moved forward because I thought we could hold the English here and not where we were. Now, sir, stand aside. The attack is coming."

Puységur saluted again and rode a few steps to the left. There he paused as he was about to wheel back through the ranks; paused breathless, transfixed by the urgency of the moment; for the first lines of the English, marching in almost perfect formation, had just come over the ridge of the hill and stood face to face, at about thirty paces' distance, with the first lines of the French. The English order "Halt!" was echoed down the line, and their men formed shoulder to shoulder with imperturbable regularity as the ranks behind them moved up.

The French officers dressed their line as sharply and quickly as possible, and Chabannes gave the order to the drums to beat for the charge. At this moment, when the pulses of ten thousand men leaped together with the beat of the drums, and the red line faced the white across an interval narrow as the narrow gate of death, there occurred an incident that appealed instantly to the myth-making faculty of the French officers, trained as they were on the romances of chivalry.

A young English officer in blazing red coat and white breeches—Lord Charles Hay, it was, of the Coldstream regiment, although Puységur and the others on the French side were not to know this fact for days, if ever —stepped in front of his men and brandished what looked like a silver flask. It was his flask of brandy or whisky, which he had found useful in the long march since the mists of early morning.

"French Guards!" he shouted in a lusty voice that carried over the roar of cannon and the roll of drums. "We are the English Guards! And mind you stand still now and give us a fight instead of running away as you did at Dettingen!"

To the astonishment of the French, a rumble of laughter came from the red-coated ranks.

"What does he say? What did he say?" the French asked each other.

The Comte d'Anterroches, a lieutenant of the French

Guards, was directly opposite the English lieutenant. D'Anterroches prided himself on some knowledge of the English tongue. When Puységur asked him what the Englishman had said, D'Anterroches answered:

"He is telling us to fire first. Inviting us to fire."

Puységur's veins hummed with the magnificence of it.

"Ah, the noble souls!" he said. "Aren't you going to answer him?"

D'Anterroches, removing his plumed hat with a great flourish, shouted back at the Englishman:

"Non, c'est à vous de tirer les premiers, Messieurs les Anglais!"

Whether the chivalrous reply was taken as an order by the nervous front rank of the French, or whether their discipline was unequal to the effort of waiting, the result was the same: a jerky, uncertain rattle of musketry broke out from the white-coated French line. Instantly the order to fire echoed down the now perfect lines of redcoats from Barry to Fontenoy, and was followed by such a crash of muskets as had not yet been heard. Point-blank, at thirty paces, the English fired, and of the front rank of the French Guards not more than one man in two was left standing.

The pandemonium that now broke loose gave Puységur no time to think of the glories of war or the niceties of chivalry. The cannon were still roaring; but no cannon and no drum could have drowned out the shrieks of agony that broke out among the French, to be followed immediately by the terrible mob yell of panic.

Seeing their front rank halved by one volley, the back ranks of the French Guards broke at once, turned and fled. Some of their officers remained in the front rank, attempting to form it again; others attempted to stay the flight of their men by yells, curses, and by beating them with the flat of the sword. Puységur on his horse—which had leaped mightily into the air with the English volley, and now plunged in terror through the fleeing men—was swept far back from the front line. He struggled to regain control of his terrified mount and to turn its head again towards the front. All around him men were throwing away their muskets and ammunition and running for their lives. Puységur burned hot with shame and horror. In a minute and a half—less rather than more—the French Guards had been turned into a frantic mob struggling with fury to escape.

Puységur got his horse round and drew his sword. He was by now far behind the front line, but he could at least do something towards stopping the panic. He flashed his sword in the air, but before he could bring it down a musket was smashed hard against his elbow; in his pain and astonishment he dropped his sword. All around him the white-uniformed men were running away with determination, with fury. His horse plunged in excitement.

"Back! Back, you cowards!" he yelled, hoarse with shame. "Back, damn you, back!"

Three bayonets—French bayonets—reached him at once: one in the thigh, one in the flesh of the right side, and one in the arm with which he was trying to control his horse. He fell heavily, and with his brain reeling. He was conscious, although confused and hot with horror. He could see one of the fleeing soldiers extricate his useless foot from the stirrup; he could see his horse plunge away into the mob. The soldier bent over him and rapidly, with practiced fingers, ran through his pockets and extracted the money to be found there. Puységur groaned with rage, shame and shock. The soldier was a leatherfaced peasant like hundreds of his own peasants at home.

"Shame!" Puységur said through his clenched teeth. "Shame, shame, shame!"

"What's the matter, my pretty?" the soldier said. "We won't leave you here. Don't worry. Jean! Louis! Hey! Come help me drag the pretty little officer down to the ambulance. Somebody has hurt him."

Three of the Guards—they were all veterans, men who had served for years—stopped in their flight to pick up Puységur and carry him, helpless and raging, towards the field hospital behind the lines. As they hurried along, making no special effort to preserve their burden from jolts, the horror and loss of blood overcame Puységur: his consciousness surrendered and was engulfed in the dark.

§

The almost instantaneous rout of the French Guards was followed two or three minutes later by the flight of the Swiss Guards who occupied the next position on the left. The plain was filled with the hurrying forms of the uniformed mob, some of whom still kept their weapons and used them to make a passage for themselves. The cavalry lines behind, already in turmoil through the excitement of their horses, were further disordered by the impact of the fugitives. Some of the cavalrymen attempted to stem the tide, and the fleeing Guards stabbed with bayonets as they fled. The weird shriek of wounded and dying horses was added to the noises of the plain.

"Let them go, let them go, for God's sake don't attempt to stop them!" Maurice shouted. "Clear the field, get them out of the way, let them run to hell if they want to! Clear for a cavalry charge, gentlemen! Clear for a cavalry charge!"

He was galloping down the line of the cavalry regiments, and even the panic-stricken Guards got out of his way: he and his horse were both monstrously big, and his corpselike face was set and terrible. One of his aides, Chavigny, caught up with him at this moment.

"The King's compliments," he shouted, riding along beside the Marshal, "and he says he sees no point in the officers of the French Guards remaining where they are, to be killed uselessly, as the men have all run away."

"Go and tell Chabannes that, the bloody fool," Maurice answered, without slackening his pace. "Tell him the King orders him to retire. His officers are to join the nearest infantry brigades. His own men have nearly all gone and we want to clear for a cavalry charge. Hurry."

He rode on alone, cursing and talking to himself.

"Um Gottes Willen——! I knew the fool would get it if he moved, and yet he would move. Herr Jesus! If I could get hold of a few of these—— Herr Jesus! Will Normandie get here in time?"

He stopped to speak to the commanding officers of the Cravattes regiment.

"You will have to charge, and then charge again, and then charge again," he said, keeping his voice to its coolest and lowest level by an effort. "Later we can bring up the left and give them an infantry attack, but it is up to you now."

"We are handicapped by the Swiss Guards now, my Lord. They are—as you see."

"Wait a few minutes. They'll clear off. If they don't, ride them down, ride them down, man. They deserve no better."

The Swiss had broken flat on to the lines of the Cravattes regiment, throwing the latter into considerable disorder and fighting to get through them; the fugitives ran beneath the horses' bellies and between the nervous animals, stabbing without mercy when the way was barred to them. Maurice's desire to let them escape as quickly as possible—since they were obviously of no further use—was ill understood by the French nobles, with the notions of "honor" and "prestige" which constituted their chief military intelligence, but by endless repetition the orders were at last understood, and the effort to stop the flight was gradually—within about fifteen minutes from the outbreak of the confusion—abandoned all down the line. Maurice rode on to the Vaisseaux regiment, which held the position to the left of that which had now been abandoned by the Swiss.

"You will have to keep up a musketry fire on their flank," he said here. "At intervals, when you can do so effectively, charge them and give them the bayonet. Keep it up all the time. You have them on the flank. The brigade of Guards is gone, but as soon as the field is cleared we are charging them with cavalry. Understood?"

"Yes, my Lord."

An officer brave in red coat—the red coat of the Irish, not the English—rode up at this moment. It was Lally-Tollendal, whose regiment occupied the next position to the regiment of Vaisseaux. He was wild with excitement, his blue eyes snapping and his voice imperfectly controlled.

"Monseigneur, Monseigneur!" he said to the Marshal. "For the love of God and his Holy Mother, will you bring the Irish into action? There we have been the whole morning doing nothing, and the men are aching for it. Will you give us an order, sir?"

Maurice looked at him for a moment, and a grim smile came over his white and sweating face.

"You will get your chance, good Lally," he said. "You can tell Lord Clare from me that he can deploy his men now; they do not need to remain in Barry Wood; it is in no danger. Bring them up on this side of the wood, and in time they will get their chance."

"Now God be praised!" said Lally, riding off.

Maurice looked after him for a moment. There was something of his own vanished youth in that slightly absurd figure. No matter. He was glad the Irish were there. He turned his steaming horse—which, like its master, had not ceased to sweat since their ride to and fro had begun—backward into the center and rode for Notre-Dame-aux-Bois.

I must just make sure of the King, he was thinking: all those courtiers around him will begin to squeak and gibber the moment they see the English coming on and the Guards running. They will pronounce the battle lost before it has fairly begun, the fools. The King is not a coward, but he knows nothing of this business, and he may be jostled into doing something foolish—ordering a general retreat, or otherwise intervening; or else running away himself . . .

The Cravattes regiment was lined up in better order now, and ready to charge. The drums were already beating, and the horses plunged eagerly in their tracks, waiting for the trumpet call. The men called out a long cheer for Maurice as he thundered heavily past them, his great sweating beast and his own swaying body as conspicuous as the red line of the enemy. Maurice gave them a sign of the hand and went on. Time was when he would have charged with them, but if he went now there would be nobody left to keep this army together and execute his plans—his plans which he was determined would not fail.

Mézières caught up with him as he was passing the Cravattes regiment and rode alongside, reporting in a shout.

"The Irish and Scots are leaving Barry Wood and filling up the positions close to Vaisseaux," he said. "Lord Clare and Lord John Drummond say their men are anxious to engage in the action."

"They will have their chance," Maurice answered. "I am going to the King now; ride with me. I shall have more work for you presently."

Mézières rode along without speaking further. He had meant to tell the Marshal of the sights he had seen among the Irish; of their savage impatience to be in the fight; of the efforts their officers were making to keep them quietly in line and waiting. He had wanted to repeat what Lord John Drummond had said to him:

"My Highlanders are not like your French troops. They do not move in parade formations and they do not often run away. To be so near a battle and not to be in it drives them crazy. Look at them! It is all my officers can do to hold them from running out there to attack the English."

But there was no use saying these things to Maurice now. He seemed so sunk in gloom, so preoccupied, with his corpselike face frowning and sweating and looking neither to right nor to left, that any information given him would have been half unheard. Marshal and aide, they rode on past the musketeers and the bodyguards until they reached the little plateau of Notre-Dame-aux-

Bois where the King and his courtiers had been installed
as spectators since the early morning. Just as they reached
it Maurice's experienced ears heard a new trumpet call
from the plain: Cravattes and Fitzjames were sounding
the charge.

Maurice stopped in his tracks to watch. The whole
plain was visible from this slight eminence. The regiments
of redcoats had advanced steadily until they were now
in the place which had been occupied earlier by the
regiments of Swiss and French Guards and Aubeterre.
Part of Aubeterre had reformed to the right; none of it
had run away. The English column thus had Vaisseaux
on their right (the French left) and Aubeterre on their
left (the French right) with the cavalry regiments in
front of them. The artillery fire to which the English had
been subjected for nearly an hour from the heights of
Fontenoy and the redoubt at Barry Wood had never
ceased. The redcoats, advancing, were thus surrounded
on three sides by whitecoats of great strength, and if
they advanced much further they ran the risk of being
completely surrounded. In spite of the desperate danger
of this position, and the continuous fire to which they
were subjected, the lines of redcoats were still firm, and
still moved slowly forward, halting to fire at the order as
coolly as if the whole thing had been a maneuver on
parade.

Against the solid red body thus thrust into the middle
of the French army the cavalry was now let loose: a magnificent charge, the horses thundering over the plain

while the trumpets shrilled. But it was over in less than two minutes. For as Maurice watched, and Cravattes and Fitzjames rode, the redcoats leveled their muskets and fired another of those deadly sharpshooting volleys, and the French cavalry was thrown into limitless confusion at thirty paces from the enemy. Many horses and men fell; others stumbled and crashed over the fallen; the remainder of the horses were crazed with terror and lashed out madly with their trembling legs, running in all directions beyond the power of their riders to control them. Part of Cravattes and Fitzjames wheeled off in time and retired with a semblance of order, but a good part of the battalions scattered in confusion or lay in their own blood on the field. Wild, riderless horses could be seen running in terror towards the farthest extremities of the plain.

Maurice sighed heavily.

"Ça y est," he commented. "Cavalry can't get near infantry; not a disciplined infantry with plenty of ammunition. Impossible."

He seemed to be talking to himself.

"But we must do it," he said in an argumentative undertone. "There is nothing else to do now. We must try it again and again. When Normandie gets up, and the Irish . . . No. There is nothing else to do now."

Mézières kept a respectful silence. The Marshal's head sank slightly, as if by its own weight, and he made a grimace of pain; then, straightening up again, he rode slowly across the plateau towards the group of spectators at its edge.

What he saw was not unlike what he had expected to see. The courtiers and gentlemen in waiting were, most of them, so pale that the paint on their cheeks stood out with startling distinctness. The Marquis d'Argenson was walking up and down at one side, apart from all the rest, in some interminable colloquy with himself. The Dauphin, on his knees under an elm tree to the left, was counting his rosary with bloodless lips. The King alone, standing at the edge of the plateau, retained his full composure. He turned and waited for Maurice to ride up to him.

"I beg Your Majesty's leave to stay on my horse," Maurice said. "If I dismount I may not be able to mount again."

"It is you who command here today, Marshal," the King said. "Our fortune does not seem to be good, up to now."

"If the Dutch were the equals of the English, we should be lost indeed," Maurice said. "But they are not. Look, Sire. The whole right wing of our army is comparatively idle. The Dutch do not even come within range of our guns on that side now. Fontenoy is safe; they have been beaten off there three times. No attack is made on Barry Wood to our left. We have therefore only the one attack to fear, that which Your Majesty sees in the center."

"However, it is a severe one," Louis observed.

"It is a severe one, but most of our army is intact and Your Majesty sees that we must win. The English cannot stay there forever. If they advance they will be cut off, and if they retire they will have lost."

"Our men do not seem to be able to stand against them, sir."

"If Your Majesty wishes to retire to Calonne, the army will be glad to know its sovereign is safe, and I shall continue the action until we have won it."

"There is no question of my retirement," Louis said severely. "I shall stay here, sir, until the end."

The old Maréchal de Noailles, who was pale and seemed in considerable discomfort—according to the tale told by the army, he had fouled his breeches three times during the morning, from fear—intervened at this point.

"I have urged His Majesty to retire," he said. "Nothing can stand against those terrible English infantrymen. Nothing will stop their advance. They may even reach this place, and seize the person of the King himself."

"We have English infantry of our own," said Maurice dryly. "We also have French infantry which will not run away. We have Scots and Irish who have not yet been used. The Normandie regiment is on its way up now from Rumillies; if you look you can see it. Vaisseaux and Aubeterre are standing firm. All those who wish to retire to Calonne are at perfect liberty to do so."

"But look!" Noailles cried in a sort of elderly whine. "Another cavalry charge! The noblest troops of France, sir, and they can do nothing."

Maurice looked out over the plain. It was true: the regiment of Clermont-Prince, with remnants of Cravattes and Fitzjames, were charging again, and with the same results as before. The thunder and the dust, a volley of musketry, and inextricable confusion. The English stood their ground unmoved.

"It is a terrible sight," Maurice said slowly. "Those who wish to avoid seeing it may retire. The bridge over the river is perfectly safe."

"I put my full confidence in you, Marshal," the King said in a loud voice, so as to be heard by everybody on the plateau. "I shall stay here. You are in unquestioned command, and will do as you see fit. Any man who disobeys you, whatever his rank, shall be answerable for it."

"Thank you, Sire. Have I leave to return to the field?"

The King, straight and still, his face pale with anger at the importunities to which he had been subjected by his courtiers, acknowledged Maurice's salute with a slight bow. The Marshal turned and rode away, Mézières at his heels.

"You see that King, now," Maurice said in mild, conversational tones, as he and Mézières descended the slope towards the lines of musketeers. "He is worth ten of those pipsqueaks he has about him. Oh, I know you can't trust him, usually, and he has a terrible weakness for the petticoats, but just the same he is the best of the lot. I dare say they have been at him for the past hour to get him to run away, or to order a retreat, or some bloody nonsense of that kind. He has more sense. After all, he must know that I know what I am doing. And if he opens his eyes he can see that no matter how many filthy cowards we have in our army—and between ourselves, Mézières, I don't blame any troops for being cowardly; it's purely a matter of how they have been trained—the superiority of our position must count in the end. What gripes me is to see all those red-heeled old women around him. That Noailles—ugh!"

Mézières was silent with astonishment. In spite of his adoration for the Marshal, he could not get used to the coarseness of language which had occasionally appeared in his talk today on the field; and it was a shock to hear anybody, even the Marshal, speak with such irreverence of the King. Perhaps Maurice was aware of the effect he was making on the young man; he shot him a look, and laughed. It was not a very mirthful laugh.

"To the gallop, Mézières," he said. "We must get back down there."

§

To those who had no firm grasp of the general line, the confusion and disorder of the French army now appeared to be complete. The Royal and Couronne brigades, marching according to the Marshal's orders, had been ordered to retreat by their own officers and re-tired in confusion behind the lines of cavalry. The cav-alry regiments had charged three times, the last two over many of their own dead and dying, and had been broken

into fragments so that no single company could be
formed together. Drums, trumpets and banners could
not conceal from any man on the field the fact that the
whole center of the French army had collapsed. A movement of flight was taking place in the best of the regiments there, and the road to the bridge over the river was
crowded with fugitives. The field hospitals were unable
to move in the turmoil, and the wounded lay where they
had fallen, to be robbed or ridden over or killed by their
own compatriots. With the courage of despair, the valid
remnants of Cravattes, Fitzjames and Clermont formed
and charged again over the encumbered field, and broke
again at twenty paces from the line of redcoats. A general terror seemed to have broken out over the whole
plain.

Maurice and Mézières, riding down towards the center
of the plain, encountered two of the Marshal's chief
aides, Valfons and D'Espagnac, both of whom had the
look of defeat on their harassed faces. They were not allowed to speak.

"Bring the Piedmont regiment up towards Notre-
Dame-aux-Bois, Valfons, and hurry. Tell them I want a
solid formation in the center there, doubled. The English will not reach that point for an hour yet, if ever, but
I want Piedmont there."

"But, Monseigneur——"

"Off with you. Hurry."

As Valfons turned and galloped off, the Marshal
belched loudly and said:

"There goes another son of a bitch that thinks the battle is lost."

To D'Espagnac, riding alongside, he said:

"Ride towards Rumillies and get Normandie to hurry up a bit. No disorder, mind you—keep them fresh, but we shall need them within half an hour or so."

D'Espagnac, greatly daring, said:

"Shall we be here in half an hour, Monseigneur?"

Maurice cursed violently in German for a moment.

"Get on and obey your orders, man, and leave that to me," he said. "We'll be here when you come back."

When D'Espagnac had gone he cursed continuously and obscenely for some time. This seemed to afford him relief, for when he spoke to Mézières again, it was in relatively mild tones. Mézières, almost stunned by the outburst of vulgarity from his chief, was riding along with jaw clenched.

"You see, Mézières, they all think we are done for," the Marshal said. "They only see part of it. They don't know that this is exactly what I expected and that nothing has surprised me, except when my orders are not obeyed. I described this battle thirteen years ago, Mézières, in a book which I may give you to read some day if you have not read it. Our center has gone, but our left and right are intact, and we shall soon have a new center, and in the meanwhile the poor devils of English are in a hell of a position. They are brave and disciplined men, Mézières—the best soldiers in Europe; you should be proud of them—but that Hanoverian sow who leads them has put them into a position which they cannot possibly hold. They can't move in any direction, and the best of my men have not yet been used."

"I hope you are right, Monseigneur," Mézières said through set lips. It was as much as he could do to speak. At his age, with an imagination fostered on romantic military traditions, honor, chivalry and the like, and with a hero worship for the Marshal which had been unshaken until this day, the events of the past half-hour were not easy to stomach. He had seen the French Guards behaving like wild dogs; he had seen officers beating their men to keep them in line, and men stabbing officers in order to escape; and he had heard his idol, the Marshal, talk like a stableboy in the midst of appalling disaster. Mézières was, for the moment, stunned; it seemed to him a colossal egotism that could look on the present confusion of the field and imagine that anything good could come of it; and he was sickened by some of the expressions Maurice had used—expressions of such strength that the most debauched of the troopers would have hesitated to pronounce them. Was this all it was, he was wondering suddenly with part of his mind—the splendor and glory of war—nothing but filth, cowardice, blood and treachery?

As they approached the place where some remnants of the Cravattes regiment were trying to assemble again, the Duc de Richelieu rode towards them.

"Monseigneur," he said excitedly, "Monseigneur——!"

Maurice did not allow him to continue.

"I know, I know," he said, shouting him down. "The center is routed, and so on and so on. I have something for you to do, Monsieur de Richelieu. Nobody in this army can do it so well. You will wait upon His Majesty the King and keep him from leaving this field."

Richelieu's horse, pawing the air as he was pulled up, nearly unseated the glittering duke.

"Very well, sir," Richelieu said. "Does His Majesty wish to leave the field?"

"He does not. But he is surrounded by a lot of old women in the last stages of panic. It is absolutely essential that he remain here now. You know that I did not want him to come here; you know that I tried to get him to retire early this morning. He would not do so. Now it is too late. If he retired, the whole army would be seized by a panic."

"It seems to me that a large part of it is already in panic, sir," Richelieu said, laughing. His laugh won Maurice, in spite of an ingrained dislike.

"Well, so it seems, but remember, Richelieu, the King must not move from where he is for the next hour. Will you make certain of this?"

"I will, sir, I will do it. I have charged twice with the Cravattes, and damn me if I can see any more men to charge with."

"You can be most useful with the King now, Monsieur le Duc. Do your best. It is absolutely essential."

Richelieu made off to Notre-Dame-aux-Bois and Maurice resumed his course. He was skirting the center of the field and making for the Vaisseaux regiment on the left. The bullets were singing through the air here, and Mézières, in spite of himself, could not help ducking now and then over his horse's mane. Maurice glanced at him and made a sort of grimace that might have passed for a grin.

"You are new to this kind of work, Chevalier," he said. "It does no good to dodge bullets, you know. By the time you have dodged the bullet has passed. They are cleverer than you are. They get you when you least expect it."

Mézières did not reply; he was mortified to the depths. What did those keen eyes not see, bloodshot and half shut with pain as they were? He wondered. His horse jumped nervously when it could not avoid the dead or wounded in its path. The corpses of horses lay here, too, and the air was filled with groaning and shrieking. The Marshal rode up the slight slope to the left and into the Vaisseaux regiment. The men cheered him loudly as he passed. They were grimy, sweating and bloodstained, but they were more or less in line, and their field hospital was still working, so that their wounded did not lie among them. Maurice and his aide passed behind the first three lines and came up through the center to Guerchy, who commanded the regiment. The Prince de Croÿ, the intrepid and handsome, brilliant in his white uniform, sat his horse beside Guerchy.

Mézières's spirits suddenly bounded high. All was not lost, then: this regiment held its lines very nearly as well as the English themselves, and there were Guerchy and

Croÿ, the bravest of the brave, to remind a sick and despairing witness that there was plenty of courage left in France. Mézières swallowed hard and tried to keep his face expressionless.

"Eh bien, eh bien, Monsieur de Guerchy," Maurice said, drawing up beside the Colonel, "you have done well. If all had done as well—but never mind that. Congratulations, sir. How many times have you charged?"

"We have made four attacks, Monsieur le Maréchal. In accordance with your orders, I have broken off the attack each time and retired after a few minutes, so as not to be too deeply engaged. We are keeping up a steady fire of musketry, and we shall continue to attack from time to time. But I do not understand what the English are doing now."

"Hm . . . Hm . . . If they had good sense they would go home," Maurice replied, with a joviality which rang a little false to his listeners. "However, let us see. They appear to be going through some kind of parade maneuver. Damn me if I have ever seen troops like them. There they are under a heavy artillery fire from both sides, with plenty of musketry peppering into them, and they are forming and reforming like a lot of toy soldiers. They don't seem to mind the fire no matter how many of them are hit. Now let's see. What the devil *are* they doing?"

He watched them for some moments through his glasses. They had advanced so far now that they occupied the center of the French army, impaling it upon a solid red-coated mass which nothing seemed able to shake. In front of them there was confusion and terror, but on their flanks they had the white-coated regiments that had not been broken, and above all they had the great redoubts of Barry and Fontenoy with their batteries of heavy artillery. The Duke of Cumberland had apparently reckoned upon frightening the French so that they would abandon these flanking positions as the English column advanced; but, since this had not happened, and both Barry and Fontenoy continued to belch destruction into the English ranks, he had now called a halt and was performing some kind of maneuver for reforming his army. Protected by lines of grenadiers on each side, which kept up a steady fire, the redcoats were marching imperturbably and forming new ranks.

"He is putting them into a hollow square, as nearly as I can tell," Maurice said slowly. "We have heavy business before us now, gentlemen. He seems to have a front of something like three battalions there, to the center, and he will have three on each side, I suppose. Yes, that is what it is, a hollow square, and what the devil does he mean to do, I want to know? Is he going to stay there for ever? They will be slaughtered."

He dropped his glasses impatiently. His regard for the Duke of Cumberland—the "fat boy", or the "Hanoverian sow", as he often called him—was not great; his regard for the English infantry was unbounded, and it seemed to him that to contest an impossible position with such stubbornness was stupidity itself, a kind of deliberate massacre. The danger was not that the hollow square could clear the field—which Maurice was convinced it could not—but that a persistence in that place, for some hours to come, might produce such panic in the French army that it would abandon the field in spite of everything. Maurice sighed heavily.

"You will have to attack again, Guerchy," he said, "while they are busy with this folderol of new formations. Can you get round to the right, Mézières, and tell Biron to attack again as sharply as possible while the English are maneuvering?"

Maurice turned and walked his horse slowly back through the lines of Vaisseaux towards Barry Wood beyond. He wished he could go to his tent and have another brief session with the sallow, lugubrious little doctor; but there was no time. It was now a little past eleven o'clock in the morning, and it had taken the English no more than half an hour to rout the French center, cause great damage, occupy the center of the plain and capture three batteries. In what seemed, to those who lived that tumultuous half-hour, no more than a minute and no less than a day, the face of the battle had changed. Maurice alone knew that the advantages gained by the English were in fact disadvantages, since by them the red-coated mass was placed in an untenable position; but to the thousands of frantic Frenchmen now engaged in running away, this truth was not apparent. To hold the English in place by repeated attacks until fresh troops could come up—Normandie, Piedmont, the Irish—and to make sure that the final attack should not fail . . . Well, he must keep up for an hour or so more before he could see the doctor. He urged his horse into a trot and groaned loudly as his watery carcass shook in the saddle. Valfons came riding up to join him.

"Did you give the orders to Piedmont?"

"I did, Monseigneur."

"Were they being obeyed?"

"I did not wait to see, Monseigneur."

"I hope no infernal prince of the blood or duke of the chamber pot interferes to prevent it, sir. Piedmont is wasted down there, doing nothing."

"Yes, Monseigneur."

Maurice glanced at Valfons. The aide was riding beside him with downcast looks, pale and worried. Maurice grunted and said nothing. He was attached to Valfons because of their kindred profligacies, their love of strong drink and low company; but even so it was clear that Valfons had somewhat lost his sanguine and boastful temperament this morning.

As they left the zone occupied by Vaisseaux, the rain of musketry dwindled and vanished. They were now coming to the slopes of Barry Wood, which were covered with the red-coated Irish and kilted Scots deploying regularly to take up new positions. Maurice looked at them with satisfaction, and even Valfons seemed to experience a slight quickening of the pulse; his color began to return. Maurice, surveying the slope, picked out the banner of Lord Clare and rode towards it. As he passed through the Irish—it was Lally's regiment—they cheered him in a wild mixture of Gaelic, English and French. He touched his cocked hat to them and grinned.

"They are savages, Valfons, but mind you, very useful," he said. "They always remind me of the men I had up North."

For a moment he saw the yelling charge of Russ and Lett and Finn over the white snow, and their blood spilled under the pine trees. That was long ago, in his youth, before Adrienne died. He drew up before Lord Clare.

"You understand your orders, my Lord?" he asked. "I had not time to come and tell you myself."

"I believe so, my Lord. We are to support Vaisseaux and align beside them."

"Not exactly. That will do for the moment, until you can get your full force up. What is there here, on this side of the wood?"

"My regiment and Lally's and Lord John Drummond's Scots."

"That will not be enough. I want the whole Irish brigade and the Scots. Every regiment. When they have all passed down here to the left they can form a column and attack the English left and center—that is, passing to the right of Vaisseaux. Understood?"

"Yes, my Lord."

"How long do you think it will take to get the whole force down?"

"Half an hour, Monseigneur. Perhaps a little more.

Some of them are pretty far beyond the redoubt on the other side."

"That will do well enough. Meanwhile we shall worry the English by repeated attacks. Vaisseaux on this side is doing very well. If you can get your force down to the right of Vaisseaux in half an hour to forty-five minutes, do so, form them, and wait. It is very important to wait for the order to attack, as we want to make it general."

"Yes, Monseigneur."

"I count on the Irish and Normandie. Where is Normandie?"

"We have seen it coming up, sir. It cannot be far away now, on the other side of the wood."

"Better halt here until you can get your whole force down. Normandie can come round on your right. Yours will be hard work, with the bayonet. You will not fail."

"No, sir."

Maurice and Clare saluted gravely. The Marshal turned his horse and made off again at the gallop.

"Come along, Valfons," he said. "We must get round to the right again quickly and see what we can do with Carabiniers."

Clare turned on his aides and sent them scurrying off on a variety of missions. The order to halt went echoing down the lines. When Lally received his orders he was near to an outburst of weeping.

"In the name of God and all his saints, O'Hegarty," he said, "are we never going to get into this battle at all? I thought we were on the move at last, and now we have to sit on our haunches again, twiddling our thumbs. Give the orders, man, give the orders. I wish I had a pack of cards with me. Devil a fine kind of battle this is, with the Irish sitting useless on the side of a hill like a herd of grazing cows."

Alexander MacCarthy of Drisbane, in Clare's, when he had given his orders, collected himself darkly and spoke to Davoren.

"There's some dirty work in this, Davoren, you can depend on it," he said. "It's the filthy French and the dukes and traitors among them. They've conspired together to take all the honor and glory of the battle away from the Irish. And we here since the break of day, panting to get at the throat of an Englishman. Devil an Englishman have I seen all this day, except the ones in our own ranks. There's treachery and conspiracy in it."

The trumpets rang and echoed for the halt, from the near slope of Barry Wood through the wood itself, to the redoubt of Chambonas (where remnants of the French and Swiss Guards had taken refuge) and to the regiments of Roth, Berwick, Dillon and Bulkeley beyond. Patrick Cusack in the first company of Dillon's blew mightily; Rory MacNaughton blew in Lally's; Michael Gilcannan blew a blast for Clare's. While the troops stopped in their tracks, the aides rode busily to explain the new orders, and Lord Clare himself turned back into the wood to speak to the other commanders. But it was Lally who—fuming in his impatience with nothing to do—thought of the four Swedish pieces, the battery of field artillery.

"O'Hegarty, O'Hegarty, quick, man! Is there not a field battery of four pieces down there by the redoubt, doing nothing? Jesus, Mary and Joseph! And not another field battery left in the whole countryside. They told us the English had silenced or captured them all. Would you nurse the regiment, man, while I go tell the Marshal we've guns to give him that all but I had forgot."

O'Hegarty's lantern jaw relaxed a little.

"Would it not be better," he asked, "to speak to Lord Clare?"

"He's gone over the hill yonder and it would be quicker to reach the Marshal," said Lally, seizing at any excuse to get a view of the field of action. "My horse! I'll be back before you've finished twiddling your thumbs, O'Hegarty."

He jumped into the saddle and was off. O'Hegarty stood, grim and silent, and watched him go. The men stood at ease or crouched or sat on the ground. The unholy din of battle before them had ceased to astonish their ears; they had grown used to it; some of them began to shake dice as they waited. Behind them, in the woods and the plain, the further regiments of the Irish, having received full orders, began to close up. In the upper slope, behind Clare's, some of the Highlanders began to dance to the piercing wail of their pipes.

"Whisht, look at them," said Alexander MacCarthy of

Drisbane, deeply disgusted. "There's a pack of wild men for you, squawking and prancing on the brink of death. Isn't it a fine thing now to send Christian men into battle beside the likes of them?"

§

The Duc de Richelieu came on to the plateau of Notre-Dame-aux-Bois full tilt; he had raced his horse to get there. Fop, courtier and timeserver though he was, he had courage and to spare; his pride was immense, his sense of military "honor" as acute as the training and tradition of his caste could make it. When Maurice de Saxe appointed him to keep the King on the field of battle, the choice was good; no other but Richelieu could have exercised the kind of pressure needed to overcome the emotionalism of a whole court.

The plateau was crowded now. Officers who had had ill-defined functions found them easy to leave; courtiers who had attached themselves to this regiment or that, this prince or that, had fled in the confusion to the center of all power; and the area was packed with babbling creatures in elaborate dress, all, apparently, of one mind. Up until fifteen or twenty minutes ago they had all been prepared for the greatest victory of the century; now they were engaged in a united effort to induce the King to retreat. Maurice de Saxe had gauged them well.

Richelieu dismounted when he reached the King, and not before. With an arrogance unequaled even in that world of arrogance, he plowed through the silken mob, straight for the King. There, on the edge of the plateau, he dismounted and knelt. His eyes, so used to the theater of Versailles, had seized in one moment what was now happening; he saw Noailles and the Comte d'Argenson and a dozen others on their knees near the King, and his instinct for the behavior of his species was so strong that he did not need to think. The voices that had been raised were silenced when he knelt, for the King spoke over them, clearly:

"Monsieur de Richelieu, what have you come to tell us?"

"I have come to implore Your Majesty for the honor of France not to retire until the battle is won."

"But they tell us now, sir, that the battle can never be won."

"Even so, Sire, for the honor of France I implore you to remain in the field, whatever the outcome."

"To die?"

"Yes, Sire, rather than to retire."

"These are extreme alternatives, Monsieur de Richelieu. We can still hope that there will be no necessity to choose between them. At any rate I shall not leave the field. I have never intended to do so and I shall not allow myself to be persuaded."

Louis paused and looked with intense dislike at the circle of kneeling forms.

"I wish all you gentlemen would get up," he said. "You

will not persuade me to leave this place, whatever happens."

The circle rose, and Richelieu with them.

"Monsieur de Richelieu," the King said, "come here."

Richelieu obeyed; the King moved as far as possible from the crowd and spoke in an undertone.

"Tell me as frankly as possible: how bad is it, Richelieu?"

"I don't know, Sire. It is bad enough. As you can see for yourself, some of our best regiments have melted away. But more troops are coming up from the left, and it is not possible for Your Majesty to retire without creating a panic."

"I do not intend to retire, sir. It seems to me I have spent the day saying nothing else. It is all I can do here, but I can do that. The losses have been frightful—is that true, Richelieu?"

"Only a small part of the army has been directly engaged, Sire, but in that part the losses have been frightful. Yes. It is quite true. But there have been many whole regiments not exposed to fire at all, and we have fresh troops to use. Everything is not lost. Even if it were, Your Majesty's place would still be here."

"We are agreed. You know, Richelieu, I had counted much upon this battle, upon a victory here."

"Yes, Sire. So had we all."

"I had counted on it for France, for the honor and advantage of the kingdom, for the suitable peace that may be obtained if we win."

"Yes, Sire."

"I had counted on it for another reason, Richelieu. You know that my military experience has not been great. I have not done much to increase the glory of my family."

"Sire——!"

"Don't interrupt. It is true. Well, I had thought to—to make a beginning; to do something; to show a little courage for the race of Henri IV and Louis XIV."

"You have done it, Sire, by being here."

"Hmm . . . Well, there is one to whom I hoped to be able to report a victory today, one in particular. You understand me?"

"Yes, Sire."

"It will be one of the pleasures of the victory, that report—or one of the agonies of the defeat. It is my custom to send a courier in that direction every day at noon, Richelieu. By posting with energy, the messages reach their destination two days later at about noon."

"I see, Sire."

"Would it be best to send no message at noon today? That is what I do not know."

"It would be best to send no message today," Richelieu said, marveling, in spite of his unequaled experience of the pettiness of the great, that this should be the King's preoccupation at such a moment.

Louis XV was silent, looking out at the disordered plain.

"Yes," he said at last, with a sigh, "I suppose so. There is nothing to say now. Later—how much later?"

"I do not know, Sire. Before the day is over, certainly."

The King sighed again and put out his hand.

"You will be needed down there, Richelieu," he said. "Tell the Marshal or any other you see that I shall be here until the end. And thank you."

Richelieu knelt to kiss his hand and retired towards the crowded plateau where a young officer was holding his horse for him. The King, turning his back with determination upon the horde of courtiers, gazed at the plain and saw its lines and colors blurred. What he had told Richelieu was the strict truth. One of the pleasures of victory, if not its greatest pleasure, would be the joy of announcing it to one in particular; one of the agonies of defeat would be the thought of her. For nearly six months—since the night of a masked ball at Versailles when eight trimmed yews had emerged upon a balcony —he had been involved in the progressions of an amorous but doubting nature towards the moment of the recognition of love. He reached that moment now, with a kind of wonder: it seemed to him that for the first time, at the age of thirty-five, after a variety of experience determined by the intrigues of others rather than by the strength of his own feeling, and in spite of the permanent structure of doubt and distrust which, occupying the core of his intelligence, weakened every secret response of nature, he not only loved, but was in love. That was it; he could not doubt it now; for the field of battle had grown hazy before him, and through the shifting lines of a scene he no longer observed, piercing its urgency with an even greater urgency, he could see the hands of love stretched out towards him. It was his heart itself that leaped at last; he said aloud, in an astonished whisper: "Jeannette!"—and hastily looked round to see that none had heard him.

He covered his eyes with his hand and listened to the plunging of his own heart.

§

The day had begun well at Etioles. Madame rose at eight, as usual, and spent an hour and a half over her chocolate and her toilette. The time thus passed was a tribute to pleasure not necessity, for her skin and hair and hands required no embellishment; but she loved the going and coming of her two maids, the weighty discussions that took place on the choice of a ribbon or the texture of a powder, the critical manipulation of a brush and the adjustment of a curl. She did not dress elaborately here, and the wardrobe which she was rapidly accumulating was destined to be used in other scenes. When she had finished her toilette she was as charming a sight as any to be seen in France. Her golden-brown hair was lightly powdered, her eyes bright with youth and good humor, her skin only a trifle touched up to enhance its natural glow. Her dress was simple enough, but had been chosen with the greatest care; it was of white silk with sprigs of pink flowers scattered over it, and had a kerchief of foamy lace knotted over the bosom. She wished to look her best today—without undue pretension or elaboration, for her taste was sound—in honor of her visitors.

She was in high spirits for a number of excellent reasons. In the first place her dear mother, to whom she hoped she had been and might always continue to be a dutiful daughter, had returned to Paris the day before after a visit of two full weeks. Mme Poisson was not well, and her conversation even in health was not such as to make her company treasured by the finer spirits of the day. Mme Poisson was, in fact—although Madame her daughter admitted it only obliquely and in the deepest recesses of her secret thoughts—a good deal of a bore, effusive, garrulous and incapable of assimilating, thus late in life, the tone of the good society to which Madame her daughter had every key. But the departure of Mme Poisson had been accompanied by an even greater blessing: Uncle Tournehem had gone with her. And the two of them had taken the child—known as a rule by no name except La Petite—with them.

Madame regarded all these ornaments of her family with affection. For La Petite, her baby daughter, she had a passionate, adoring love which made her reluctant to produce the child before strangers: it was unmeasured, and Madame wished to do all things in measure and with grace. For Mme Poisson her feelings were perhaps a little more mixed; filial love and gratitude were not without some strong leavening of embarrassment, especially in company. And as for Uncle Tournehem, there was no doubt that he was a dear, good man, and extremely generous with his money, but a more vulgar or boring one could hardly have been found in the whole kingdom of France. He would eat and drink too much, and above all he would talk too much, and about the wrong things, and in the wrong way. Uncle Tournehem had spent his whole life working for the financial and social aggrandizement of his family, and was unable to forget it. He would talk about finance, and taxes, and banking, and army contracts, to people who shuddered and grew deaf at the very mention of the words. He would boast of his possessions, and of his niece's beauty, and of the numbers of grand people who sometimes came to the house. Madame had a good heart, she hoped, and would never forget what she owed to Uncle Tournehem, but she knew that his mere presence was enough to throw a blight over any conversation. And there must be no blights today.

"Free from the family, the whole family!" she said to herself as she went down the stairs, laughing at the thought.

She went out into the garden and breathed the air of the May morning with fresh and unalloyed pleasure. She had the château and gardens of Etioles to herself for the first time in many weeks.

"I am going down to sit by the lake," she said to a

manservant. "Bring anything that comes to me there. If the visitors arrive show them down there."

There was a charming terrace with trimmed yew hedges and a fountain; beneath it a walk led between elm trees to a little artificial lake. Beside the walk, set out in careful borders, were an army of tulips in every color and variety known to the century. Madame walked along, humming a song to herself. Suddenly she let out the full power and brilliance of her voice in a great roulade from the air of *Armide*—Lulli's *Armide,* one of her favorite operas, which had the merit of suiting her voice and her dramatic talents to perfection. The trill and run startled a pair of gardeners who were at work among the tulips, and they straightened themselves up to stare. She laughed at them and showed her perfect teeth. They returned to work, smiling. Like the other inhabitants of the place, they thought well of Madame.

She passed on to the lake and drew a garden chair out from the little summerhouse beside it and sat down. It was sometimes a little puzzling, she thought, what was to be done about her family. She was fond of them all, and determined, like a good daughter and niece and sister, to advance their interests, to make their fortunes, to surround them with every attention as they grew older. But the fact remained that she often found them a source of embarrassment. They were, to begin with, a rather peculiar assortment of relationships, and difficult to explain on any usually accepted basis. There was Papa: François Poisson, once a tax collector, now retired and living with Mamma and with Uncle Tournehem. Now, the fact was, and a very large number of people in Paris knew it, that Papa had been tried and condemned for embezzlement in the grain shortage of 1725, and had saved his skin only by a flight to Germany. During his absence Mme Poisson—Mamma—had consoled herself, and provided for her daughter's tuition with the best teachers of talent, by successive friendships with Paris-Marmontel, the army contractor, and with Uncle Tourne-hem, a rich farmer-general of taxes. When Papa returned from eight years' exile in Germany, having obtained an appeal on his condemnation, Mamma was thus happily established, and Papa had taken the only course open to a reasonable man by joining the ménage. Papa, Mamma and Uncle Tournehem had lived together in the utmost harmony, and when it came time for Jeanne-Antoinette to be married it was only natural that they should wish to knit the family even closer together by choosing Uncle Tournehem's nephew Lenormant d'Etioles as the bride-groom. So, there it was, an odd assortment of relation-ships, and Madame was not surprised when, at times, the more strait-laced among her acquaintance showed no en-thusiasm for her family.

A little needed clearance had been made in this thicket of parentation. The husband—married by arrangement, but passionately attached to his lovely young wife—had been sent off a month ago to travel in the southern prov-inces, by royal order. Mamma and Uncle Tournehem had now gone back to Paris, and it was obvious that neither intended to follow Jeannette too closely on the road that now lay before her.

"Ma petite Reinette," Mme Poisson had said, using the pet name which Jeanne could no longer hear with pleasure, "I am neither young nor well, and I shall not be alive much longer. You are going to fill a very great position. I never thought I would live to see my daughter a marquise and installed at court, but it is certain that if I survive another six months I shall see it. All I ask of you is to come and visit me when you can. I should not be suited to Versailles. I am a bourgeoise and don't know how to follow the talk of such people. I am happier in Paris among my own friends. But remember that if you have lovely manners and a perfect education, and know how to sing and dance and act and talk and write like nobody else in France, it is because I and your Uncle Tournehem—and, of course, your Papa as well—have seen to it. We have spent a great deal of time and money making you the beautiful and talented creature that you are. We gave you a good husband with a good position, and you were to be Uncle Tournehem's heirs, the two of you, and I'm not at all sure that you wouldn't be better off like that, living the life of a bourgeoise. Not at all sure. But there it is—love, and ambition, and all the rest of it; and they've sent your husband off packing and Uncle Tournehem says the young fool is so wild with jealousy that he wishes never to see you again; so it's clear that you have only one road to go. But when you are in Versailles among all those fine ladies and gentlemen,

never forget your Uncle Tournehem, your Papa and me,
or you will suffer. You must keep your good heart and
your good sense, and you can have no happiness unless it
is based on love, gratitude and kindness."

Jeanne, overcome by the length and solemnity of the
address, had burst into tears and embraced her mother
fondly, swearing that nothing should ever come between
them. Mme Poisson—a very fine-looking woman, darker
than her daughter in coloring, and without the delicacy
of articulation which made Jeanne exquisite—received
this assertion with unusual reserve, in view of her native
garrulity, and merely added:

"I hope that is true, Reinette, but whether it is or not,
remember what I have said."

Jeanne-Antoinette—Jeannette, "Reinette"—moved her
small feet restlessly over the gravel. She had a good heart
and a good head, she considered, and intended to keep
them; she disliked the assumption on anybody's part
that the gratifications of worldly ambition could cause
her to forget her origins. And yet she had already seen
enough of a certain kind of privileged society to be aware
that neither her mother nor Uncle Tournehem could be
unaffectedly welcomed there. She had been to Mme
Geoffrin's house in Paris, for instance, and had seen the
company go into its shell at each ill-judged remark of
the unfortunate Mme Poisson. She had met, at Mme
Geoffrin's and in other houses, most of the well-known
literary and philosophical figures, Fontenelle, Crébillon
and the like, and knew that their pleasure in talking with

her was great (for she was young, pretty, intelligent and
deferential); but they, too, wasted no effort on Mme
Poisson or Uncle Tournehem. Except occasionally Crébillon, and he was paid for it—paid very well, by the
generosity of Uncle Tournehem, for all the lessons in
declamation and dramatic art that he had given Jeannette. The aristocratic principle of exclusion (which
ruled at Versailles) had nothing to do with this attitude
on the part of liberal-minded society in Paris. In the
salons of Paris persons were welcomed for their own
qualities, and not for the prestige of their ancestors. Men
of all sorts frequented the houses of Mme Geoffrin, Mme
Ferté-Imbault, Mme d'Estrades: lawyers, writers, philosophers, courtiers, soldiers, diplomatists, men of high rank
and men of no rank at all. They were alike only in one
thing, that they did not excessively appreciate Mamma
and Uncle Tournehem.

Well, if this were so—and Jeannette had seen it for five
years of somewhat fruitless effort—how much worse
would it be at Versailles? At Versailles it was going to be
difficult enough even for Jeannette, with the most irresistible power on her side, to obtain a foothold. For
Mamma and Uncle Tournehem it would be clearly impossible. Jeannette had seen the women of Versailles;
some of them came to Paris at times to visit bourgeois
salons for the sake of the conversation or the food. Jeannette had even been presented to two or three of them,
and those not the most important. The results had always
been the same: a cold, searching look, an imperceptible

elevation of the eyebrows, a general air of uninterested inquiry. "Who is that young woman? D'Etioles, d'Etioles —nonsense, my dear man, there is no such name. What is her *real* name? What was she *born?*" Jeannette had once overheard a woman saying just those words in a cool, friendly undertone, at Mme Geoffrin's house. She also overheard the man's reply: "Oh, my dear, she wasn't born at all."

That was the way they talked at Versailles. You were not born at all unless you happened to have been born into one of the families the existence of which they recognized. This question of birth preoccupied them so much that once it had been established—once a person could be said to be "born", really "born"—they could talk for hours about the intricacies of relationships, and how this made Héloïse a second cousin to Jean-Robert, and how in consequence somebody was entitled to such and such a quartering.

Well—and Jeannette laughed as she looked over the cool lake shining in sunlight—what could the answer be?

"I was born the daughter of a tax collector, if he was my father, which doesn't seem altogether certain; he was also a grain contractor, an embezzler and a fugitive from justice, and I love him very much," she might say. "My mother was of higher rank; her father was a successful butcher with a market contract of some importance. My mother spent a lot of money on my education and then married me off to her lover's nephew——"

No, it wouldn't do. Decidedly it would not do.

Jeannette laughed aloud. Mamma and Uncle Tourne-hem were right, as always. She would have to leave them behind when she went to Versailles, and thereafter visit them at times privately, as they wished. And then, as for "birth", she would simply have to provide for herself, and accept rebirth at the hands of fate under her new name: Mme la Marquise de Pompadour. It was a pretty name; it suited her taste; it was slightly *nacrée,* with delicate suggestions of gaiety and a southern sun in it. It had happened to be the only extinct marquisate availa-ble at the moment, and the King had not precisely con-sulted her taste in the matter, but she pronounced it over critically and found it good. The difficulty was going to be to recognize herself under this exquisite new label. Nobody called her by the name yet—only the King's letters, coming every day at noon, addressed her in that way, and she had not yet got over the feeling, as she opened them, that they just might be meant for some-body else. Her own servants and relations called her Mme Lenormant d'Etioles, as was right; she had no in-tention of laying herself open to ridicule by assuming a title before it had been officially bestowed upon her with every legal form executed in full. She had even refused to have coronets embroidered or engraved in places indi-cated by the eager merchants who now frequented the house. No. She must be sensible, moderate, and intelli-gent, as nature and education had made her, and take each thing in its turn, supported by the inconceivable good fortune that had befallen her, but not overcome by it; deriving all things from love, gratitude and kindness, as her mother had said; for there could be no other happiness.

Love. Yes, she derived all things from love, first and last. Mamma's love for her, and Uncle Tournehem's love for Mamma, and now—the final, permanent miracle— the love that lay between this garden and the fields in Flanders where, even now, at this moment, while the morning sun touched the little lake to brilliance and the gardeners dug in the tulip bed, there was war and the danger of death.

She dropped a sudden hot tear and quickly caught it with her handkerchief before it could impair her face. With her other hand she fished a letter out of her bosom: yesterday's letter from the King. She read it through twice and kissed it and held it over her heart; these were the customary movements of a passion which—although it did not occupy her whole mind all the time—was un-affected, sincere and strong. She loved the King and had never loved anybody else and would never love anybody else so long as she lived. She was quite clear on that point. She had loved him long before he became aware of her existence; it seemed no more than yesterday that she had first seen a portrait of him, as a child of eight in her convent at Poissy, and burst into tears; it was cer-tainly only yesterday that she had driven out in her calèche day after day in the neighborhood of Etioles, when she knew him to be hunting the Forest of Sénart, for the delight of one glance from him as he rode unthinking by. She knew that this passion for Louis XV was extremely common among Frenchwomen, and there were probably thousands upon thousands of them unknown to him who had gone through much the same distresses and delights for years, exactly like Jeannette; but she differed from all the rest in that she had, at last, attracted his attention—attracted it, and held it, and would never (here she kissed the letter again) would never let it go.

"Madame la Marquise! They told me you were down here and I lost no time . . . Do I interrupt?"

She turned, charmingly startled, bright-eyed, with heightened color; she could not avoid coquetry, which was as natural to her as breathing, and it was with perfect unconscious coquetry that she held her head on one side and put out her hand to be kissed.

"Monsieur l'Abbé!" she said. "What a pleasure to see you! You surprised me a little; I was reading a letter . . . But you must not call me Marquise, you know. I am not a marquise—yet."

The Abbé de Bernis followed her nod and got another garden chair from the summerhouse; this he put beside hers and sat down.

"All Paris calls you that, Madame," he said. "But it shall be as you wish. Have you news of the army in Flanders?"

"You should be the one to give me news," she said;

for her good sense had warned her never to refer to the King's daily letters, even to Bernis. "You come from Versailles?"

"I do, Madame, and a very dull place it is without its sun. There is no news there; there are a thousand rumors. It is persistently stated that a great battle must be fought during these days; some people say it has already been fought, that it was a great victory for the English, and that the news is being concealed from us. I do not believe it."

"Nor do I, Monsieur l'Abbé—nor do I," she said hastily, and then blushed again and added: "But I know nothing of such matters. What is the other gossip of the court?"

Bernis smiled. He was a small, soft man, with clear blue eyes and a sensitive mouth and chin; there were intelligence, receptivity and even a sort of feline beauty in his face, but no great strength. His face was expressive enough to convey what he meant now without words. It said: You should know by now, Madame, that the court has no subject of gossip except yourself, and that it devours every slightest item of information about you with avidity, and that the court is, in fact, holding its breath in terror of the day when you, a totally new and unknown power, may be installed in its midst.

The words he said were quite different.

"The poor court," he said, "is without subjects of conversation nowadays. What subjects can there be when the King is not there?"

"Her Majesty the Queen is well?" Jeannette asked solicitously.

"She is well, Madame, and prays a great deal, most of the time in fact, for the lives of the King and the Dauphin. She is a good woman, our Queen, and we must look upon her with deep respect."

"I do, sir, I do sincerely," Jeannette said; and she meant what she said to the full, for in her eyes to be married to Louis XV and yet obliged to live separated from him was the culmination of human tragedy. "I have the deepest respect for her and the greatest sympathy for her sorrows."

Bernis sighed. He had not taken full holy orders, and did not regard himself as a priest; he was, in fact, a man of courts, theaters and society, a writer of verses, a member of the French Academy, a critic, a wit, anything but a religious; yet there was something in him, some ancestral impulse towards austerity, which made him at times regret the relaxation of manners in the world about him. He would have liked to see Louis XV and Marie Leczinska living in exemplary domestic happiness for the edification of their subjects; but as this was not possible, he did not think Mme la Marquise de Pompadour— he must get used to calling her that—a bad compromise. Here she sat, the exquisite girl, twenty-two, twenty-three at most, expressing sympathy for Marie Leczinska, totally unaware that the devout and melancholy Queen would have regarded the statement as the height of impudence. It was a strange world, Bernis thought, and strangest of all in its aptitude for constant, reciprocal and internecine cruelty.

"What you say does credit to your good heart, dear Madame," he said gently. "But I must warn you that if such expressions are repeated, and get to the ears of the Queen, she will not be pleased. Forgive me for telling you."

"No, no, don't ask forgiveness," Jeannette said. "I want you to tell me things. I am young and ignorant of such matters and I do not know Versailles. Why would the Queen not be pleased?"

"She would—forgive me again—think it presumptuous. If I may advise you, Madame, let me say it would be best for the present to mention the Queen as rarely as possible, and then with the greatest respect, but with no expression of sympathy, or words of that kind, whatsoever. It would not be well received, and of course whatever you say is sure to be much repeated."

Jeannette digested this in silence, and as she did so her extraordinary eyes filled with tears. The eyes were the most remarkable feature in that lovely face, Bernis thought again, watching her: they had the faculty of changing all the time, so that it was quite impossible to tell what color they were, and no two portrait painters could ever agree on what they looked like. They were darkened now to a soft, luminous black, all one color, the color of grief; but they could brighten to blue, or blue-gray or blue-green, and flash and sparkle as they

melted now, a whole gallery and répertoire and army of
eyes in that one young face.

"I suppose," she said, "that to the Queen I am—or
would be, if the Queen had ever heard of me—a very
wicked woman. Is that it?"

Bernis stirred restlessly and chose his words with care.

"The Queen is a pious Christian who obeys every law
of the Church," he said. "I do not know that all these
laws were meant to be obeyed to the full by weak human
creatures. In any case, you are not a wicked woman, dear
Madame, and I doubt if anybody, even the Queen at her
most pious, could imagine you to be that. It is a question
of time. You must wait."

Jeannette dried her eyes.

"I am to be presented to the Queen," she said. "You
know that. I have to be presented to her if I am to live
at court. We have discussed it often enough. But will she
look upon me as a wicked woman when I am presented
to her? What will she say?"

"She will very probably say nothing at all," Bernis answered gently. "It may be a very long time before she
addresses a word to you. She does not speak to everybody who makes a courtesy before her. You must be
prepared for that, Madame."

Jeannette had apparently not been prepared for it; in
her ignorance of Versailles she had supposed that any
woman presented at court must be on some kind of
terms, good or bad, but terms of communication, with
the Queen. The idea that the ostracism of an offended

wife might be added to the envy of court ladies (which she fully expected) and the disapproval of priests (which she discounted) was new: it required thought. She could not think it out with any other person, even the friendly Bernis, who was, by the King's own request, her tutor and guide in all these matters: she must think it out alone. Abruptly she changed the subject, and her smile danced in her eyes as she spoke.

"I have a new parasol, dear Bernis," she said. "I must show it to you at once. It is a jewel, my dear; I am entranced by it. The handle is made of cornelian and jasper, and has a barometer set in it."

"No!" said Bernis, laughing; he delighted in her changes of mood. "It is not possible."

"A barometer, my dear Abbé, I assure you, and what is more, it works. I can tell whether it is going to rain or shine, or blow or chill, just by looking at it—that is, I can when I have learned to read it. You shall see. Come along. We may go back to the house and look at some of my acquisitions. Oh, I have had a merry time with the milliners and the lapidaries and the rest of them, I can tell you!"

She touched his arm lightly as they walked up between the tulip beds. Bernis looked upon her with a kind of affectionate and wondering admiration. When he first met her he had thought her a ravishing creature, full of charm and talent, a living proof of the theory that money (the money of the Paris bourgeoisie, well spent on teachers) could do anything, could produce all the effects

which it was the Versailles tradition to believe inseparable from birth and breeding. He had not then supposed
that the opinion would be shared in such high places.
He had been stunned—like the rest of his caste; for he
was a noble and nothing could eradicate his inherited
prejudice—when he first heard that the King's favor was
falling upon a bourgeoise, any bourgeoise, even upon this
enchanting girl; he had refused to believe it. He had believed it upon the King's word alone, and not until then.
He had received the King's request to visit and instruct
her, and had obeyed. Once a week now, for the past six
weeks, he had been coming here to answer questions, to
tell her what the court was like, how she should behave
there, who its officials and what its ceremonies were,
and what was the delicate balance of the powers, so many
of them invisible and at first imperceptible, among
which she had now to take her precarious way. And
every week he paid his visit more willingly than the week
before, until now it had come to be one of the keenest
of his pleasures, to be thought about for days before and
afterwards. The courtier's caution and his priestly robe
protected him from a more direct enslavement to her
charms; but tranquilly, pleasurably, without the tumults
of desire or the agitations of jealousy, he felt himself to
be, in a mild, platonic way, half in love with her; enough
so that he could take the clearest enjoyment in the sound
of her voice when she called him "my friend."

"Tell me," he said as they walked, "before we inspect

your new treasures and the miraculous parasol, who is coming down today?"

"There will be Monsieur de Voltaire, as I said in my letter," she answered, "and the Comtesse d'Estrades. Monsieur de Voltaire is to stay the day and Madame d'Estrades will be here for a week or more. We have already agreed, as you know, that she will go with me to Versailles when I go."

"Yes, I know," Bernis said thoughtfully. "She is a kind, good woman . . . But Monsieur de Voltaire . . . Why, exactly, did you ask him?"

"He wanted to come. You literary gentlemen are so suspicious of each other——! Why should I not ask Monsieur de Voltaire when he expressed the desire to come? I think it an honor to receive him here. He has been here once before, for a meal as he was passing by, but Uncle Tournehem was here and monopolized his conversation."

"Yes," Bernis said, still thinking it over. "Yes, I see."

"Now, my dear Abbé, you are not going to scold me for asking Monsieur de Voltaire here. I have been learning his poems all my life; I can recite hundreds upon hundreds of lines from his tragedies; I have applauded them in the theater and read them at home ever since I was old enough to read anything. I have even acted his *Zaïre* myself, in our little theater here. How could I refuse to receive a man who is so great, so good and so clever?"

Bernis nodded his head as he listened to her spirited

tones. She had plenty of life and fire, this girl; she knew what she was talking about; but even so, even so . . .

"I must warn you, whether I wish to do so or not," he said with decision. "His Majesty asked me to advise you in any matters which come within my competence. I think I may fairly say that Monsieur de Voltaire is a subject within my competence. I have known him for years. He is an immensely clever man, but I am not sure you are right in describing him as either good or great. His powers have been devoted, ever since I have known him, towards the advancement of his own fortunes, and to nothing else. He is capable of any form of flattery or deceit to attain his ends. He will praise you to the skies on Monday and murder you with ridicule before Tuesday night. He is false and ambitious. I feel quite certain that he makes no visits, pays no compliments and cultivates no acquaintance unless the aims of his personal ambition can be somehow pursued by that means. He is also inquisitive, gossipy, and vengeful, with a tongue that cuts like a knife and cares nothing for either truth or mercy. I think you should beware of the friendship of Monsieur de Voltaire, Madame."

"I do not see how he can harm me in any way," Jeannette said, pouting a little as she reflected over the problem. "Nor do I understand how I can be of any use to him in his ambitions. What does he want? He is a very celebrated poet. What else can he desire? He is not a young man."

"My dear," Bernis said, dropping his official and

admonitory manner to smile at her, "take my word for
it. I know him. He wants something. To be a celebrated
poet is not enough for a man like Voltaire. He also wants
honors, appointments and pensions. Like most people,
he wants money. He would give the eyes out of his head
to get into the French Academy, for instance; fortu-
nately we have excluded him so far. But in coming to see
you today, he wants something. You can take that upon
my word."

Jeannette's lips had begun to curve in a smile which
now turned into frank laughter.

"Oh, dear," she said, "now you *are* going to scold me!
The fact is—the fact is——! I hardly know how to break
it to you, but the fact is that he has already obtained
something."

"From you?"

"From His Majesty the King, dear friend, not from
me. But it is just possible," she added demurely, "that a
few words from me to the King may have helped."

Ah, Bernis thought, ah, she has started early; it has
begun.

"What has Monsieur de Voltaire obtained?" he asked
evenly.

"Now, don't scold me, please, dear Abbé! I only
thought something should be done for him—our greatest
poet, a glory of France. Only think, dear Abbé, of that
immortal epic, the *Henriade!* So long as men have eyes
to read with, and poetry is cherished, the *Henriade* will

be valued as one of the sublimest efforts of the human genius."

Bernis cleared his throat with a dry, crackling noise.

"It is a great poem, perhaps," he acknowledged. "But I am not among those who think it better than the works of Homer. At any rate, Madame, what favors have you bestowed upon Monsieur de Voltaire, exactly?"

"I have bestowed none, sir. They come from the King. The King in his bounty, and in his concern for French literature and the humanities, has made Monsieur de Voltaire the free gift of the first place as Gentleman of the Bedchamber that shall fall vacant."

"My God!" Bernis exclaimed, astonished. "My dear lady, are you mad? A free gift? People pay all sorts of sums for those appointments. The post is valued at about sixty thousand pounds."

"I know," Jeannette said demurely. "I have been told so. But it is not too much for the poet of the *Henriade*."

"I confess that I do not see the connection," Bernis remarked, "between epic poetry and the post of Gentleman of the Bedchamber."

"That also occurred to me," Jeannette went on, a trifle nervous at what she still had to reveal. "Consequently, to make the rewards more suited to the nature of Monsieur de Voltaire's talents, the King also has granted him letters patent as historiographer to the court, with an income of two thousand pounds a year."

Bernis was stupefied. For some moments the pair walked along in silence; then they reached the upper terrace, near the house, and the Abbé saw a stone bench that might support the weight of his agitation.

"Let us sit down for a moment, Madame," he asked. "I am feeling a little stunned at these sudden favors. I want a moment to breathe."

"Poor Abbé," she said innocently. "How can the favors granted Monsieur de Voltaire affect you so much? There are still many gifts in the King's bounty, and he will not forget a friend like you."

"That isn't it," the Abbé said weakly. "I don't resent the good fortune of Monsieur de Voltaire. I am not inordinately ambitious—not so much so as to resent the favors granted to others. It is only—it is only——"

He waved his small white hand feebly in the air.

"You must know, Madame," he said, "what Monsieur de Voltaire represents. He is thought to be an atheist, although he does not disdain to pay court to religion too, when his ambitions demand it. The Church as a whole distrusts and dislikes him. Moreover, his friends, and all those writers who are influenced by him—the so-called philosophers—have become almost a party of recent years. They have their point of view, and it is not a point of view favorable to the institutions of the State as we have known them. They have a great and growing power in their hands: it is the printing press. In granting favors and honors to Monsieur de Voltaire the King may be offending all the people who are most devoted to the monarchy, and pleasing only its enemies. That is the truth, Madame. The truth is that Monsieur de Voltaire is a viper."

"Please, dear Abbé, don't be cross with me. And don't exaggerate, above all, or you will feel ill. Monsieur de Voltaire is a charming man, and doesn't in the least resemble a viper, although I'm not sure I know what a viper looks like. Come into the house and let me show you my new parasol with the barometer in it. Please do. You know I do everything I can to please you, but Monsieur de Voltaire has been very charming to me, and I can't agree with all the terrifying things you say about him. I'm sure you don't mean them, of course. You couldn't."

The rich complexity of this logic defeated Bernis; he lifted his hands and let them fall again, sighing.

"Very well, Madame," he said. "Let us go in and see the new parasol."

It seemed to him, as they left the sunny terrace and went into the long, cool salon of the house, that the feminine principle—and Jeannette was the feminine principle if it had ever taken single form on earth—was the least comprehensible of the forces that surrounded the struggle between nature and man: least comprehensible because it followed no known rule, exerted its power when least expected, and determined actions with unimaginable results in the unending concatenation of cause and effect. To make Voltaire the court historiographer, to raise him to high favor, and with him the whole band of the "philosophers", was to offend the Church, a large

part of the aristocracy, and above all the Jesuits. Once
that sort of warfare had begun there was no telling where
it would end, and the whole social environment was
at the mercy of such dictation by the feminine principle
at any time, anywhere; it was a condition of life, like its
brevity and its transience, not to be argued against by a
good Christian—not even, in fact, to be understood. If
Bernis had been alone just then he would have fallen on
his knees and prayed—not for himself and not for the
persons or groups involved in the struggles he now fore-
saw, but for all living. While the moment lasted he was
filled with sadness.

"You see," Jeannette said, picking up her new parasol
from a sofa where it was displayed, "I was not deceiving
you; it has a barometer in the handle, a perfectly good
barometer. Isn't it lovely? It's even prettier when it's up,
but we mustn't raise it in the house; that brings bad luck.
I'll take it out when we go into the garden again. Now,
you're not angry with me any more, are you, dear Abbé?
Come and look at the other new things. There are several."

Yes, there are several, he thought, gazing at the astonishing array of objects on the big table in the middle of
the room; there are several, and I'm not at all angry with
you, clever, foolish, beautiful and charming Jeannette;
such a thing is impossible; I am only a little sorry when
I think of the results that will ensue, in a chain stretch-
ing to a time unknown, from the careless gestures of
those exquisite hands . . .

"I'm very fond of porcelain," Jeannette said, showing off a vase of English *chinoiserie*. "I think the King should have a porcelain factory of his own, a royal factory on crown property, as I believe they do in Germany. It would make money and would supply him with beautiful objects. I have suggested founding one at Sèvres."

Bernis tried to take up his role as mentor again, although in a less confident tone now that the name of Voltaire had revealed the extent of Jeannette's independence.

"Your taste and judgment in all these matters cannot be surpassed, Madame," he said. "I hope you will continue to interest yourself in them. French art and industry cannot be too much encouraged."

Jeannette laughed at him with her head on one side; her eyes were brown now, and merry.

"Stick to my porcelain and art and industry," she said, "and leave appointments and politics to those who understand them better? Is that it? Dear Abbé, dear Abbé . . . I am not such a fool, you know. I am only a trifle ignorant in some matters. But you have only to instruct me, and then I shall be ignorant no longer; isn't that true?"

Bernis was deeply discomfited; he felt that she was laughing at him, but he was not sure why. He abandoned all pretense and returned to the subject which had most powerfully aroused his curiosity.

"Does Monsieur de Voltaire know the amount of his good fortune?" he asked.

"I think he knows well enough, as we have discussed it," she said. "He does not know that the letters patent have actually been signed."

She paused, with her lips parted, as if discretion had stopped her, just in time, from telling more. Bernis thought: *she has the letters patent here and is going to give them to him today.* It was clear, in a flash, exactly as if she had told him.

"Shall I show you a charming letter I have had from Monsieur de Voltaire?" she asked. "I think if you read it you will see how you misjudge him. Nobody could write like that if he did not have a good heart. I have it here, in this desk. Let me read it to you."

She found it in a moment and put it on the big table in front of Bernis.

"I should explain," she said, "that he has written a poem on Caesar and Cleopatra, and sent it to me. A delicate attention, I thought. The poem was accompanied by this letter."

Then they read it side by side, Jeannette aloud and Bernis to himself.

"I am persuaded, Madame" [the letter said], *"that in Caesar's time there was no Jansenist malcontent who would have dared to criticize what ought to be the charm of all honest men, and that the almoners of Rome were not fanatical imbeciles. I should like to have the honor of talking to you about this before I go to the country. I interest myself in your happiness more than you think, and perhaps there is nobody in Paris who*

takes a livelier interest in it. I am not speaking to you now as an elderly gallant, a flatterer of beauty, but as a good citizen; and I ask your permission to come and say a few words to you at Etioles or at Brunoi during this month of May. Have the kindness to let me know when and where. I am, with respect, Madame, of your eyes, of your face and of your wit, the most humble and obedient servant."

The suggestion of this letter that Louis XV and Jeannette were in some way like Caesar and Cleopatra made even Bernis—hardened, as he was, to the grossest flattery of a shameless court—doubt his own eyes. He read the letter over again in silence.

"It is a pretty letter, isn't it?" Jeannette asked. "Now, sir, could I have refused to let Monsieur de Voltaire come here, after a letter like that? Especially as it was accompanied by a poem which, although it mentions nothing of our modern doings, is obviously inspired by warm feelings towards the King? And then look at those words *as a good citizen*. There is a compliment in that which I appreciate, dear Abbé, because I also wish to be a good citizen. The compliments of a man like Monsieur de Voltaire are worth something."

"Apparently," Bernis could not resist saying, "they are worth an appointment of sixty thousand pounds' value and another with two thousand a year."

"Oh, Abbé——! That was unworthy of you. I see that you do not like Monsieur de Voltaire and nothing will convince you that you are wrong. Well, let it be so. But please, dear friend, don't show him any unkindness here today. I should not like to hurt him in any way; I regard him so highly."

Bernis laughed aloud, shortly, sharply.

"If you think anything I said or did could conceivably get beneath the skin of Monsieur de Voltaire," he said, "you have not known the gentleman long. It is impossible to hurt him. One can only make him angry, which is not the same, and I don't want to bring any of his fiendish little epigrams upon myself. I shall be very polite, Madame, you can be sure."

He paused and reflected a moment, growing calmer.

"As a matter of fact, it is easy to be polite to him when he is in good humor, as he will be here today. He can be the most agreeable company in the world, and we have not been unfriendly in the past. He—ah—he has sound reasons for cultivating my friendship. I am in the French Academy and he wishes to get into it. He never will, but to a man of his colossal and unreasoning vanity that plain fact will not become apparent until the hour of his death. No—no, Madame, I never meet Monsieur de Voltaire without a great display of amiability on both sides."

"Then—forgive me, but I don't understand—what have we been talking about all this time? Why do you warn me against that amiable man who is also the greatest of our poets?"

Bernis gave it up. He might have attempted further admonitions, even so, for his distrust of Voltaire was profound and his regard for Jeannette was sincere; but he could hear a stir of movement in the courtyard and hall, and was sure that somebody had arrived. He made up his mind swiftly.

"Forget that we have ever discussed it," he said, "and do whatever you wish for Monsieur de Voltaire. Only remember that he is not to be trusted too far; no secret is safe with him; he is as inquisitive as a monkey, and never ceases to take notes. That is all. And what I said, dear Madame, was said only in your own interest—and in that of the King. Somebody is coming."

It was, indeed, the Comtesse d'Estrades, in plumed hat and velvet coat and a vast furbelowed muff, who stood in the doorway giving the last voluble order to her maids about her luggage. The lady was not beautiful, but she had a kindly and pleasing face, a good figure, an air of grace and authority. She was a little older than Jeannette, had befriended her a good year ago—before the beauty's unexpected fortune—and was depended upon to be more useful than ever now. The Comtesse d'Estrades was almost the only woman of position available for the necessary steps that now lay before Jeannette: the official presentation at court, the installation in apartments at Versailles, and the difficult exploration of a new world. It was with more than her usual eager amiability that Jeannette hurried across the room to embrace her. Jeannette was without the talent for feminine friendship, and had often been made to feel that other women were aware of it; the Comtesse d'Estrades was an exception.

There was a flutter of "my dears" and "my cousins" in the entrance to the room. They called each other "cousin" because Mme d'Estrades was, by happy accident, a distant cousin of Lenormant, Jeannette's husband, and could thus add the respectability of parenthood to her friendly protection.

"Who is here, Belle Cousine?" the Comtesse asked. "Is that Bernis that I see on the other side of your crowded table? And what have you been buying, you wicked child? Good day, Bernis, you are looking well. Have you come from Versailles?"

Bernis kissed her hand and said he had come from Versailles which was very dull.

"I from Paris, which is duller," she said. "I am dying of thirst, Belle Cousine. I wonder if the resources of your charming household would extend so far as a little lemonade? And what are all these objects on the table? Upon my word you are an extravagant child. What will you do with so much porcelain, so many boxes and fans and bits of carving?"

"I like them, dear," Jeannette said tranquilly. "They are not all for me. I shall give some of them away."

"That alters matters," the Comtesse said, putting up her lorgnon to stare at the crowded table. "Who knows, perhaps one of them may even come my way. Oh, my dear cousin, I have completely forgotten to thank you for the bracelet! How thoughtless of me! Come here and let me kiss you again. It is lovely, quite, quite lovely, and I have brought it with me to wear tonight at supper.

Only imagine, Bernis, this child sent me a bracelet of diamonds and sapphires, set in the most exquisite design imaginable. I wish I had more relatives like you, my dear! I can't think there are many . . . Now show me your pretty things."

Bernis, watching them as they embraced again, and Jeannette displayed her treasures and the Comtesse chattered in continuous comment, said to himself that this relationship would soon be changing its form and context. The Comtesse d'Estrades had been kind to little Mme Lenormant, the pretty and talented bourgeoise who was married to some sort of distant relative of her own; but it would not be possible to be "kind", in this tone of good-humored condescension, towards Mme la Marquise de Pompadour. The day was not far distant when the roles would be precisely reversed, and Bernis, judging them as he watched, paid the two women the tribute of thinking that they would reverse their roles with ease and grace and without acrimony. What was more, he thought, they must both know this already; they must both have foreseen and planned; they must now, at this very moment, be aware that Mme d'Estrades was no longer the sole bestower of favor, that diamond bracelets did not grow on trees, and that the acceptance of condescension was merely Jeannette's graceful and temporary acknowledgment of an obligation that approached its term. It was, for the moment, the merest play acting; but there was enough genuine kindliness and good sense beneath Mme d'Estrades's affectations to ensure that she would accept the adjustment of positions without a murmur. For the moment she enjoyed what was left of her stage as patroness, and Jeannette—the clever, sensible creature, Bernis thought—allowed her to do so, adding a shade of deference to the customary charm of her discourse.

"Let me leave you now, dear cousin," the Comtesse said at last, "and get rid of my traveling things, and of a little dust, as well. I may rest a little, and change, and come down again in an hour or so. Don't dream of coming up with me. My maids are unpacking, and I know my way. Stop here and keep our dear Abbé in good humor. I am sure you have many things to talk about, and you will have no opportunity after Monsieur de Voltaire arrives."

"Don't speak ill of Monsieur de Voltaire, or you will only encourage the Abbé," Jeannette said, taking Mme d'Estrades's arm to go with her to the door. "He has been warning me not to trust the great man too much."

"Very sensible advice," the Comtesse said, smiling at Bernis. "We know our Voltaire, don't we, Monsieur l'Abbé? Still, he is most agreeable company, and I am glad he is going to be here. Don't come any further, dear cousin; I know my way perfectly. Console the Abbé. He does not look too happy just now."

Jeannette returned to Bernis, but before they had resumed their "lesson" (for it was as lessons that his weekly visits were planned between them) a clatter from the courtyard announced the arrival of the last visitor.

The house at Etioles was not large, and when its main doors stood open on the courtyard, and the doors from hall to salon were likewise folded back, it was easy to hear the rumbling and creaking of the carriages.

"It is Voltaire," Bernis said a little sadly. "The lesson is over for today, dear Madame! Even though he uses a carriage with the new system of springs invented by Réaumur himself, he seems to make a great deal of noise. Must we greet him on the threshold?"

"Indeed, yes," Jeannette said, laughing at the Abbé's doleful face. "And cheer up, please. It's no great hardship to talk to him, as you have admitted yourself. Come along, good friend."

She took him by the hand and led him across to the hall. The menservants stood there waiting until their services should be needed with luggage. A big carriage, painted dark blue, with coats of arms embossed on the doors, had drawn up before the door; the man on the box had descended to open the carriage door, and M. de Voltaire, cursing gently to himself as he moved, was clambering out. He was only fifty years old, but a variety of maladies made him a touchy and difficult traveler, even though he spent a great deal of his time on the road. There were rugs, cushions and shawls in great number to be kicked or pushed out of the way before he could get out of his carriage. When he stood on the cobblestones of the courtyard and could raise his head again he saw Jeannette and Bernis.

"Ah!" he said in that sharp, crackling voice. "The divinity of the place! And our friend the Abbé in attendance, no less. Dear Madame, only the thought of your kindness in letting me come here has sustained me on the way. I have the most comfortable carriage I could find in Paris, built to Réaumur's design, and nevertheless I am shaken like the bundle of old dried bones that I am; I think it must be the fault of our roads, which are well known to be the worst in the world . . . Never mind. Never mind. Everybody in this house is well, I hope? Above all its exquisite chatelaine?"

While he spoke he came up the steps, kissed Jeannette's hand, bowed to Bernis, and turned again to Jeannette.

"I am very well, thank you," Jeannette said, smiling at him with her head on one side and her eyes shining, "and better still now that I see you, sir. Do you come from Paris?"

"I come from the Duke and Duchess of La Vallière," Voltaire said. "They, like everybody else in France, live only for the day when they can meet you, Madame. Have you heard news from Flanders? They say a great battle is to be fought during these days. Perhaps it has already been fought."

"I know nothing of such matters, sir," Jeannette said, "but I do not believe the battle has been fought yet. The army is besieging Tournai, is it not?"

The three of them moved on into the salon; the menservants attacked the problem of M. de Voltaire's luggage, piled it up in the hall and closed the doors.

"I hear frequently, very frequently, from the Marquis d'Argenson," Voltaire said. "He is the most constant of correspondents, the most amiable of men. It is a pity he is so long-winded, but I suppose that comes of being a minister. He says the English are unquestionably marching to the relief of Tournai, and Marshal de Saxe will fight them off in a pitched battle. These are great events."

"I pray for the army, the Marshal and the King," Jeannette said.

"That will no doubt make a considerable difference," said M. de Voltaire. "My dear Marquise, if I may call you that——"

"Not yet, sir, please," Jeannette said.

"Very well. Dear Madame—although the title of Marquise becomes you, none better—I wonder if I might have a negus? My valet knows how it should be prepared and can tell your people. I am much shaken up and full of pains and aches after my journey, which, at that, was not very long."

Jeannette went and pulled a bell rope.

"And you, Bernis, my old and devoted friend, I hope I see you well?" M. de Voltaire said with a wry face, sinking into the most amply cushioned chair he could perceive in the room. "Those last verses of yours were very creditable, very creditable indeed, sir. It is a perpetual source of astonishment to me that anybody who can write as correctly as you do should be a member of the French Academy."

"You overwhelm me with kindness," Bernis said. "As for the Academy, I think it can boast of several members who are not wholly illiterate."

"Indeed?" said M. de Voltaire with interest. "Their works must have failed to capture the attention of my wretched bookseller. He never sends me anything nowadays that I can make my way through. But I see that the Marquise is laughing at us—we must find less prickly subjects to talk about, dear and respected Abbé. If you are telling that man about my negus, Madame, be sure to make him consult my valet. It is a very special sort of brew, of which he has the secret."

"Monsieur de Bernis and I shall drink a glass of wine meanwhile," Jeannette said, "to the health of all present, and of French literature, and of the French Academy. After which I think we might speak of something else, or there will be battles nearer than Flanders. What do you hear from the Marquis d'Argenson, sir?"

"The usual sort of thing," M. de Voltaire answered. "He inclines to a somewhat descriptive style when he has a good pen and plenty of room for his elbow. The birds and the flowers, you know. I skip those parts. The good D'Argenson is not precisely Vergil. But he tells me the King is well, and as courageous as we always knew him to be. Maurice de Saxe is dreadfully ill. Poor Maurice! I saw him the day he left for Flanders, and he was unable to sit up in his carriage. I am willing to admit that one may write novels, epics, tragedies and comedies, anything you like, the entire range of possibilities, in the midst of every illness that can afflict a human body. If this had not been so I should never have written a word. But I doubt if battles can be won in the same condition."

"The Marshal has a very good mind, even though he is ill," Jeannette remarked with some timidity. She was always a little afraid of M. de Voltaire.

"Mind? He has less mind than anybody I have ever known," Voltaire answered. "He may be said to have no mind at all. He has a sort of genius, which is something altogether different. He hits upon the right thing. By a series of such happy accidents he has become a Marshal of France and commander in chief of our armies. Have you ever seen a letter from him? There is no organization, no thought, no system of statement. I don't even speak of the language, which is a form of Chinese unknown to me. I believe they are proposing him for the Academy, Bernis. No doubt because of his literary accomplishment."

"The Marshal has no need to write well, sir. What he does need is what he has—a military genius."

"Perhaps you are right," Voltaire said, looking out of his pinched, pale face straight at the Abbé. "Upon my word, Bernis, you have uttered a profound truth. Here comes my negus. I shall digest your wisdom while I drink it."

Bernis, who was as pale with fury as Voltaire was pale with fatigue, accepted a glass of wine and drank it off swiftly.

"You must have letters also from the Duc de Richelieu," Jeannette said. She spoke of these high matters without much confidence, for—as yet—she knew none of the people, and derived most of her own information from the King himself.

"Yes, Richelieu often writes to me," M. de Voltaire said, sipping his negus a trifle noisily. "His are very polished letters. He has an astonishing combination of talents, perhaps too many. To tell you the truth, I believe my correspondents in the army are more assiduous than usual just now, because of what they expect that I may write about their deeds. I hesitate to attribute such low motives, Madame—it is very alien to my nature—but Monsieur de Bernis, as a literary man, will appreciate the plausibility of the suggestion."

"What do you propose to write about the campaign?" Bernis asked.

"That depends upon how the campaign turns out," Voltaire said. "I can hardly write an epic about a defeat. If there should be a battle, a battle of importance, in which the French arms are victorious, I propose to give some account of it. I can hardly do less, in view of— in view of certain kindnesses that have lately come my way. But a defeat is another matter. I confess that the effort of imagination required to turn a defeat into a victory would be very taxing to me just now. In case the work required is of that order, perhaps I might resign it into your hands, dear Abbé. You enjoy better health than I do, and your character is equally warlike."

"You must stop teasing the Abbé," Jeannette said. "We

know you are old colleagues, but you really mustn't . . .
Monsieur l'Abbé is one of the dearest of my friends, and
I shall protect him."

"There is nobody on earth, Marquise, who would not
be safe from me under your protection. But for that matter Bernis needs no protection. We meet as fellow scrib-
blers who have known each other some years, under a
roof where all is love and kindness, and I can already feel
my rheumatism fading away. This negus was very good,
Madame. If the Abbé permits——"

"The Abbé permits everything," Bernis said swiftly.
"What good would it do him to refuse?"

"Ah! with a leave so graciously given, I wish to read
some verses I have written for Madame."

Jeannette clasped her hands together and looked at
the great man with starry eyes. Her love of poetry was
sincere, and had been cultivated by long years of reading
and recitation. To have verses written for her by M. de
Voltaire was a delight so new that she received it in a
transport of pride. M. de Voltaire pulled a sheet of paper
from his pocket and held it close to his eyes as he read
forth:

> "*Sincère et tendre Pompadour*
> (*Car je peux vous donner d'avance*
> *Ce nom qui rime avec l'amour*
> *Et qui sera bientôt le plus beau nom de France*),
> *Ce tokai dont Votre Excellence*

Dans Etioles me régala,
N'a-t-il pas quelque ressemblance
Avec le Roi qui le donna?
Il est comme lui sans mélange;
  Il unit comme lui la force et la douceur,
  Plaît aux yeux, enchante le cœur,
  Fait du bien et jamais ne change."

Jeannette's great eyes filled with tears of happiness.

"Oh, it is beautiful, beautiful!" she said, clasping her hands more tightly over her neckerchief. "Read it again, Monsieur de Voltaire, read it again. I have never heard anything that pleased me more."

Voltaire obligingly read the verses through again. His voice, dry and cracked, was not precisely made for poetry, and seemed—to Bernis, at any rate—to underline the flattery of the lines with a mocking ironic contradiction. No such subtleties troubled Jeannette. She took the sheet of paper from the poet's hand and read the verses over again to herself, trembling with pleasure.

"I shall send them to the King," she said. "Oh, Monsieur de Voltaire, what great and wonderful gifts you have, how kind you are, how lucky I am to count you as my friend!"

She pressed his hand and smiled at him through her tears. The poet, who perceived that his stroke had by no means been wasted this time, exposed his yellow teeth in an amiable grimace. Bernis was unable to bear any more of these cajoleries; he credited Voltaire with no sincerity of any kind, except the sincere desire to advance his own interests by flattering the new favorite; moreover, the verses were not good, and their cleverness afflicted Bernis with a sense of the irresistible talent that had thrown them off. It was lamentable that such a talent should be lodged in such a man.

"I ask your permission to retire for a while, Madame," Bernis said. "I have not yet got rid of the dust of my journey. My compliments on your verses, Monsieur de Voltaire. They are, as you said of mine awhile ago, creditable—very creditable indeed."

"Thank you," Voltaire said dryly. "The praise of a colleague is as welcome as it is rare."

"Of course you must go upstairs if you wish, dear Abbé," Jeannette said. "You know your own room? I hope everything will be as you wish it. If not you have only to ring."

She accompanied the Abbé to the door, her hand on his arm. She had been fully aware of the acrimony that lay beneath the words spoken by her two guests, and was anxious to show that her own heart was still warm towards them both. As soon as the Abbé had vanished she turned and came towards Voltaire with rapid, scurrying steps.

"I have something to give you, dear and honored sir," she said. "I am especially happy to give it to you today, after these exquisite verses. One moment; it is here in my desk."

She unlocked her writing desk with a key from the chain at her waist, and pressed the catch for a secret drawer. From it she took two large documents hung with official seals.

"Here, sir, is the gift of your King."

Voltaire accepted the documents and looked at them. The wrinkled, pointed mask of his face was unchanged; his lips were pressed firmly together. Here it was, at last, the court favor and fortune which he had pursued with unflagging zeal for thirty years. He had stooped low indeed, at times, to obtain something like this, and had been forever cheated by circumstance, by the malevolence of priests, the jealousy of rivals, the whims of those in high places. Once before he had been on the verge of obtaining some such honors through the influence of Mme de Prie, the mistress of the Duc de Bourbon, and had failed because Bourbon died and was succeeded by the pious, economical Cardinal de Fleury. A vast epic poem, many tragedies and histories, a lifetime of indefatigable literary proliferation, had brought him little except the popular fame which seemed to him almost worthless; and the things he had always wanted—money, a fixed income, an appointment at court—were his now by virtue of a few rhymed compliments to a lucky grisette. There was a dry, furious bitterness inside him. He rose from his chair and fell on one knee before Jeannette. She gave him her hand to kiss.

"I am so overcome by the King's generosity and your

kindness, Madame," he said, "that I can hardly speak now. I am your devoted slave forevermore. But I am so agitated that I want to ask your leave, like the Abbé, to go and remove the dust of my journey."

"Go, sir, you are at home in this house," Jeannette said, exalted by the occasion. "Every favor you receive is deserved, as you must know, by your works which are the glory of our literature. The King asked me to give you these because I have spoken to him so much of you. These papers are the mark of the first favor I have ever asked him to grant. I am proud that it should be for you."

Voltaire felt the instinct of the actress rising in her as she stood with her head high and her cheeks flushed; he rose and bowed very low, his hand on his heart. Beneath the gesture there was, at the moment, nothing but the gusty sigh of an anger of fifty years. That is the way it happens, he thought: everything comes too late and for the wrong reasons; we are rewarded for the worst in us when the best has been disdained; it is from such hands as these that the greatest poet of Europe is to receive his due.

"Madame," he said, "I am forever yours."

Jeannette's dramatic sense preserved her from any attempt to prolong the scene, although she had been so excited by his verses and her own generosity that she could have gone on for half an hour. She stood silent, her hands folded on her bosom, as the poet left the room.

When he had gone she picked up the sheet of paper from the table and read it over again eagerly.

Sincère et tendre Pompadour

.   .   .   .

Ce nom qui rime avec l'amour.

It was true, and she had never thought of it before, perhaps because she had spent most of her time for the past three weeks trying to accustom herself to the thought that she was to be called Pompadour in future. The rhyme was obvious, but it was Voltaire who first pointed it out to her; she would not forget that.

The clock ticked from the wall: tick-tock-tick-tock. She had been listening to it for some time without being aware of why. Now she heard it afresh, and went to ring a bell.

"It is after midday," she said to the manservant. "Has the courier not yet arrived?"

"Not yet, Madame," he said.

She went out into the hall, agitated suddenly by the thought of the King in Flanders and of the courier who had not yet arrived. What might it mean? The battle had perhaps been fought? The King killed? The French arms of no use against the English? *The King killed?*

The notion so undermined her composure that she could no longer think of Voltaire, his verses and his honors, of Bernis and his grievance, of the house or of the servants in it who watched her with avid eyes. She had been told that one among them was in the pay of the Prussian ambassador. She had been told that at least two of the others were regularly employed by the English Embassy. It made no difference. She walked up and down in the hall—where she was much out of place, according to the etiquette of the house—and looked through the opened doors into the courtyard. The courier had been due at noon. Sometimes he came at eleven in the morning. He was seldom later than half-past twelve, and now it was twenty minutes to one.

She could see the King now with a stain of blood on his white and silver coat. His noble head, so grandly planned, with the high straight brow and commanding nose and sensitive mouth of his family, was not visible to her at all for the moment: it was turned away, hidden, one arm flung up to conceal it. What she saw was his white and silver chest with the terrible red stain upon it. The tears that came to her eyes now were allowed to flow without hindrance; she could attend to her complexion afterwards; for the moment she was beside herself with anxiety. The great clock in the hall ticked even louder than the one in the salon, and with its solemn count her heart, erratically leaping, could not keep pace. She went back to the salon and sat down by one of the windows looking on to the terrace. She must try to be calm or she would begin to believe the visions conjured up by her sudden alarm. The courier might have been delayed by any one of a dozen minor accidents; post horses were not always ready and fresh, even in the King's service; there might have been rains in the north

to wash the roads away. She sat with her hands folded
and stared at the terrace and garden outside. Her tears
ceased, and she waited.

It was one o'clock when her maître d'hôtel came in
and delivered the package.

"Here it is, Madame. The man has just this moment
arrived."

Jeannette cried out with joy as she snatched the packet
from him.

"Give the man wine and food," she said, "and ask him
why he is an hour late today. He only comes from
Amiens; he could have been on time."

She unwrapped the silken packet and took the letter
from it. It was dated two days before—May ninth—as
was right; it was long and filled with the words she
loved to read. Reserved, secretive even in his love-
making, Louis XV seldom employed a language that
would have seemed even faintly amorous to those who
did not know him. He addressed Jeannette as "Madame", and the warmest of his expressions were wrapped,
like his letter itself, in the silks and satins of propriety.
But she knew him so well by now that she could trans-
late as she read, and the polite, colorless phrases slipped
easily into the passionate accents of poetry and the
theater on their way through her imagination. She read
the letter through three times before she rose from her
chair. Then, kissing it with fervor, she thrust it beneath
the neckerchief which already concealed its predecessor,
the letter of the day before. All was well; the battle was

still to be fought; the army was waiting and the King loved her. She went upstairs to remove from her face the traces of her tears. It would soon be time to meet her guests again for dinner.

§

Richelieu, riding down into the plain again, thought: at such a moment, when the outcome of a battle of capital importance, perhaps of a whole war, is in the highest degree uncertain, the King's chief worry appeared to be whether or not his courier should be sent off to that common little woman Lenormant. The notion shocked him, not altogether because of its pettiness in the midst of great events, but because the woman did not have the honor to meet with his approval. He had personally suggested a number of ladies of high degree, including his own nieces, to the attention of Majesty, and it was galling to reflect that a grisette from nowhere had succeeded where the beauties of Versailles had failed. Moreover, it was a little disquieting: if she exercised such dominion over the King's mind that he could think of the battle itself chiefly in relation to her, what would happen in the days or months to come, when she was to be, by all accounts, installed at Versailles? Everything might come, in time, to depend upon her—appointments, favors, pensions; rank, preferment, distinctions; the honors of the French Academy; issues, even, of peace and war. Richelieu reflected that he had perhaps been wrong in not taking her seriously enough. If he had seen the danger earlier, and combated it with vigor, something might have been done. It seemed now that there was little that could be done; her dominion over that strange, secretive creature, the King, was obviously more complete than anybody had imagined possible.

Tomorrow, Richelieu thought, tomorrow I shall write to my friend M. de Voltaire (who, I believe, knows the woman) and sound him out about her . . .

As he rode down into the plain before Notre-Dame-aux-Bois his eye lighted upon something that changed his train of thought in a flash. It was a battery of field-pieces *à la suédoise,* the last in the possession of the French. It had been over in Barry Wood, but somebody must have transferred it here in front of the plateau where the King and court were installed. It was, or might be, worth its weight in gold in the next hour or so.

"Forward!" he yelled to the young lieutenant who appeared to be in charge. "Move that battery forward and wait for orders from the Marshal!"

The young man, who had been leaning on one of his guns and watching the confusion of movement before him, saluted and gave his orders. Richelieu saw that the movement would be executed (which was not always so certain) and rode on at the gallop. He had two things of consequence to report to Maurice de Saxe, and for the moment his mind was swept bare of all those tangled impulses of jealousy and intrigue which infested it: he wanted one thing only, to see the battle won. He had to ride through three cavalry regiments which had been shattered by successive charges, and the efforts now being made to restore order in their ranks were not altogether successful. Richelieu groaned, but plowed on through the riot of men and horseflesh. The officers of Clermont-Prince told him he would find the Marshal further to the right, directing an attack of Carabiniers, and he turned his horse in that direction. As he came out into the open plain in front of the French line he could see the redcoats calmly drilling under fire, reforming again, but not advancing. For a brief space, to make speed, Richelieu rode across ground which was swept by the bullets of both armies. Then he plunged behind the lines of Aubeterre, on the right center, and found the Marshal.

Maurice was still on his horse, coming back from the positions near Fontenoy, and his ghastly face looked towards Richelieu without expression.

"So," he said, "you are back. What have you done?"

"I have spoken to His Majesty. He pledges himself to stay where he is, whatever happens."

"Good, good," said Maurice. "That is one uncertainty removed."

Before Richelieu could speak again they were interrupted by a red-coated officer who drew his horse up from the gallop and flung himself off, all fire and fury: Lally-Tollendal.

"What's this? What's this?" Maurice said, controlling his own huge beast with difficulty. "Not so fast, man. What's the matter?"

"I have to report, Monsieur le Maréchal, that there is a battery of fieldpieces intact, down on the left," Lally said with a flourish of his hat.

"Where the bloody hell have they hidden themselves, then?" Maurice bellowed. "Fieldpieces going to waste, when we have not one in the whole field?"

"They were there half an hour ago, in Barry Wood," Lally said, not at all dashed. "I thought you should know about them."

"Should know about them——! In God's name, what kind of an army is this?"

"I think they must be the same fieldpieces I have just now ordered up, sir," Richelieu said, without undue emphasis on his eagerness. "They were stationed at Notre-Dame-aux-Bois and I thought they would be useful. They are coming forward and should be somewhere in the center now."

"They were at Barry Wood, and I thought everybody had forgotten them," Lally said, only slightly put out at the news.

"Very well, Lally, very well," Maurice said. "You did well to tell me. And you, Monsieur le Duc, did well to order them up. Let us go and find them at once, before they disappear again. Herr Jesus! Every mobile piece in the field silenced hours ago, and there's a battery doing nothing all the time——! Herr Jesus!"

He started off at once at the gallop, passing behind the front line, with Richelieu and Lally riding beside him and two aides behind.

"You see how important these pieces are," he shouted at Richelieu. "We have no others. In the general attack we may be able to break the English lines with them. Nothing else has succeeded in doing so."

"What is the state of the field, sir?" Richelieu asked, in what was very nearly a tone of respect.

"Hell and damnation," Maurice said briefly. "Just as it has been since eleven o'clock. Nothing can shake the English, and our cavalry is useless."

"What are we going to do, sir?" Richelieu went on.

"Attack with infantry on three sides, as soon as we have any infantry. That's when your fieldpieces will find work to do. We've got them on the flanks all right, but we have no center. Lally, where are the Irish?"

"Coming up, sir, coming up as fast as they can."

"Well, the faster the better, so long as they keep their order. You will rejoin your regiment, Lally, and thanks for the bit of secret information about the battery. If I knew who had hidden it away I would have him castrated. This army has all the discipline of a herd of goats. Richelieu, did you see anything of the Piedmont regiment?"

"No, sir."

"Well, what's happened to it, I wonder? It should have been in the center, in front of Notre-Dame-aux-Bois, at least half an hour ago, and you've just come from there

. . . Valfons! Valfons! You ordered Piedmont up, didn't you?"

"I did, sir," Valfons said from behind.

"Well, then, go and find them. They are not where they are supposed to be."

Valfons swung his hat in the air and turned back to the right again.

"I wanted a center," Maurice explained to Richelieu as they rode. "After the Guards collapsed and the cavalry was no good, I wanted a new center, using Piedmont, Normandie and the Irish. Now Piedmont has got lost, or disappeared, or disobeyed orders. How can I be everywhere at once? Herr Jesus!"

They rode through a sudden hail of bullets, to which neither Maurice nor Richelieu paid any attention.

"If the attack is to be of infantry only," Richelieu asked, "staff officers can dismount and advance with the men, I suppose?"

Maurice looked over at him with a grimace of unwilling respect.

"You can, sir," he said. "I doubt if many of the others will be so anxious. You can advance with any infantry body you choose. Was the King much beset by that mob of old women up there?"

"He was," Richelieu admitted. "But he has now made up his mind to ignore them. He is pledged to stay to the end, whatever it may be."

"That is good work," Maurice said. "I thought you could do it. What's that I see? I believe it's your famous battery, Richelieu, the mythical battery, the disappearing battery. Let's see what they have to say for themselves."

They reined up before the four guns of the battery *à la suédoise,* which had been coming forward at a trot. The young lieutenant saluted them smartly.

"Where have you been all day?" Maurice shouted at him.

"Stationed beyond the Chambonas redoubt in Barry Wood, Monseigneur," the young man said. "Those were our orders from Monsieur du Brocard."

"Du Brocard had his head blown off in the first ten minutes of action!" Maurice roared. "Herr Jesus! What an army! You stayed there, then, without moving?"

"We were waiting for orders, Monseigneur. An aide from the Count of Clermont told us to move down to Notre-Dame-aux-Bois half an hour ago, for the protection of the King."

"Um Gottes Willen——! The King is in no danger, sir. Stay where you are, exactly where you are, without moving one hair's breadth from that spot, until I give you an order to advance. You will draw no attention to yourself by firing or by any movement whatsoever. Your battery is precious and will be used when I say it must be used. Disobey any order coming to you from anybody but me."

"Yes, my Lord."

"Unless, that is, I get my head blown off too, like Du Brocard," Maurice added, his white and sweating face suddenly creased in a grin. "Just stay where you are, sir, and I'll come back before long, head and all. Richelieu,

if you could help the remains of our cavalry to form and
retire slightly, it would be useful. Fitzjames may be in
trouble. The English are not doing much at the moment
—at least they are not moving, although they seem to
have plenty of ammunition. I don't see how they can
have carried so much. Damn me, their musketry fire is
an education in itself."

"You want the cavalry to retire, Monsieur le Maréchal?"

"They can't retire far, or the English may think the
field is theirs and stop maneuvering. So long as they stay
where they are I can get an attack going soon. Just bring
the cavalry back a bit. Normandie and the Irish will have
to advance in front of them. Do what you can, Monsieur
de Richelieu. The poor devils have charged a good many
times, and no wonder they are in some confusion."

The corpse on horseback thundered on. When he
rounded the left edge of the plain and approached the
slope of Barry Wood he saw that most of the Irish brigade had been brought out of the woods now and was
forming a column in the open. Best of all, to his anxious,
bloodshot eyes, was a white column coming up on the
lower plain to the left of the Irish, from behind Barry
Wood: the Normandie regiment, and with it the banner
of his friend, Löwendal the Dane.

"Now God be praised!" he said. "Do you see, Mézières? Here they are, they have arrived at last."

§

M. de Voltaire came downstairs in much better humor. He had rested; he had even engaged in some tentative and partial bathing; he had changed his clothes. He was aware that a slight acerbity had marked his earlier conversation with the Abbé de Bernis, and was now resolved to soften his tone towards that amiable cleric if the opportunity presented itself. After all, he had nothing against Bernis, except the general objection he made towards all literary men, members of the French Academy, and poetasters of the drawing room. He was at intervals, and for his own purposes, a poetaster of the drawing room, but he could conscientiously assure himself that his efforts in this kind were accomplished with his tongue in his cheek; whereas Bernis— well, poor Bernis . . .

"Ah, the Abbé, our friend the Abbé!" he said, coming into the salon. "I hoped you might be here. Could we not take a turn in the garden before dinner?"

"With pleasure," Bernis replied, recognizing at once that the vinegary edge of M. de Voltaire's temper had been taken off by the trip upstairs. "The garden is charming here. You have been here before, I believe?"

"I have, once," M. de Voltaire said, "and I hope I may be here often again. I am devoted to the divinity of the place. Between ourselves, Bernis—as men of the world we need not speak in riddles—have you ever known or heard of a King's mistress who seemed more ideally suited to her position than our charming hostess?"

Bernis, who was not accustomed to this frankness of speech, tried to smile.

"I hardly know," he said. "I am no authority——"

"Well, think," M. de Voltaire ordered. "There was Mademoiselle de la Vallière, who supplied us with a poetic and melancholy legend, but appears to have had all the intelligence of a kitten. There was that apppalling adventuress Madame de Montespan, who cared for nothing but money and the advancement of herself and her brood of bastards. And there was the sniveling old hypocrite Madame de Maintenon, a priest-ridden she-devil with a heart of ice. That was what the old King presented us with, as you know very well."

"I ought to tell you," Bernis said tentatively, "that our present hostess has a lively admiration for Madame de Maintenon, and reads everything she can find about her."

"Perhaps," Voltaire said. "Yes, I can see how that would be. Madame de Maintenon was so correct, so respectable . . . Yes . . . Quite so. But I do not think we need worry about any fundamental resemblance between this charming lady and that old witch."

"No," Bernis said hastily, "of course there can be none."

"Well, what has his present Majesty, the Well-Beloved, given us in this realm of ideas? A trio of duchesses with the morals of the gutter; three beautiful and worthless intriguers, self-seeking and false to the last degree."

"I have heard you speak well of Madame de Mailly in the past," Bernis remarked. They were walking down between the tulip borders now, and M. de Voltaire had taken the Abbé's arm to lean upon.

"Yes, no doubt; she was the best of them," Voltaire said indifferently. "But there was no hope in any of them. There is hope in this present lady, Bernis. She is educated; she has received an admirable instruction in the useful and beautiful arts; she recognizes merit when she sees it, and is alive to the judgments of history and literature."

Bernis thought: Ah, she must already have presented him with the patents of his new appointments. Merit——!

"It is not by such means that she has won the King," Voltaire went on. "But, having won him, by those personal attractions which I am sure neither of us would deny, she is about to occupy a position of very great importance, in which she will be able to affect the course of events, the distribution of favor, even the administration of the laws. I think it is a notable fact that in this case—and, mark you, Bernis, only in this case, as never before—our King has elected to honor a lady who is by no means an imbecile."

He paused to inhale a noisy pinch of snuff.

"By no means an imbecile," he repeated.

"The delicacy of the compliment would enchant her," Bernis said.

"Perhaps. But you are not such a fool as to repeat it. The fact is that it is rare in any company, at any time, to find a young woman of twenty-three who possesses all the qualities of Madame Lenormant d'Etioles. (When shall we be allowed to call her Madame de Pompadour? The other name is an offense to the ears.) She has beauty, wit and accomplishment, but without all those terrifying pretensions which make it difficult to deal with the learned ladies of Paris. Between ourselves, Bernis, I am not very fond of learned ladies."

"I am glad to hear it, sir," Bernis said. "But I am wondering one thing. That is, why do you enlighten me with this particular discourse? I am already well acquainted with our hostess and admire her deeply."

"No doubt. In fact, they tell me you are a frequent visitor here, once a week, a sort of tutor, they say, in the ways of the great world? Never mind. Don't answer if you don't want to. No; my reason for speaking to you like this is of another order. I know you admire the lady deeply, although no more deeply than she deserves. What you may not know is that I also admire her and that I base great hopes upon her. It seems to me that in a time when so much is changing and so much is bound to change, when the laws and habits of mankind are shaken, attacked, defended and re-examined, it is no small thing for the forces of enlightenment to have a friend at court."

"I will not engage in that argument with you *à fond,*" Bernis said, "but I think you may realize that I don't agree with you about the forces of enlightenment. They may seem to me no more than the forces of anarchy and chaos."

"My dear Abbé!"

"I am not a priest, sir, but I am a faithful son of the Church, and I contemplate going on to take full holy orders in time."

"When you have had your fling, I suppose."

"I do not have the honor to understand you, but no matter. I won't argue about the forces of enlightenment, except to point out to you that we may not agree in the least upon what they are."

"Very well, let us disagree," M. de Voltaire said. "But even so, you know now why I come to Etioles, Monsieur l'Abbé. It is because in an intelligent and well-meaning lady, in this position of great power, I see the promise of some encouragement for certain principles in which I firmly believe. She is a ray of hope."

"*Your* hopes, at least, will not be disapppointed, sir," Bernis said in a tone filled with meaning.

(So, Voltaire thought, the soft little neat little Abbé has claws!)

"My hopes for myself are not great," he answered. "If the King wishes to reward a lifetime of scribbling by some form of pension or annuity I should not refuse. But I was talking of something rather more extensive in significance than my own poor fortunes. However, I sup-

pose it is too much to expect that anybody will understand that . . . Anyhow, my dear Abbé, are you yourself above all that sort of thing? You would not be
averse to a Cardinal's hat, would you? Think, Bernis, a
beautiful red hat with tassels on it—a Prince of the
Church. It is within our hostess's power to obtain that,
too, you know, and it would not be the first time that the
holy signs were bestowed for rather droll reasons."

"Enough, sir, enough," Bernis said, flushing with anger.
"I think this conversation has gone far enough. If you
have no more decent subject to discuss, I think we might
return to the house and wait for the ladies."

"Oh, no. Oh, no," M. de Voltaire said, delighted.
"They will not be down for some time yet, and I enjoy
your company, dear Abbé, I take great pleasure in the
wit and wisdom and agreeableness of your commerce.
Let us walk around this little lake and stroll back at our
leisure. Example: you might now tell me your opinion
of the work I intend to undertake on the great battle in
Flanders. Shall it be a pamphlet? A dramatic poem? An
epic poem? A ballet? An opera?"

"You seem to have a wide choice of forms," Bernis
said. "I hardly think a ballet would suit the subject.
Beyond that I have no opinion."

"Providing it is a victory," Voltaire said, "I think I
shall write an epic about it. Yes, decidedly, an epic of
sorts, but brief and to the point, to come out in pamphlet form in the streets as soon as possible after the
battle. You know, Bernis, that sort of thing is no trouble

at all to me, no trouble at all. The only trouble is that there are sure to be a large number of fools who will complain because it is not a masterpiece."

"You have been afflicted by them before, I believe, sir."

"I have, sir. For the past thirty years I have never published a sheet of print that was not instantly judged to be unworthy of me. In its way, it is a sort of compliment, but grows wearisome with repetition. You have no such anxieties, dear Abbé. You have only to read a bit of rhyme to the Forty Immortals—your pardon; the other Thirty-nine Immortals—and it is crowned by acclamation. That is what it is to be a gentleman who writes from time to time for his own pleasure and the edification of others. A miserable scribbler who can scribble and do nothing else is not so fortunate."

"If you will forgive me for saying it, there are those who think you scribble too much. I have used your own word. The poet of the *Henriade* should not rush to the printers with an epic every time there is an event to justify it."

"I do not agree, sir. Writing is a foolish pursuit when it is taken to be an end in itself. As a means it is not wholly to be despised. I believe the time will come when events will be reported in the gazettes almost as soon as they have happened; there will be a thousand times as many printing presses as there are now, and all busy turning out material not greatly different in kind from all these scribblings of mine that you deplore. There will be an immense production of printed work, to be examined or rejected by whatever intelligence the future may develop. The good will remain, or some of it will, and the bad—the false, the worthless, the ephemeral—will perish. This means that most of it will perish, of course, but on its passage through the minds of its readers it may make some slight difference."

Bernis sighed deeply. The thought of a world filled with printing presses, all clacking away busily at narration and comment and discussion, jangled along his nerves like a discordant noise. He looked across the peaceful little lake with the swans sailing silent and white upon it.

"I do not think your world of cheap print would please me much," he said. "It seems to me that there are already too many books, too many pamphlets, too many plays and too many gazettes. And I still do not think that a man of your talent can serve any useful purpose by writing so much. How many volumes would your work fill, up to now?"

"Fifty or so," M. de Voltaire said cheerfully. "That is, of course, a rough guess. So far no printer has been mad enough to want to collect it all. But there are two things, my dear Bernis, that you don't understand about me, and I am forced to believe that you will never understand them. The first is that I could not stop writing if I tried; and the second is that, as I said before, there are certain principles in which I firmly believe, which somehow or other, through the good, the bad and the indifferent, I will serve before I die."

Bernis walked along silently. They were returning to the house now, and the warm sun of the early afternoon, filtered through the elm trees, suggested that the dinner hour might be at hand.

"I think you are speaking the truth," he said at last, "and I wish it were not so. The principles in which we believe are not the same ones."

M. de Voltaire took snuff noisily and sneezed at a bed of yellow tulips.

"That sounds almost like a piece of flattery, Bernis," he said, cackling and nodding his head. "You have not given me the habit of hearing such words."

"It is no flattery," Bernis said somberly. "That is one thing you need never expect from me, Monsieur de Voltaire."

As they approached the terrace Jeannette saw them and came down the steps, holding her skirts out prettily while she half danced towards them. It was a sort of pas de ballet that she did, for she was as accomplished in that direction as in singing and declamation.

"Messieurs, Messieurs!" she said. "I hope you have not been quarreling up and down the garden walks. Why is it that you men of talent are so rude to each other?"

"We have been like a pair of cooing doves," Voltaire said with another raucous cackle. "Have we not, Bernis? The Abbé was singing your praises, and I sang them back to him again, until you would have thought us a duo from the Italian opera. Where is the resplendent Comtesse? I thought she was to be here today."

"She is in the salon, sir," Jeannette said, walking between the older poet and the Abbé with her fingers lightly, coquettishly poised on theirs. "If you will come there with me you shall see her, and you shall have a glass of the Tokay which you praise so beautifully in verse."

She deepened her voice slightly with a shade of mock-heroics and declaimed:

> *"Ce takai dont Votre Excellence*
> *Dans Etioles me régala,*
> *N'a-t-il pas quelque ressemblance*
> *Avec le Roi qui le donna?"*

Bernis looked upon his pupil with favor.

"You see," he said to Voltaire, "she has already learned it! There is flattery for you, sir."

To himself he added: and more than the wretched little bit of rhyme deserves.

"Oh, but I can say it all," Jeannette protested. "I learned it at once. As you know, I learn poetry with ease, and even if it had been difficult I should have memorized this at once. I shall say it all through for Madame d'Estrades. She has not heard it yet."

Bernis reflected that it might not be considered in the best of taste, in other company, for her to recite verses written to herself; but he did not dare read her a lesson on that point today.

The three of them entered the salon, where the next five minutes were taken up by bows, courtesies and compliments between Mme d'Estrades and M. de Voltaire. Jeannette waited with impatience until they had finished; then, making her *révérence* to the company, she recited again the poem about Pompadour and the Tokay. Bernis said to himself, with wry patience, that she could not possibly recite it more than another two or three times in the course of the day, and perhaps, with luck, she might be diverted on to some other work of the master.

"I am sure Monsieur de Voltaire would like to hear you in one of his dramatic or tragic works," Bernis said after the flurry of congratulation was over. "You have performed his *Zaïre,* and I do not believe he has heard you do so."

"After dinner," Jeannette said, head on one side, "I shall recite anything Monsieur de Voltaire wants. This poem is another thing—in honor of the day, the company, and the Tokay. Why, is it not good Tokay, Monsieur l'Abbé?"

"It is not the Tokay that annoys the Abbé," M. de Voltaire said, grinning crookedly at Bernis. "It is the poem, which suffers from the misfortune of not having been written by himself. Believe me, Madame, there is no keener annoyance."

Go on, between you, Bernis thought, mock at me and enjoy yourselves; yours are temporary things, and mine are eternal; I have at least a kinship with the Church of God.

"Dear Abbé," Jeannette said, putting her exquisite

hand on his arm, "pay no heed whatever to Monsieur de Voltaire. Drink your Tokay in a good intention—to the King, to the army in Flanders!"

§

Richelieu rode through the frightened mob of courtiers at Notre-Dame-aux-Bois and flung himself on his knees before the King.

"Permission, Sire," he called out in a loud voice, the voice for great moments, "to charge with the King's Household!"

Louis XV stroked his chin and was silent. He had just passed two of the most anxious hours of his life, with a defeat of the first importance, involving perhaps imprisonment or exile, staring him in the face; he was surrounded by people whose only thought since the early morning had been to induce him to escape into safety; and to his unpracticed eyes the English seemed to be unattackable, unshakable, and the French army a mere rabble in disorder around it. The dramatic appeal of Richelieu, reinforced by every emphasis of voice and manner which that accomplished performer could produce, did not stir him because he did not understand it.

"Why, sir?" he asked coldly.

Richelieu replied with passion, the words tumbling out fast and loud.

"The decisive moment is here," he said. "The Marshal

has ordered the general attack. In ten minutes we shall be victorious or defeated. Is the King's Household not to share in the glory of the day?"

Louis looked up, distracted. The Duke of Harcourt and the Comte d'Estrées had followed Richelieu and were also on their knees. A movement of sympathy stirred through the crowd on the little plateau. Even the Marquis d'Argenson, nursing his smelling bottle, looked mildly interested. Louis was averse to being pushed or hurried into action, and wished above all things not to give orders which did not suit the plans of the Marshal. Moreover, little as he knew about military affairs, he was well aware that all these dukes had their appointed places and their appointed duties. The Duc d'Harcourt and the Comte d'Estrées were both lieutenant generals with armies under their command. What were they doing here?

"Has the Marshal ordered you to come here? Has the Marshal ordered my Household to charge?"

"No, Sire," Richelieu said boldly. "He has forgotten us. He has planned a general attack of infantry with some cavalry support. But is the aristocracy of France to count for nothing on this day? Is Your Majesty's Household to sit by and watch the battle won or lost by Irish and Normans? I asked the Marshal's permission to advance on foot with the infantry, and he gave it. That is what he thinks of the peers and marshals of France. I ask you urgently, Sire, to give us permission to charge at once."

Louis XV's big nose quivered with discomfort. To make a decision was always difficult; to make a decision like this, in one moment, was almost impossible. But what was he to do? He knew the pride and vainglory of the great nobles, their extreme touchiness at any slight, real or imagined; he knew exactly how troublesome they could be. If one of the duchesses was accidentally passed over in a court ceremony, or had a tabouret a quarter of an inch lower than another duchess, the whole gaggle of dukes rose in wrath, and there were petitions and recriminations and complaints from morning to night, until life became insupportable with them. There was no limit to their capacity for annoying everybody—sovereign or peasant—who did not accept the claims of their rank. If this was so in ordinary court matters (with which he had had bitter experience) what would it not be if they felt themselves slighted on a day of battle? He groaned a little when he thought of it.

"Monsieur de Richelieu," he said, "you know that the Maréchal de Saxe commands in this field."

"He is busy, Sire; he has no time; and we have no time. He is over on the left, with the Irish. I demand permission to charge with the Household now—to advance with it, and charge when the Marshal's general infantry attack begins."

"It is our right, Sire, and it cannot be denied," the Duc d'Harcourt declaimed.

"It is due to the shades of our ancestors," D'Estrées said.

I wish they were all dead and buried with their infernal ancestors, Louis thought, frowning with the effort to make up his mind. What if they charged? Would it do any harm? He looked away from them, towards the vast confusion of the field, where his eye could discern no shape or form whatever except the red block of the English square thrust into the middle of his army.

"Charge, then, gentlemen," he said, keeping his voice as firm as possible, "and may God and Saint Louis and Saint Denis charge with you!"

The dukes got to their feet at once, and, with the miraculous spontaneity of long training, everybody present cried out "Vive le Roi!"

Louis XV leaned forward and said to Richelieu in an undertone:

"But remember, sir, you are not to get in the Marshal's way."

§

"I have had dinner put in the little room on the garden side," Jeannette said. "It is very pretty on a sunny day like this, with all the flowers. Shall we go in now?"

§

There was a great sudden thrilling of trumpets, and the drums beat loud from Barry Wood to Fontenoy.

Patrick Cusack in the first company of Dillon's regiment
blew mightily; Rory MacNaughton blew in Lally's;
Michael Gilcannan blew a great blast for Clare's. Every
man had put on his iron skullcap beneath the three-
cornered hat; every bayonet hung ready at the crossbelt;
every firelock was primed. Keeping their double line in
good order, the Irish and the Normans advanced at a
jog trot, the Normans at the extreme left and the six
Irish regiments filling the rest of the left and left center.
On the other side the trumpets had called the Carabiniers, Aubeterre and the remains of Royal and Couronne.

Mézières could not see them go without him. He had
ridden since before dawn, and had taken part in no
fighting. The Marshal was, for the moment, alone, all
his aides scattered on missions or gathered in by field
hospitals; but Mézières could not be still now.

"Mon Maréchal," he said stiffly, "have I your permission to dismount and advance with the Irish?"

Maurice frowned at him, furious at the distraction.

"Go wherever you like," he shouted. "Go on, go with
Lally's."

In another moment he was roaring orders at a fragment of the Swiss and French Guards which had been
rallied and brought back to take the right of the Irish.
The fate of Mézières concerned him not at all. It was
now, in this moment—in the next five or six minutes, at
most—that his destiny would be decided, and as he saw
his plans coming to the point of life and death before
his eyes, he was cold with a fury of determination. The

English would be broken now, now; he turned and galloped towards the center, alone, in full view of the whole
English line, to give his decisive orders to that one small
battery of fieldpieces *à la suédoise*.

Mézières got off his horse and gave it a slap on the
rump. "Au revoir, César," he said, and the horse, exhausted by a day of unceasing movement, turned back
without enthusiasm towards the green trees and grass of
Barry Wood.

Mézières ran forward and found a place for himself in
the front line of Lally's, next to a vast sergeant with hal-
berd and sword, who cast a grim look at him.

"This is no work for the likes of you," the sergeant
said, "but come along, then. Draw your little bodkin!"

Mézières drew his sword and said nothing.

For hundreds of yards on the whole left side of the
red square the Normans and Irish were advancing at a
trot. They kept their line well, and held their fire. The
stolid redcoats watched them come, motionless, and
there was a moment when no bullets fell at all, and the
space between the two red-coated lines—their uniforms
much alike, for the Irish had kept the livery of the
Stuarts—was like a lane of peace. Then the order sounded
off down the line, and there was a sudden blinding roar:
thousands of muskets had spoken almost at once, on
both sides, at a distance of about twenty paces, and at
the same time the wild Irish and the wilder Scots set up
their unearthly yells as they plunged onwards. In the
moment's interval they clipped their bayonets on, and

over the bodies of their dead and wounded they hurled
themselves at the English ranks.

Mézières in his white uniform was a conspicuous object among so many red coats, but fortune seemed to be
on his side; the first Englishman that he encountered in
the moment's sharp mêlée was already slightly wounded
and it was no trick at all to make him drop his firelock
and bayonet by a thrust of the sword. Mézières was
armed with the sword of a French officer, and the Englishman, once he had lost his musket, was equipped
only with the short sword—hardly more than a big dagger
—of the infantryman. There was a blind clash of steel,
and the Englishman went down with Mézières's sword
through his chest. And already, as he drew it out again,
the trumpets were shrilling and the drums beating as the
officers yelled: "Get back, get back!" It was no part of
Maurice's plan to let the Irish and English get completely
mixed, for their uniforms were so similar that a confusion of slaughter would result, and the English in their
superior regularity might easily hold the field. The front
line of the Irish got back, raggedly, quickly, leaving
many of their number behind; the English were reload-
ing for another volley, and were ready for it just as the
second line of the Irish moved forward and fired, almost
muzzle to muzzle. In the hellish noise Mézières could
hear no more orders. The mêlée now, at least in this part
of the field, was general and would certainly continue to
be general for a few minutes; he ran on with the rest,
almost choked with the smoke and noise, and with the

blood pumping violently in his chest and ears. He prayed to fall upon an English officer, for the inequality of weapons between the ordinary guardsman and himself was too great.

Alexander MacCarthy of Drisbane, leading his company forward in Clare's, was praying too. "Lamb of God who takest away the sins of the world," he prayed, "give us peace." He thought of Arlette and of MacGuire, who had loved her, and brushed the thought away again angrily. Still, he was glad he had shaken hands with MacGuire, after all. His lips moved swiftly as he said aloud, over and over again, "Lamb of God who takest away the sins of the world, give us peace." Clare's line clashed with the line of the Coldstream Guards, and Alexander MacCarthy of Drisbane found himself face to face with an English officer whose face was streaked with blood but whose sword was still ready. Alexander MacCarthy was fresh to the battle, and the Englishman had been marching and fighting for hours; it was easy enough. As MacCarthy's sword, swift and strong, disarmed the Englishman in one thrust and slit his arm, he was still praying. He brought the sword up again and cracked it down with all his might along the Englishman's jaw and throat. As he pulled it up, blind with blood and excitement, he barely noticed the figure that now lay dead before him, the face that would never see Kent or Devonshire or the hills of Sussex again. He did not at all notice that a trooper just behind the officer had leveled his musket straight at Alexander MacCarthy of Drisbane from a distance of three paces. "Lamb of God that takest away the sins of the world," he was beginning again, when the musket roared out and the prayer was not finished, for the hour of his death had come.

Trooper MacGinnis and his friend Rory O'Neill charged side by side, and it was MacGinnis who fell first, O'Neill who plunged over his body with a howl of animal grief and rushed upon the English bayonets. Trooper Wogan of Lally's, bayoneting an officer, had the presence of mind and the immense good luck to find fourteen golden sovereigns in his belt, then and there, without interference. MacGillicuddy of Roth's cut a man's head clean off with his sword, but it did him no good in the end, for there was a loaded English musket in the right place, and his own head went next.

O'Hegarty fought with the grim coolness and caution of an old hand, who knew that this kind of man-to-man conflict was of its nature brief and decisive; if he accounted for one or two of the English he would have done his share, so long as he kept his men at it too. That was the difficulty in a mêlée like this: officers and men were lost among the enemy, orders were neither given nor taken, and the very desperation of the business made it next to impossible to keep the troops from engaging too deep. He tried to maintain the fiction of order, croaking hoarsely at the men nearest him, and fighting off death as well as he could for himself. There was a great hulk of a guardsman who made at him with a bayonet, and would have got him, too, but for a providential mistake: the man was shot from behind by one of the English muskets. O'Hegarty guarded himself with his great heavy sword, and croaked at his men to keep back, not to get in too far; he croaked as MacCarthy had prayed, automatically, unthinking, with his head bursting and his nostrils distended with the smell of blood and smoke. But his luck was not in; he had stood four or five minutes of the hellish mix-up when the heavy butt of a musket crashed down upon his skull and he sank like a slaughtered bullock. For the second before complete blackness overtook him he could feel the boots of his own men trampling over his body.

Mézières found the officer for whom he had prayed—an officer equipped like himself, with a sword, and, like himself, young and quick. For the better part of a minute it was like a fencing match. In spite of the terrible tightness of his nerves, the suffocation of smells and the tumult of his own blood in his head, Mézières almost enjoyed the first half minute of the conflict. Then he succeeded in getting his sword under the other's guard and slashed him in the breast; the other was weaker now, but fought on, staggering slightly. Perhaps he had already been wounded in this day which had been even longer for the English than for the French. Mézières laughed aloud and called out in English: "Now for it!" His thrust was strong and exact: it cut the great artery in the other's throat and he fell slowly, first to one knee and

then to the ground. For the first time Mézières saw him
—saw his face, unbelievably young, and the look of surprise in his glazing blue eyes. It was the face Mézières
knew best in the world although he had never once seen
it in waking life. He was shaken by an unknown horror,
and strange suffering sounds came from his own throat.
He leaned over the red-coated boy on the ground.

"Your sister!" he said, his voice torn out of his throat
painfully and yet without much noise. "Your sister! Is
she your sister?"

The young face looked up at him without expression.
The eyes were glazed in death, and still looked very surprised.

Mézières's legs gave way under him, and he, too, fell
on his knees. For the briefest space of time, no more than
two or three seconds, the battle and the whole waking
life of man existed no more: he was looking through the
dead young face before him to another that he would
never see again. Then the sword of an Englishman came
down on his own head and he fell. His blood was mixed
with the blood of the boy he had killed.

§

Maurice de Saxe thundered down upon the placid lieutenant who commanded the battery *à la suédoise.*

"Up, now, at the gallop," he said, "and open fire with
all you've got on the center of the English line. Keep at

it while there's any grapeshot left. Quick. You may make a hole—you should be able to make a hole."

He rode ahead of the fieldpieces and sought out the Prince de Croÿ.

"That battery will either break the English line at this point or will attract all their fire upon it," he said. "It doesn't matter which. As soon as it has opened fire you must charge."

Without waiting for a salute Maurice was off again to the right, to Carabiniers. The attack was already begun left and center, and was about to begin center and right. He no longer worried about the regiment of Piedmont, the orders that had been disobeyed or the movements that had gone wrong; this time he was sure, and the cold fury that possessed him would endure for ten minutes, at least—ten minutes was all he wanted.

§

Richelieu led the King's Household up, the whole body of men cheering in the wildest state of enthusiasm, and directed them upon a point between the battery *à la suédoise* and the Prince of Croÿ's regiment. The cavaliers galloped forward with the utmost gallantry, were greeted by a volley of musketry at twenty paces, and fell back in confusion, their horses crazy with fear at the hail of bullets. Then Richelieu, moved by frantic necessity (he *would* strike a blow in this battle; no German bastard

could keep him out of it) shouted the order to dismount.
Harcourt and Clermont-Gallerande and D'Estrées and
the rest of the noble volunteers took it up: "Dismount,
dismount!" The Gentlemen of the Household dismounted and beat their horses back. Forming in some
rough approximation of an infantry body three or four
deep, they ran forward with drawn swords. The exhausted English guardsmen on whom they now fell were
armed only with muskets, bayonets and short swords;
their ammunition was nearly all gone and they had only
the bayonet to depend upon, for their short swords were
of no use against the long swords of officers and gentlemen. The wall of bayonets might have stood if the men
behind it had not been shattered by many hours of
marching and fighting, an unceasing artillery fire and—
latest of all—a demoralizing shower of grapeshot which
had plowed lanes among them. As it was, weakened and
bled white, they could not stand any more. Their lines
broke into confusion and fell back quickly into the middle of their square. All over the red square the trumpets
sounded for the retreat: to the right, to the center, and
especially on the left it was giving way, and there was no
time to lose if Cumberland expected to get his army out
of the field in reasonably good order. Maurice de Saxe,
clinging with desperation to his saddle (if he could hold
out for a few more minutes it would be enough) saw the
charge of the King's Household and made his corpselike
grimace, the substitute for a smile.

"There go the dukes," he said to Valfons, "without

orders and without order. Never mind. We could have done it just as well without them."

§

At Notre-Dame-aux-Bois the crowd of courtiers were shouting "Vive le Roi!" The Comte d'Argenson, Minister of War, knelt to the King and said: "Your Majesty has won or is about to win the greatest victory in the history of France. The English lines are broken and they are retreating."

Louis looked out at the field. Even he could see now that the English were in rapid retreat, their red lines falling inward and backward as their once impregnable square was broken. At first he had been unable to distinguish much, especially as the Irish and English looked exactly alike from this distance; but once the white-coats of his own household, Croÿ's men and Aubeterre had been engaged, he could tell by the colors that the English were being beaten back. It had taken between seven and eight minutes from the sounding of the general attack—seven and a half minutes during which his heart had very nearly ceased to beat from the sheer anguish of a decision so great.

He looked down at D'Argenson.

"Rise, sir," he said. "I hope you are right. Where is the noon courier, the courier who should have gone at noon? My own courier? Find him, somebody. D'Ayen, can you find him, quickly? He should have gone at noon . . ."

If it is true, Louis thought, straining his eyes to see what was happening on that rapidly altered field, if it is true, the first news must go to her, for she has wanted it and prayed for it, and it is to please her that I am here today; the victory, if there is a victory, is hers and must be laid at her feet.

§

M. de Voltaire was attacking a handsome soufflé with considerable pleasure, in spite of his many digestive ailments and the bad state of his teeth, which made eating —even of a soufflé—sometimes painful to him.

"Yes," he was saying, "it is a poem I shall write about the battle; nothing but a poem could do it justice, if I understand my correspondence correctly. It is to be a grand battle in the open, a sort of happening we have not had lately."

"But, sir, it will surely require all the resources of even your talent," Jeannette said, "to describe a battle you have not seen. How can you manage to do it?"

"That is a professional secret," M. de Voltaire said, smacking his thin lips with pleasure. "If the Abbé does not object, I might tell you, Madame, but let it go no further: all battles are exactly alike. Numbers of men set upon and kill numbers of other men. That is all there is to it. But there are always deeds of gallantry, great per-

sonages in danger, anecdotes of a curious or heroic nature
—you may depend upon it that the Marquis d'Argenson
will supply me with a quantity of all these materials by
the next courier. With a touch of Boileau and a great deal
of Voltaire it should be possible to produce a very reada-
ble epic in a very few days. It took Boileau no longer to
write his masterpieces in the same kind. I do not need
to recall to you, Madame, those great works, the *Prise de
Namur* and the *Passage du Rhin.*"

"You have consulted them lately, no doubt," Bernis
said smoothly.

Voltaire looked at him and cackled. He knew what
the Abbé had in mind and did not trouble to refute it.

"Naturally," he said. "As nobody has taken the trouble
to read that sublime master, Boileau, for the past twenty
years, it would be a service to literature to bring him back
to life. I may even go so far as to borrow a rhyme or two.
Why not? My sincerest compliments on your cook,
Madame."

"For my part I hope your poem, whatever it is, is all
Voltaire and no Boileau," the Comtesse d'Estrades, having finished her soufflé, said with decision. "Between
these four walls I am free to declare that Boileau bores
me to madness."

"Only because he writes of things that happened before
our time," M. de Voltaire said, smacking his lips and putting down his fork at last. "Substitute modern names and
scatter a few contemporary references throughout, and
the *Prise de Namur* would be read as eagerly today as it

was in the days of the Old King. It is astonishing what people will read so long as it contains some sort of reference to themselves or their friends."

"I begin to see," the Abbé observed, "the outline of your poem on the battle."

Voltaire cackled. By now he was in high good humor, for the plates had been whisked away and the fumes of an enormous *poularde* cooked in white wine scented the air of the little room.

"Never mind, good Abbé," he said. "Even if I do lean rather heavily on Father Boileau, only you and I and your Thirty-nine Immortal colleagues will ever know the difference—and I greatly doubt whether most of them will. You take all these things, battles and poems alike, much too seriously."

Yes, Bernis thought, I take them too seriously, you mountebank; I take them too seriously, when they are paid for in human flesh and written in blood.

The Abbé bent over his plate. His pale, delicate face, with the sensitive mouth and chin controlled to immobility, was hidden for a moment from M. de Voltaire's eyes—those eyes like the claws of a monkey.

§

"Now Glory be to God in the Highest!" Lally was shouting as he led his men on. "Glory be to God for the day! Long live Ireland! Long live King James III!"

His sword was bloody and so was his smart new uniform; he had lost his hat; he was slightly wounded in the arm, the cheek and the side; but the English line had been broken, well broken, and after two or three minutes of the wildest rout and confusion, during which the Irish had chased them with savage ardor, the broken lines had formed again, but only to retreat with the utmost speed. The English were, in fact, running away—running away in miraculously good order, stopping every hundred paces at their officers' commands and turning to give a volley of musketry, but running away just the same. For all his spirited bragging and his predictions of victory, Lally had never really hoped to see the day when the backs of the red coats would be turned to him in battle. He yelled with nearly as much savagery as any of his men as he took up the chase.

"Long live Ireland!" they yelled in English and in Gaelic. "Long live King James III!"

An aide-de-camp in a glittering white uniform rode up to Lally—who had been dismounted and fighting since the beginning of the attack—and flourished his hat in the air. It was Valfons.

"Retire, Comte de Lally, get back at once," he shouted. "The Marshal does not wish you to pursue the English. Retire!"

Lally looked up in amazement and disgust. The nearest English back was no more than ten feet away and rapidly moving off as the once hollow square solidified into a column on the run.

"Jesus, Mary and Joseph!" Lally said, his blue eyes dull with horror. "Move back now? Monsieur de Valfons, Monsieur de Valfons, this must be a mistake! We have broken the English for him—surely the Marshal does not want to cheat us now?"

"You have heard the Marshal's orders," Valfons said harshly. "Stop the pursuit at once and retreat to the left near Barry Wood. You will take up your old position. The Marshal says that if you pursue the English too far you will run into an artillery trap at Vezons. Let them get away. They have lost and they will not stop running for a long time."

The aide-de-camp wheeled his horse and rode off to repeat his orders to Lord Clare. He had given them first to Lally because Lally's came first in his path, but once he had given them to Clare there would be no hope; the trumpets and the drums would carry the message throughout the brigade; it was over.

Lally turned to bawl out his orders. His heart was filled with amazement and disgust. It was the Irish who had broken the English and turned their victory into a defeat; it had cost the lives of good men; and now they were to be thrust back into the woods again while the hereditary enemy calmly ran away in good order, unpursued. Lally's face was black with misery. He had seen O'Hegarty fall.

"Let me get at that Marshal," he said, "and would I not tell him something?"

§

Lord Clare protested stiffly, sword in hand, as Valfons delivered the order.

"We are still in excellent condition and can continue the pursuit for hours," he said. "In five minutes our brigade has done more than the rest of the army in an entire day. Why, sir, must we withdraw now?"

"The Marshal asks me to tell you, my Lord, that the English have very strong artillery at Vezons and beyond. If we continue the pursuit we lose our order and our positions and run the risk of being defeated on a new ground. That defeat would be a rout. We have won the battle. The Marshal thinks that is enough. Will you stop your brigade at once, my Lord?"

Clare was in a white rage.

"I will, sir," he said. "Tell the Marshal I obey his orders although I have not the honor to understand them. Good day, sir."

The trumpets shrilled suddenly forth and the drums beat; Michael Gilcannan and Rory MacNaughton and Patrick Cusack blew mightily; in Clare's, in Bulkeley's, Roth's, Dillon's, Berwick's, Lally's, and in the Scots of Lord John Drummond, the men halted in their tracks and took the bayonets off their firelocks and cursed. For eight minutes they had been face to face with the despoilers of their lands, the murderers of their parents and grandparents, the black Protestant English who had driven them from their homes across the sea; in the clash of arms they had vanquished; and now they were told to draw back and let their prey escape. The air of the summer afternoon, stinking with smoke and the reek of torn human flesh, was filled with their curses in the two kinds of Gaelic and in English. The Scots pipers set up a wild wailing tune. They were cheated again.

§

It was then that Dillon fell—just as the trumpets called their unwelcome orders and the men were drawn to a standstill, aghast and cursing. Some of the English in front of Dillon's were firing as they ran, and a musket ball hit James Dillon between the eyes and he fell. A howl of horror and rage broke out from his men; it was all the officers could do to keep them from avenging his death by a general disobedience of orders. Dillon, severe and just, owned the oldest regiment in the brigade, and there were many men in it—especially now, after some minutes of hand-to-hand fighting—who would have willingly given their own lives to avenge him.

"Back, back!" the officers shouted, brandishing their swords. "Get back! Get in line! Get back!"

§

It had taken the English two full hours to march into their position in the midst of the French army; it took them only a few minutes to vanish from the field. The Hanoverian foot soldiers had preceded them in flight by a good six or seven minutes, and fled in such disorder that the English cavalry, coming up at last to cover the infantry's retreat, was at first thrown into confusion by the fugitives. By desperate effort the officers of the English had succeeded in restoring fairly good order in their ranks, but the whole army was retreating with the greatest possible speed, leaving field guns, the big guns that had been brought to the middle of their square, and many caissons of munitions behind them. Some of the men threw away their muskets as they ran, and the field that had once seemed a solid block of red-clad men was now strewn with the spoils of victory.

Maurice watched the flight of the English through his glasses. A grim excitement possessed him. If he could enforce his will and make it stop at this, he would have achieved a victory in open battle over an English army—a thing unknown for hundreds of years on the continent of Europe. It would be his victory, won according to the exact principles he had laid down thirteen years ago in his *Rêveries,* and even the English had behaved exactly according to his rules. But the question was whether he could make it stop here; the Irish were enraged—as he knew, having received Clare's message—and there was all the pride and fury of the French dukes to contend with, the bravado of the Marquis de Clermont-Gallerande, the fire of the Duc de Biron and the Comte d'Estrées, the importunities of Richelieu. They surrounded him now, protesting.

"My Lord, it is impossible——! Monseigneur, you cannot mean——! Marshal, the honor of France demands——!"

"I have given my orders," he shouted suddenly, unable to endure the din of objection around him. "I tell you if we pursue the English from this field we get into a totally different position, in which they may well be able to turn and defeat us. They have plenty of heavy artillery at Vezons and beyond. I tell you we must stay on this field. See to your men, get them into their old positions. There will be time to pursue the English tomorrow if they are still retreating."

He suddenly dropped his voice to a conversational tone.

"And to guarantee that they keep on retreating, Monsieur d'Estrées, you might just harry them gently with a squadron of cavalry. It is essential that the rest of the army return to its positions, at least until tomorrow."

D'Estrées, glad of the exception which enabled him, at least, to continue the action, flourished his hat in the air and made off quickly before Maurice might change his mind.

There they go, he thought exultantly, the last of the English: I can barely see their red coats through these glasses, and in a few minutes they will have disappeared altogether from this field which seemed their conquest until a quarter of an hour ago. I, Maurice de Saxe, have done it: I, the German bastard, the nameless one, the miserable hulk and ruin of a man, I have done it. If Adrienne were alive she would be proud today.

"Where are all my young men?" he asked suddenly. "Where is Puységur? Where is Mézières? Now the bad part of the business begins, gentlemen. We have now to count our losses."

His face clouded over as he spoke. This would be a bad business; there would be thousands of the dead to count and bury, thousands more of the wounded to be treated. He had attended well to the hospital service and thought it would be done with more care than was usual in the makeshift services of the day; but it would have to be done soon. The hot sun of the May day was already busy upon the fields of flesh and blood, and although Maurice's nostrils were not sensitive, he could see that many of the officers around him had had recourse to their smelling bottles lately to overcome the stench of human carrion.

§

Over the whole field from Barry Wood to Fontenoy
the sun picked out the flashing points of lances and the
white silken sheen of banners; the trumpets called
proudly; the army was returning to its original positions,
leaving the pursuit of the already vanished English to a
handful of cavalry. Louis XV stood alone on the edge of
the plateau of Notre-Dame-aux-Bois and stared down at
the field of victory. Now that it was over he could hardly
believe it; he realized now that he had never fully believed it would happen; he had done what neither his
great-grandfather nor Henri IV had done—he had defeated the English in a great open battle. He thought of
St Louis; such a thing as this had not happened since
St Louis, and then the foe had been of a different breed.
The army flowed easily, triumphantly, into its old positions, and the French Guards and the Swiss Guards returned to the place from which they had been routed in
the morning. The auxiliary services were all busy now,
the hospitalers collecting dead and wounded, the Q.M.
amassing the booty the English had left behind. Louis
obeyed a sudden impulse to pray. He did not go on his
knees, conscious as always of the silken mob behind him;
but he closed his eyes and prayed to St Louis and St
Denis, the protectors of his fathers since the dawn of

their greatness; his soul was, for one moment, filled with awe.

A cough behind him made him turn round. It was the Duc d'Ayen.

"I have found the courier, the noon courier, Sire. He is ready to go whenever you like."

"Ah, good, good. Give me paper and a pen, please, D'Ayen. I shall use him at once."

He sat down on a wooden bench that had been dragged out for him. His first words came haltingly, and then he wrote with speed, the words falling over each other in his excitement. It was victory, and it was hers: for her. When he finished he addressed the paper in a bold script:

> À Madame la Marquise de Pompadour,
> À Etioles.

That was her name now and henceforth, and he would proclaim it as soon as possible. But for her, he would never have been here today; he would have missed the glory of his reign. He held the letter for a moment in his hand, as if to impregnate it with the feelings of triumph and love that raced through the secret places of his being, and then thrust it at D'Ayen.

"Get it off at once," he said, "and then take another for the courier to Versailles."

With brief, cold words he filled up a sentence or two of announcement, signed it and addressed it to Her Majesty the Queen. This letter, too, he held in his hand for a moment. His eyes saw her for a moment across the sunlit field: her patient, kindly face, her submissive head forever bowed, either to him or to God.

"There it is," he said to himself, "and it can't be helped."

He gave D'Ayen the letter and turned back towards his gentlemen of the court.

§

D'Argenson thought: I must write to M. de Voltaire as soon as possible. Richelieu thought: I really must find time to write to M. de Voltaire this evening. Maurice de Saxe thought: they will all be writing off to Voltaire and the rest of them as quickly as they can, to claim the credit of a victory I have won; there will be Te Deums in the churches and there will be poems in the streets; but it is my victory, and I know that in the end it must be known for what it is. Meanwhile there is work to do: the redoubts and entrenchments must be restored to their original strength at once, the field cleared and the men encamped as solidly as before; for the victory is won, but it must be made sure.

§

It was nearly three o'clock when Maurice was able to take his attention from the field long enough to ride up to Notre-Dame-aux-Bois. He had—with agony and many

curses—changed horses twice during the day, but the
third horse was nearing exhaustion now, and as for himself, nothing this side of death could have equaled the
numb unceasing torture of his body. He would kneel to
the King, if that monstrous body would permit; and
thereafter get back to his tent and the little doctor and
ride no more horses. His "cradle" was there, waiting; he
could still endure movement in the "cradle", perhaps,
once the doctor had tapped him . . .

He rode into the plateau at Notre-Dame-aux-Bois and
Valfons and D'Espagnac, close behind him, dismounted
to help him out of the saddle. D'Espagnac got his right
leg over the horse and lowered it to Valfons' bent shoulder. With white, sweating face and staring eyes, Maurice
got through the pain of the dismounting and said nothing, although his favorite curses were boiling in his
throat. He knew what was due the magnificance of the
occasion, and was willing to pay his tribute to the Versailles tradition once more before he succumbed. He paid
no attention to the cries of "Vive le Maréchal!" that surrounded him. These were courtiers, and they were always ready to cry "Vive!" in fair weather. Maurice
straightened himself and walked forward to the place
where Louis XV stood, calm and silent, waiting for him.
The plateau was hushed to silence as he drew near. With
immense deliberation and control, Maurice's vast body
sank: he was on his knees.

"Your Majesty is victorious," he said loudly. "Vive le
Roi!"

The crowd took up the cry and yelled itself hoarse. The guards beyond, and the Musketeers who were returning to their place at the foot of the plateau, heard it and echoed it back again: "Vive le Roi! Vive le Roi!"

Louis XV's face had turned dark red. He leaned forward to assist the Marshal to get up again.

"Cousin and friend," he said, with more emotion in his voice than Maurice had ever heard there, "the victory is yours. France will know how to be grateful to you."

Maurice struggled up, unable to avoid grunting. The King staggered with the weight of him, but no profane hand was put forward to aid in the task.

"Some of our officers are not content to leave off now," Maurice said. "They wished to pursue the English. I ruled against this for reasons which seem to me very sound."

"You command here, sir," Louis said. "Your orders must be obeyed. Is it possible for me to go down into the field now?"

"I was about to suggest that Your Majesty might like to visit the wounded and the whole encampment," Maurice said. "The men are exhausted, and there have been very heavy losses. It will inspirit them to see you."

"It shall be done at once," said Louis, more than glad to escape from the little plateau where he had spent the entire day. "Is there any news beyond what I have heard? The English have gone, but what of the Dutch down there?"

"As soon as they heard the English had been broken,

they vanished," Maurice said with a grin that slashed his pale face into halves. "The Dutch have been down there, doing nothing, all day long, and only wanted an excuse to run away. There is no enemy anywhere near us now. The men can sleep tonight."

Louis gave his orders; the horses were to be brought up; he was going down to the field. There was a great hustling and bustling all over the little plateau and in the clump of trees behind it, where the horses had been placidly nibbling all day.

"I have heard a wonderful story," the King said. "It was told me by Monsieur le Marquis d'Argenson, who heard it from a doctor in the field hospital down there, who got it from, I believe, an aide of yours, a certain Puységur."

"Yes, Puységur," Maurice said. "He vanished at the beginning of the English attack. What has become of him?"

"He was wounded," Louis said indifferently. "At any rate it appears that he was present when the first English came over the little hill. He heard the English officers shouting 'You may fire first, gentlemen of France,' and the French officer with him replied, 'No, you first, gentlemen of England.' Is that not a beautiful example of our ancient chivalry, Marshal?"

The Marshal's face was a study in the grimmer shades of expression.

"I do not attach much credit to such pretty stories, Sire," he said stiffly. "But no doubt by the time it gets to

Monsieur de Voltaire it will be the main event of the battle."

"There were others who heard it too," the King protested.

"No doubt, Sire. But do they understand English?"

Louis gave up.

"It is not my story, Marshal," he said, laughing. "I have done my duty by warning you, and when you read it in the gazettes or hear it in the talk of the day, you will at least recognize it."

The cavalcade began to go down the slopes towards the level field. Before they had reached it the cannonading, which had died down to an occasional far-off rumble of sound, ceased altogether, and the silence of peace descended on the living and the dead.

§

Jeannette filled in the long, lovely afternoon with those diversions to which she was most addicted—conversation, poetry and music. At the instigation of the Abbé de Bernis she declaimed a whole scene out of Voltaire's *Zaïre,* and the poet was lavish with his compliments afterwards. Then the Comtesse d'Estrades sat down at the spinet and Jeannette sang airs by Lulli and Rameau, the great aria from Lulli's *Armide* with all its decorations, acting the while, as she had been taught, in the style of the singers at the Opéra. Bernis, whose irritation at Voltaire was assuaged, or at least forgotten, in the enchantments of these efforts, had to take his leave with regret.

"If I do not go now, I shall not be at Versailles before dark," he said. "Dear Madame, it will be a whole week before I see you again. What cannot happen in a week?"

"Nothing bad," she said, laughing with her head on one side, as was her way. "Nothing at all bad, dear Abbé. We shall have a victory to celebrate when you come again."

"And another poem of Monsieur de Voltaire's, no doubt," the Abbé said, bowing to the poet.

Jeannette walked with him to the courtyard.

"When you come again," she said, "*he* will not be here, and we can work. Admit that he is the most charming of men, the most agreeable of companions. Admit it before you go."

"I think him a dangerous friend, Madame," Bernis said, his delicate face leaning towards hers as he spoke. "But it is the privilege of beauty to mock at danger. I shall scold no more."

Jeannette came back into the room, smiling at her secret thoughts.

"Shall we walk a little in the garden while the sun is still warm?" she asked. "My little lake down there is very pretty."

"I shall go upstairs and rest, dear cousin," the Comtesse d'Estrades said. "You can march Monsieur de Vol-

taire up and down the garden. I shall be better this evening for a little rest now—and when I come down again
I shall wear your bracelet, Jeannette, your wonderful
gift."

There were kisses and courtesies and bows, and Mme
d'Estrades went upstairs. The unbridled flattery Voltaire
bestowed on her young "cousin" had produced some
effect on her; she knew that Voltaire did not flatter for
nothing; the thought that such court could be openly
paid to the little Mme Lenormant took all the edge off
her own condescension. The day was near when she
would drop it altogether, and, like the rest of the world,
pay her homage to the rising star.

"I will make only one turn in the garden, if you permit," Voltaire said. "I am a lame, spavined old creature
with creaky joints, you know, and I also must rest before
the evening. We can't all have your resplendent youth,
Marquise. In fact I never did have it. I was born ill."

They went through the long windows on to the terrace.
The green young elm trees and the assertive tulips led the
eyes down gently to the shimmer of the lake at the end
of the walk. Jeannette breathed deep and began to speak
—earnestly and quickly.

"Sometimes I am afraid of what is going to happen,
Monsieur de Voltaire," she said. "You understand me—
I am young and ignorant of the world, in spite of the
efforts that have been made to teach me. I do not know
Versailles. I do not know the people there, their ambi-

tions, their intrigues and their politics. Here in my garden I am safe. Shall I ever be safe again, when I have left it?"

"Never," Voltaire said firmly. "Never. You will be exposed to every invention of spite, malice and envy. You will have to struggle day and night to maintain yourself against the intrigues of politicians, priests, women; you will be obliged to learn all about their miserable designs; you will have to learn something about politics in your own protection. But with your beauty and intelligence everything is possible."

"Usually I feel sure of that," she said gravely. "But there are times when I doubt. Only think: I do not really know why we are fighting this war, for instance. I realize that the enemies of France have combined in alliance against her, and that they want to make the Queen of Hungary govern the Empire in spite of the law. Aside from that I know nothing—and surely that is not very much. There must be more to it than that."

"There is more," the poet said. "There is the fundamental opposition of the English and the French all over the world, and this campaign in Flanders is only a small, immediate part of it. There is that great man—at least he says he is a great man, and we must believe Kings when they speak—Frederick of Prussia, who wishes to create a new power in the German north. It is a war which concerns deeper things than any of the pretexts upon which it was declared. It is the clash of nations in their rise and fall—there are those that are now rising and those that are in decline. They have met, and that is the battle."

Jeannette frowned.

"Which are the rising ones?" she asked.

"England, Madame, England and Prussia who are to-day opposed, who will be friends tomorrow."

"Ah, then you mean that France is in the decline!" Jeannette cried indignantly. "Shame, sir!"

"It is true. We have taken more, in the Americas and India and generally all over the world, than we can hold. We are a nation which cannot long survive in its present state; our system of society is rotted through, and unless something can be done to reconstruct it, we shall go down to ruin in a general cataclysm."

"I do not understand you, sir. Sometimes you speak so seriously that I am afraid. I cannot believe that the system of society, as you call it, is rotted through in France."

The poet bowed.

"I hope you may be right, Madame," he said. "In the position of great power and influence to which you are now going, I hope you will let me come and talk to you at times, and bring others who may tell you things you should know. You may learn that the people are not as happy as you think; and you may consider how dangerous and how stupid is the structure of a society based upon their incessant misery."

Jeannette shivered.

"I never heard you talk like this before," she complained. "You, the gayest and the wittiest! If the King heard you talk like that he would not be pleased. He would even be bored."

Voltaire cackled suddenly.

"That would be far worse," he admitted. "We must see to it that I do not bore him . . . But it is true, Madame, that I do not often talk like this. Shall I tell you why? It is because I, who spend my life ridiculing others, live in mortal terror of ridicule myself. I do not often speak seriously because any serious idea is regarded as ridiculous in this country. I talk to you because I hope in you—I hope that your power, which will be very great, may be used on the side of justice. In this wretched misgoverned country, where three fourths of the people are forever starved and the rest are either fools or scoundrels, the side of justice is always the weaker side."

"I declare I do not know how to understand you, sir," Jeannette said. "You should not complain of injustice. You have just benefited by a magnificent display of the King's generosity."

The poet's thin lips cracked in a crooked smile.

"I had forgotten that," he admitted. "Yes, I had forgotten that, for a moment. Perhaps you are right, Madame. Perhaps you are right. May I, having bored you enough for one afternoon, be permitted to go upstairs and rest? I shall try to be gayer this evening, and avoid speaking of these subjects which do not please you."

He bowed over her hand and went into the house. As he left her the crooked smile came again across his lined, weary face; as there was nobody to see him, and the mask of ironic mockery was not needed, the smile was weighted with sadness.

Jeannette watched him go, and turned back to her stone bench on the terrace. She sat there for a moment, troubled in spirit at what he had said, although she did not fully seize his meaning. The sun was beginning to sink, and the little lake at the end of the garden was flashing with red gold.

"I will be a good citizen," she said aloud, and then wondered at the sound of the words.

Well, she was young, beautiful, intelligent—they all said that; it must be true—and the King loved her. She would know how to face the problems as they came, for she was informed and supported by love. When the King came back, victorious, from the war——

She stood up; there was a thrilling intensity in the suddenness with which she realized the meaning of those words. When the King came back, victorious, from the war——! She would be the Marquise de Pompadour then, in sober official fact, and she would go to court, she, Jeannette Poisson, and not a minister or an ambassador would there be at Versailles who did not do her homage.

She laughed suddenly in sheer joy and turned back to the house. She would get a pen and paper and design the dress for her presentation.

§

The wounded men lay in rows at the foot of the plateau of Notre-Dame-aux-Bois, and the King, Dauphin and Marshal, followed by the pompous horde of the King's suite, rode slowly past them. Some of the men, wounded though they were, set up a feeble cheer for the King, and Louis took his hat off to them. The surgeons and dressers passed between the rows of the wounded, giving such rough, quick attention as they had time for. Maurice, scanning the innumerable figures they passed, drew up short.

"That should be Mézières," he said, turning his horse's head towards the side. "One of my aides, Sire. Mézières! Mézières! He has had a clout on the head. Is his case serious?"

A dresser looked up.

"It is a scalp wound, a hard blow," he said. "The young man does not seem to be in his right mind, my Lord."

"Mézières! Mézières! It is I, the Marshal."

The figure on the ground looked up without recognition.

"He talks sometimes, but it seems he talks only in English," the dresser said. "Also he calls out a name which sounds like Marie, only pronounced in an English way."

"Lost!" Mézières said from the ground, without a sign

of attention to the Marshal peering down at him. "Lost, lost, lost!"

"Now what the devil is he talking about?" the Marshal demanded. "What has he lost?"

"A dream, sir," Mézières said with unexpected fierceness, raising himself on his elbow. "Is that not enough for you? And what have you lost, may I ask?"

Maurice shook his head.

"Poor boy," he said, "he's crazy. It takes them like that sometimes. He'll be all right in a day or two. Take care of him, leech."

A wounded man somewhere down the line let out an unearthly yell, as if the fiends of hell were torturing him.

"Let us move on," the King murmured. "We can do no good to these poor fellows."

They turned off into the center of the plain, where the army had by now resumed its original positions and rested under arms, ready to bivouac there for the night. The warm sun of the late afternoon brought out odors which came up in waves and almost stifled the unaccustomed nostrils of the courtiers. One such wave rose to them now, and the King, the Dauphin and all the rest took out their smelling bottles and sniffed vigorously. The moaning and groaning of the wounded followed them down the field.

Louis XV's face had grown somber. From his place of vantage at Notre-Dame-aux-Bois he had been present at the battle as at a spectacle, and the details had never at any moment been clear to him. Now that he was down in the field, reeking with the horrid stench of blood and murdered flesh, he felt his gorge rising. So it was like this, a famous victory.

"We must think of promotions and gratifications," he said to the Marshal, making conversation to conceal his discomfort. "You and the other general officers must prepare lists for me. Certain regiments, Normandie and the Irish and Aubeterre, perhaps, should be specially honored. There must be general promotions among the Irish. My cousin Stuart will be glad to hear of what they have done today."

"If the Irish are to be believed," Maurice said grimly, "the Stuart family is already restored to the throne of England as a result of this day's work. The Irish and the Scots think of nothing else, poor devils."

Louis did not answer. He was trying with all his might not to be sick; for the sights he saw as they penetrated further into the field were even less to his taste than the rows of wounded men being cared for back there. Here, in the open field, there was no attempt to give the men attention; they were being collected simply and piled in the hospital wagons for transport. The men from the medical service looked at them and sometimes prodded them or turned them over to see if they were alive or dead; the living were shoveled into the hospital wagons, and the dead were piled up in heaps here and there in the open field to be removed later. The army had formed again, resting on its old positions, and this work of collecting the human carrion took place in the midst of the survivors, who looked on, for the most part, in exhausted, unhappy silence.

"Vive le Roi!" the men cheered as Louis passed. "Vive le Roi!"

They came to a great smoking heap of corpses in the center of the line where the English had once stood. Arms and legs protruded obscenely from the blackened and bloodstained mass; the smell came out with violence, like a blow in the face. Louis turned to the Dauphin, whose fat white face was puckered in the effort to keep his composure.

"Look, my son," he said, "at the price of victory. Learn how not to shed the blood of your subjects."

He was profoundly moved, for once, and the others dared not speak. They turned their horses towards the left and rode down to the Irish. All along their way the cries were taken up again and again, so that the cheering never ceased: "Vive le Roi! Vive le Roi!"

Here Maurice took his leave.

"I will not go with you, Sire, to the left," he said. "I am in desperate pain and ask leave to retire to my tent, where my doctor will know how to relieve me a little."

"You have anything you wish to ask for, even leave to go, dear cousin," Louis said. "I hope you will not try to mount your horse again today."

The cries then divided—"Vive le Roi!" for Louis as he

rode to the left, and "Vive le Maréchal!" for Maurice as he turned back at last towards his tent.

Louis came to the first of the Irish, and there in the midst of his shattered regiment was Lally-Tollendal, sitting on a drum. The lithe body of the adventurer, his uniform bloodstained at the shoulder and down the thigh, jumped to attention as the King paused beside him.

"We owe the issue of the day to you and the Irish, Comte de Lally," Louis said. "There will be general promotions and gratifications in money, and the Cross of Saint-Louis to you and as many of your officers as you recommend. You have earned the gratitude of France."

Lally was still bitter sore from the events of the day: in seven minutes of fighting he and his had won a battle, and had then been cheated of its dearest fruit, the pursuit and slaughter of some more of the English. His regiment, his beautiful new regiment, had been more than decimated, and the corpses lay in neat heaps along the field, while the wounded and the dying filled the air with their laments.

"Sire," he said fiercely, "the favors of Your Majesty are like those of the Gospel—they fall upon the lame and the blind."

Louis rode on. He could not reprove the man for sharp speech in that place, where not a breath could be drawn without the aid of the smelling bottle. This is the victory, he was saying to himself: this is a famous victory.

§

The sun was rapidly setting when the Marquis d'Argenson got into his carriage for the return journey to his quarters at Calonne. He had said good-by to the Marshal in that warrior's tent; he had visited the lines in the King's company, obliging himself for the occasion to ride upon a horse; he had seen the weary men in their thousands preparing for a night's rest in the field, while the kitchens handed out the evening soup and wine. His heart was very heavy.

"Drive slowly," he said to his coachman. "I am not sure that I shall not be sick if you go too fast."

He clung to his smelling bottle and leaned back upon the cushions of his carriage. He was Minister for Foreign Affairs, and he had been unable to do anything to prevent this battle. He wondered if he would be able to do anything to obtain a peace now that the victory had been won.

But was it won? He sat up again straight and frowned at his coachman's back. What was the use of a famous victory on one field in Flanders? The English would retreat; Tournai would fall; the Channel might be open; all Flanders would be overrun by Maurice de Saxe's army; perhaps an expedition might be fitted out, and that mad young man, Charles Stuart, could be landed in England or Ireland or Scotland . . . Yet . . . Yet . . .

What of it? The English fleet was still upon the sea, and the King of Prussia was master of Germany; who could tell what was happening in Canada? It was too big to be decided by the struggle of one day. It was too big altogether—too big for him. He slumped back again upon the cushions.

The life of man, he thought, was a struggle in a space between darkness and darkness, and those who died in this day were like the powers of one man forever dwindling and dying in the struggle which filled his time on earth. Why, then, knowing as he did that it was vain, that the forces amongst which he and all those at Fontenoy on this day had contended were too powerful for such puny antagonists, that it was life itself and the treacherous thrusting surge and roll of its tides that carried men to their ends unknown, why had he not abandoned this world of effort and retired long ago to that garden he knew where there were flowers, trees, birds, and the ways of ambition were overgrown with philosophy? He did not know; it was the eternal dilemma; but he did know that this was what it came to in the end—the body lifeless and inert, the limbs that would move no more, death in the head and the heart. He had seen them piled up, the dead men, so many slabs of carrion meat piled high in the sunny field. The smell of it would never leave his nostrils until he, too, could smell no more. They had been of all ages, but mostly young; they had fought for what they conceived to be good causes ("against the King's enemies") but in fact they knew no more than did the King himself of the fundamental oppositions of interest for which they died. Those interests, he thought, would remain untouched by the issue of the battle, for it was the rising, growing, devouring, expanding and aggressive interest that had been defeated in the battle—and it was the loser who had won.

That was it; he frowned intently at the coachman's back as he repeated it: the winning side had lost, and it was the loser who had won. In the peace that he would now attempt to make, now or very soon, what would this victory of paradox mean? Nothing, he thought; nothing. The powers of the past—chivalry, aristocracy, all the notions of which the French made extravagant parade—had won by the aid of the savage exiled Irish; but the demands for colonies, land and trade were still the demands of these vigorous rising powers, the English and the Prussians, and one victory on a field in Flanders would not deflect the course of movement of the century. He saw that movement clearly: the English would get what they wanted. Beyond the seas, in the forests of the Americas, and in the rich whole world of India, they would take what they wanted, and the French King and court, dazzled by their own splendor and the easy triumphs near at hand, would scarcely even notice.

He was weary and sick at heart. The life of man, he thought, was a poor thing, between darkness and darkness, but its hope—and when he was not so weary he thought it a lively one—lay in this: that some day men might learn to fight for themselves instead of for the confusion and greed of those who governed them. There would be no end to the battle while the life of mankind endured; it was in a sense the condition of life, its permanent and prevailing character; but the time might come when men in masses would learn to choose their weapons and their cause.

He rested upon the cushions and his eyes closed. He was weary and sick, and he slept.

§

When the sun had gone and the men had settled into their camp for the night Maurice de Saxe was already sleeping in his tent; the King and the court had returned to Calonne; from Barry Wood to Fontenoy and down to Antoing the army rested in its old positions. The trumpets blew then for the bivouac: Patrick Cusack in the first company of Dillon's regiment blew mightily; Rory MacNaughton blew in Lally's; Michael Gilcannan blew a blast for Clare's. In prayers and in silence, for they were sick and sore and had lost many men, the Irish prepared to sleep. The light of fires sprang out of the dusk between the wood and the far-off river, and along the dark ridge of the hill the sentries aligned their yellow lanterns against the coming of the night.

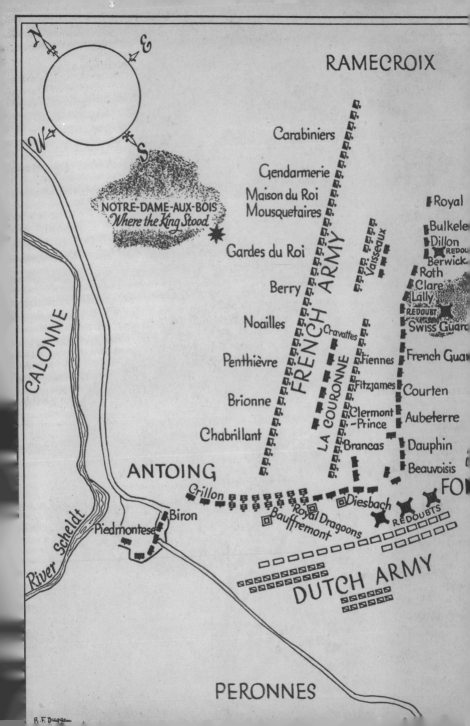